DRAGON WARS

HEATHER JEAN

Contact: heatherjspraga@yahoo.com

Cover, interior design, and formatting by Aubrey Labitigan

Contact: facebook.com/designjai

ISBN

Ebook 979-8-9921404-0-8

Paperback 979-8-9921404-1-5

Hardback 979-8-9921404-2-2

Dustcover 979-8-9921404-3-9

HEATHER JEAN

STORIES THAT TAKE YOU INTO EXCITING NEW WORLDS

"Truly an amazing read! Great world-building and character interactions. I was able to relate to the female main character who inspired me to overcome challenges and face my own doubts and fears. Highly recommend!"

- Aubrey Joy Rosales (Jai Design)
Proofreader and Copyeditor

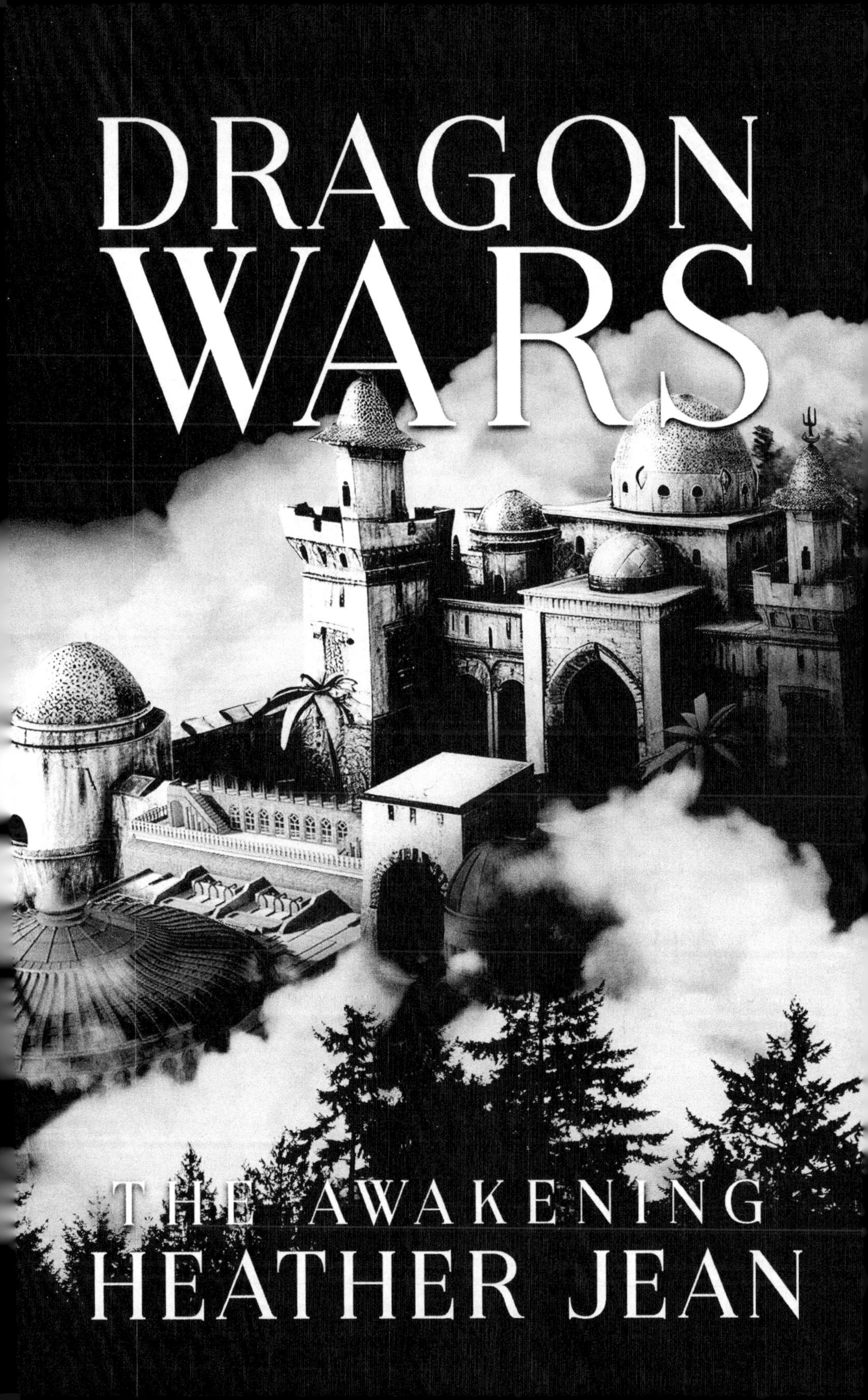
DRAGON
WARS
THE AWAKENING
HEATHER JEAN

N
W
E
S
Plateaus
Isis
Athena

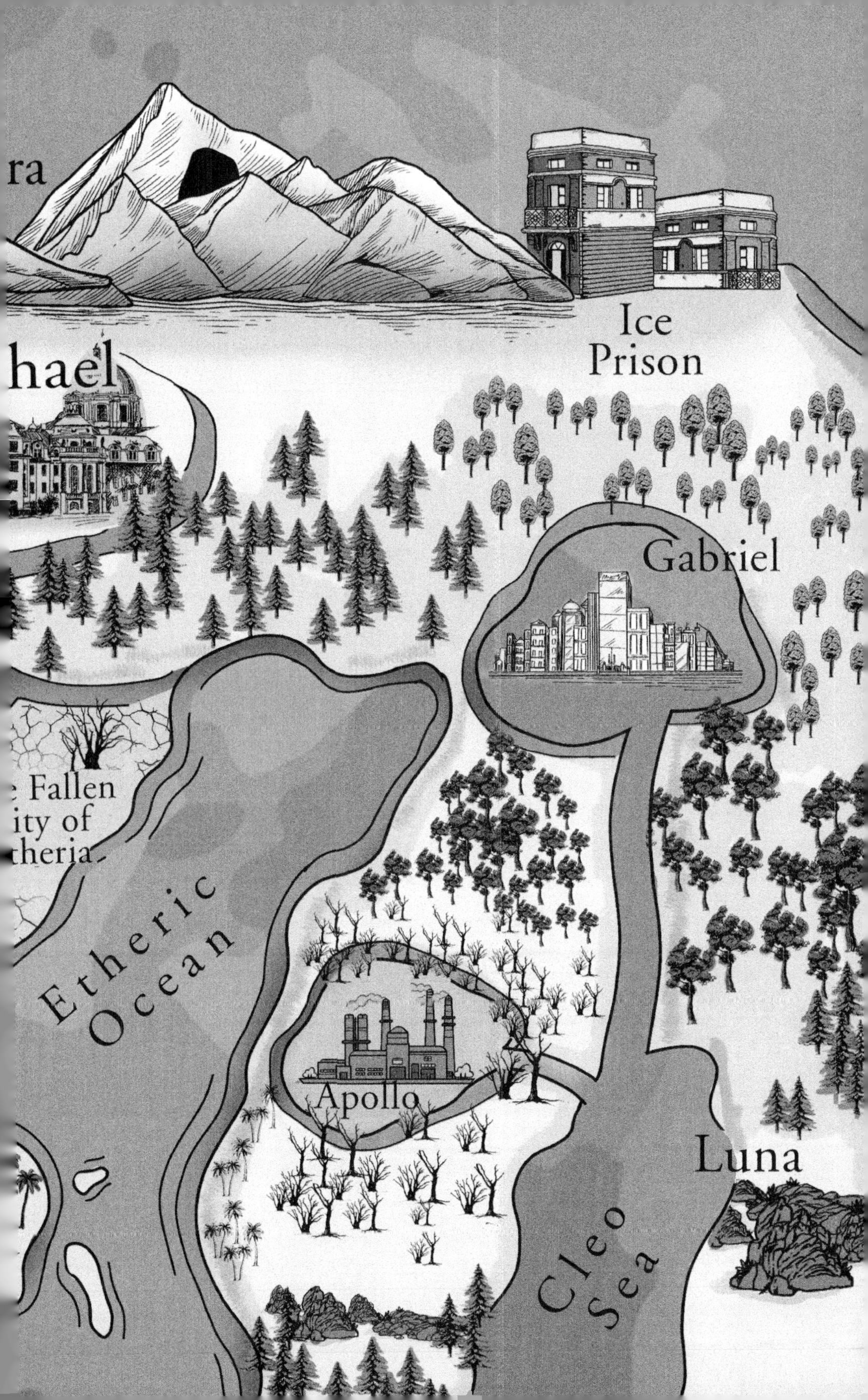
Ice
Prison
Gabriel
Fallen
Etheric
Ocean
Apollo
Luna
Cleo
Sea

CHAPTER ONE

Welcome to the Planet Anu

Dragons were peaceful and magnificent creatures, not the monsters you were told about in stories. They were the protectors of Gaia. One thousand years ago, dragons roamed freely, but humans were not afraid of them. Dragons and humans were friends. Thousands of dragons existed on the planet, but only four dragons chose to soul bond with humans. These dragons were known as the Spirit Dragons. Each dragon represented one of the four seasons: Spring, Summer, Autumn and Winter.

Kero Embers laid on a filthy mattress in her tiny bedroom, holding a picture book in front of her. The only light she had came from a lone candle that sat in a lantern on the floor next to her mattress. Gaia was the name of the planet in her story. She liked it a lot better than the name of the actual planet where she lived. The planet's name was Anu, a word that made little sense to her. Kero's eyes shifted to the next page where there was a colorful picture of a fiery red dragon with golden eyes. The dragon's eyes looked like golden flames. Under the picture was the caption, *The Crimson Dragon*. Out of the four dragons featured in the book, Kero liked this one the most because she and this dragon practically shared the same eye color. It was odd that Kero was the only one in her family with gold-tinted eyes. Her brother had light brown eyes just like their parents. Kero definitely had a distinct look as she shared the same bronze skin as many others in her colony, but stood out because of her bright copper red hair and golden eyes.

Kero paused from reading her book and crept over to the tiny window adjacent from her so-called bed. Drawing back the curtain, she took a quick glance outside. Everyone busied themselves with their morning chores. She should have been out there too, bailing hay. Kero decided not to join them yet and slunk back into the dark room. She returned to her book, continuing the story.

The Spirit Dragons, together with their soul bonded humans, also protected the gateway into the higher realm where all dragonkind dwelled. Many other mythical creatures like fairies and unicorns existed in the higher realm as well. Another race of dragons known as the Elder Dragons also protected the gateway from the other side. The Elder Dragons were seven of the wisest dragons to ever exist. They kept watch over the gateway in the higher realm, while the Spirit Dragons kept watch from Gaia. However, only the Spirit Dragons could open and close the gateway.

On the next page was a picture of a beautiful purple and blue dragon with sky blue eyes. She was known as the Crystal Dragon who breathed ice. Kero wondered why none of these dragons had names. When she was little, Kero imagined names for each dragon. This one she named Crystalina. Kind of dumb, but she was a child at the time.

Time was slipping by, but no one had come looking for her yet. Kero knew she would have to make an appearance down at the barn soon. She peered down at her book. She only had a few more pages to go.

The Elder Dragons were wise and saw a change in humanity. Humans had become more savage and began to destroy Gaia. The Elder Dragons decided to permanently close the gateway. The Spirit Dragons were sent to the four corners of the planet to slumber. Kero gazed over a picture that spread across two pages. It almost resembled Anu with the islands in the south, the desert in the west, the mountains in the north and the dense forests in the east.

It's been nearly a millennium since all of the dragons left Gaia and returned to their realm. It is said that the gateway to Gaia will open again when the four humans who originally bonded with the Spirit Dragons go on a sacred journey to awaken them. They will remember their past lives and reunite with their dragon. Once all four dragons awoken, they will open the gateway once again and Gaia will be restored.

Kero flipped to the next page to see the last two Spirit Dragons. On the left page was a picture of a dragon with golden scales and bronze-colored eyes with the caption, *The Golden Dragon.* The right page showed a vibrant green scaled dragon with eyes matching the same color as her scales. Under this picture was the title, *The Emerald Dragon.* Kero tried to remember what names she made up for them. Something like Goldie and Emmy–she wasn't sure. It sounded dumb now anyways. Thumbing back a few pages, Kero glanced over the picture of the Crimson Dragon again. She remembered the name she gave him. Phoenix. She couldn't explain why she came up with that name, but it always stuck with her.

Kero studied the front cover for a moment. Her eyes gazed at the ball of light in the middle with purple and red hues in the background. The words of the title read, 'The Spirit Dragons,' in big bold golden letters. The name of the author wasn't printed anywhere, which she always found odd.

Kero placed the book in her usual hiding spot, under the loose floorboard that was always covered up by her mattress. No one ever found it there. There were times the Patrol came to various homes to do an inspection, but there was only one time they chose the house where she and her brother lived. One officer came into her room and looked around, but never moved her mattress so her book was safe. It scared her too much to think what they would do her book if they found it. They'd probably burn it right in front of her, then punish her for breaking one of Anu's cardinal laws: *Reading a book not approved by the Empress.* In fact, they'd be surprised that Kero could read at all. They may kill her for that alone. Only scientists and medical professionals were allowed to read.

Kero took a deep breath before leaving her room. Across the hall was her brother, Darion's room. He was always up before her, helping down at the corn fields. Her eyes wavered towards the end of the hallway where her parents once slept. Neither she nor her brother bothered to go into that room since their parents died. Kero hurried down the stairs and into the kitchen where a few pieces of bread sat on a plate. Darion must have left those for her. By now, the bread was cold. Kero stuffed the pieces in her mouth anyways before heading outside.

Just as Kero exited the house, someone tapped her on the shoulder. She jumped a mile high as she spun around to face the colony's speaker, Arthur Daniels.

"Oh–uh, hi Mr. Daniels," she greeted nervously.

"Oh hi, yourself," he returned mockingly. Why aren't you at your station?"

"I was on my way. I just-uh-had to clean my room." Mr. Daniels knit his eyebrows. Kero knew he wasn't buying it. "Sorry. I woke up late." It was still a lie, but it was better for her to tell him that she overslept. There's no way she could tell him what she was really doing.

"Okay, don't worry about it. Just get out there. The Patrol will be here any minute now. Don't forget, it's Harvest Day." Mr. Daniels said.

There's no way she nor anyone else in their colony could forget Harvest Day. It was the day when the Patrol visited to inspect everything as well as take a large portion of crops and livestock and distribute it among the other colonies. Kero supposed it was fair for everyone on the planet to be fed, but the Patrol was greedy. They often took so much that her colony barely had enough food left over for themselves.

"I'm sorry–"

"Just get to yer station! Hurry!" Mr. Daniels yelled. Kero hurried off towards the barn.

While Kero ran off to do chores, her brother, Darion Embers was deep in the woods, north of the farm. The young man sat high in a tree waiting with his bow and arrow. A mild wind blew his dark curly hair into his face. Patience paid off as he finally saw a buck, large enough to feed the entire village. Taking the arrow between his fingers, Darion drew back the bow, waited a minute and let it go. The arrow whizzed through the air and struck the deer in its lung. The animal took off, sprinting through the trees.

Darion climbed down from his hunting spot and immediately scouted for the blood trail. He ran through the trees, keeping his eyes on the trail. He walked between two cottonwood trees and found the deer lying on the ground exhausted. Darion drew back another arrow, and released it. The tip of the arrow pierced through the buck's head.

Kero made it to her station at the barn. As she walked into the barn, Tyrian, one of the stable managers approached her.

"Look who decided to show up. Let me guess, you slept in? No, no, wait, I got it. You forgot which station you were at today." Kero turned to the tall, scrawny teenage boy. He was eighteen, only a year older than her, but he had the authority to have her whipped if he wanted. "Well, what do you have to say for yourself?"

Kero didn't have anything to say, well, nothing that wouldn't get her into a bunch of trouble. This guy acted like her father, but not quite. To say, he acted as her father would be an insult to her actual father.

"I'm sorry I'm late. I'll get the job done. I can get all the hay into the wagon by the time lunch is served."

"Excuse me?" he said, with a laugh. "Ya think yer gettin' lunch? No, no, no. Yer late. Yer workin' til sundown."

"I have to eat!" Kero yelled, half panicked.

"I don't like yer tone," Tyrian chastised.

"Ya can't just not let me eat," Kero spoke a little calmer.

"Now yer arguing with me?" he asked, outraged. "Oh, that's fine Karel. I'll just hand you over to the Patrol when they get here. I'm sure they'll be glad to take care of any dead weight not earning their keep." Kero decided to rope it in. It angered her that this guy was one of the managers anyways. He just got this position a week ago and now he acted like he owned the whole farm. Not only that, but he mispronounced her name again.

"My name is Kero," she said, trying to keep her voice calm.

"What?" Tyrian asked crossly.

"You said my name wrong." The tall, lanky young man stepped towards Kero, pointing an accusing finger at her.

"How does a nobody like you get such a big head? Ya think anyone cares who you are?" he sneered. "Yer a dumb farmgirl. Yer no different from any of them." he pointed at the other kids busy working in the barn. "All of ya are dumb farm kids who will never do anything important. Until ya earn the right to be a manager, just shut yer mouth and do yer job!" He thrusted a pitchfork into her hands. Kero almost punched him, but decided it would be a terrible idea. Instead, she stormed over to a pile of hay and aggressively stabbed the straw pile and tossed it into the wagon next to her.

After three hours of sweating profusely, Kero threw the last of the hay into the wagon. It was lunch time. Many other workers were tossing down their pitchforks and heading out of the barn. Her eyes caught Tyrian at the barn entrance. He told her that she wasn't getting lunch. Kero sighed, wiping her brow. Tyrian was yelling at some other kids just outside the barn doors. All that guy did was yell all day. She didn't care what he said earlier. She was going to get some food.

After placing the pitchfork against the wall, she climbed the ladder into the hayloft. Quickly, she crawled over to the window. The rope the younger kids tied up was still there. They loved swinging on the rope for fun, but right now, Kero could use it to escape. She shimmied down the rope until she reached the safety of the ground. As she ran towards the house, she noticed a Watcher close by. She quickly dodged the flying robot by disappearing into the cornfield. Each Watcher was programmed to float in a particular pattern. The spy robot recorded everything on the farm, so she had to be careful not to be spotted.

Kero emerged from the cornfield and dashed towards her house. As she approached, she noticed Darion was holding part of a large animal. She caught up with her brother as he began hanging the animal in the shed.

"What cha doing?" she asked. Darion spun around, his mouth fell open. Then, when he realized who disturbed him, his gaze softened.

"Just storing our dinner safely away," he said proudly.

"Our dinner?" she asked. He bent down to whisper in her ear. "I caught a deer."

"A deer?" Kero repeated with excitement. Darion hushed her.

"Yes, in the woods. No one saw me, so we're good."

"As far as you know. How exactly did you leave your post without anyone knowin'?"

"I didn't even go to my post," Darion replied. "I got up before anyone else and just headed towards the woods."

"Won't you get into trouble?"

Darion laughed. "No one cares." He lowered his voice, "They all know what I do. And you know why I do it, right?"

Kero nodded. She knew he did it for the people in this farm. Food was scarce. A deer meant meat for weeks.

"Yep. Everyone will bow down to your greatness," Kero smirked. "Maybe we should build a statue in your honor."

"Stop being a smartass," Darion haughtily replied.

Darion locked up the shed. "We're eatin' good tonight!"

He was certainly in a good mood. However, that changed as Mr. Daniels walked their way.

"They'll be here any minute," he announced. "We need to get everyone gathered by the mill." Mr. Daniels ran off before Darion could respond.

"Who's he talkin' about?" Darion asked.

"It's Harvest Day," Kero practically screeched.

Darion's mouth went dry and his eyes turned weary. He shook his head.

"I forgot!" He silently reprimanded himself for this grave mistake. The Patrol officers would definitely find the deer when they opened the shed.

Darion unlocked the door, and quickly unhooked the door from the ceiling. He began dragging it behind him.

"Where ya goin?" Kero called after him.

"I gotta hide this. I'll be right back."

While Darion hauled the animal towards the woods, Kero hurried towards the mill to join the other villagers. Looks like lunch would have to wait.

Everyone stood around in a cluttered mess. Mr. Daniels did his best to organize everyone, so the colony looked more presentable. Kero stood, nervously pulling on her fingers and tapping her foot. After a few moments, Mr. Daniels approached her.

"Where's Darion?"

Kero was at a loss for words. She just stared at the large

man. He shook his head. "I don't have time for this! Where is—" Before he could finish his sentence, he saw Darion running to join everyone.

"I'm here," he announced. Mr. Daniels nodded to him. He began counting heads. "--thirty-one, thirty-two, and myself is thirty-three. Good. We're all here."

Everyone turned their eyes towards the sky to see a large airship approaching the farm. The ship landed and the gangplank lowered down to the ground. Five Patrol officers in plated armor walked down in a straight line. Behind the officers came a squad of Watchers, their one mechanical eye began recording everything.

Four officers began searching the entire farm, walking into various homes, and sheds. One of the sheds was where Darion had originally hung his deer.

"Good day to ya sir," Mr. Daniels greeted the head of the Patrol.

"Good day," the man's voice echoed from behind his helmet. Kero turned her eyes away from the officer. She hated the horned helmets the Patrol officers wore. They wore full black helmets to match the black armor suits covering their bodies. No one knew any facial features or any other appearances of these men. The head officer began his speech to the colony.

"Greetings, people of the colony Athena. Your Empress has a few requests before the usual harvest." A Watcher floated above the people, displaying an image of Empress Celise. The woman stood tall, wearing her traditional white robe and dawning her golden horned mask. Everyone in the colony immediately bowed on one knee, some bowed on both knees. Kero hated this part most of all. When she was younger, she refused to bow. It didn't go well. Her parents begged her to bow, but when she didn't, an officer struck her. Kero grinded her teeth as she went down on her right knee.

"Greetings my loyal subjects, I wish to extend my thanks for all of the hard work you do." Kero rolled her eyes. "Having said that, there will be a few changes. First, instead of twelve barrels of crops, it will be sixteen."

Some murmurs rose from the villagers.

"Quiet!" the head Patrol officer growled. Everyone went silent.

"Second, I require you to give me more of your livestock. At least two animals instead of one. Please understand that the population of our world is growing and this food will feed many hungry people. Thank you for understanding."

As the Empress finished her speech, the Patrol began to chant.

"We give thanks to our Empress, the one who projects us!"

Now everyone joined in. "Thanks be to her."

Kero didn't say a word, but no one seemed to notice.

The image of the Empress disappeared and the Watcher continued surveying the area. The Patrol officers, who were done with inspection, began transporting the barrels of crops onto the airship.

"Uh, we also have a few lambs for you too," Mr. Daniels said to the head officer. "They were just born a few months ago." An older couple stepped forward, herding the lambs towards the ship.

"We raised them ourselves," the old man's voice quivered.

The officer barely acknowledged him. One of his men harshly grabbed the collars of the lambs, one in each hand, before dragging them to the ship.

"Hurry up!" the head officer yelled to his men. "We have to get through the whole Southern Region by the end of the day! The Salamand Islands are in for some storms and I don't want to deal with the harsh weather!" The officers quickened their pace.

Kero noticed how tense Mr. Daniels was, which was understandable. This was the most stressful day of the year. She hoped they would just load everything and leave, but now the head officer approached Mr. Daniels.

"Excuse me good sir, how long have you been the speaker of your village?"

"Uh-about ten years sir. I took over after my father passed away–"

"Then, you realize that you are short of the required crops."

Mr. Daniel widened his eyes. "Oh, uh–sir, we weren't aware of the Empress' changes to the amount of crops."

"Are you telling me that those barrels are the only crops you have?"

"Well no, but the rest of the crops need to be kept here to feed our colony."

"We all have to make sacrifices. We'll need four more barrels," he spoke without missing a beat. "Also, we require two more animals. Those cows in the pen will do."

"The Empress said just two animals, sir," Mr. Daniels barely spoke above a whisper.

"Those lambs you gave us barely have any meat on them," the Patrol officer argued.

"But we need those cows for our milk, sir."

"Milk is not a required source of food," the officer replied.

"We have infants and children here, sir." Mr. Daniels pointed out.

"Fine. We'll just take one, but we'll have to compensate with two more barrels of crops, so we'll need six more barrels." He nodded to the officers and they opened the doors into the mill and started taking more barrels of crops.

"Mr. Daniels, they can't take all of those!" a man complained. "We won't have enough food to get through the year!" Conflict filled the man's eyes as he contemplated how he could convince the Patrol officers not to take any more of their food supply.

"Sir, could you maybe take sixteen barrels and we'll provide you with more crops next time? I'm concerned we won't have enough food if you take all of those barrels.

"Your concerns are not my problem," the head officer answered with indifference.

As the officers finished loading the crops onto the airship, the head officer bid them farewell.

"Thank you for your patronage," he said before leaving the crowd of now very distraught villagers.

Darion began breathing easier after they left. They didn't find the deer, now he could go retrieve it from his hiding spot in the woods. He just hoped nothing bothered the animal's corpse. He rushed off just as the villagers began yelling at Mr. Daniels.

Poor guy. Darion thought to himself. It wasn't his fault that the Empire took so much of the colony's food supply. The Empire was greedy. He highly doubted that all of that food was going somewhere to feed hungry people.

Kero watched as her brother headed towards the northern

woods. Darion was going to get that deer, she realized. Kero hurried back to the angry mob crowding around Mr. Daniels. She pushed her way in between him and the rest of the villagers.

"Stop! It's not Mr. Daniel's fault!" Kero cried out. The people stopped and stared at her. "Listen, my brother went hunting this morning. He caught a deer! We'll have plenty of food."

Mutters rose from the people and they began to relax. Mr. Daniel's glance went to Kero.

"Thank you," he said genuinely.

"No problem," Kero said. "Hopefully, it won't take Darion long to find the deer he hid."

Minutes later, Kero spotted her brother heading towards their house, pulling the deer behind him. Her eyes widened as she saw the huge animal and Mr. Daniels joined her.

"That's bigger than the last one you got," he exclaimed. "Kinda risky of you to go huntin' on Harvest Day, but I'm glad ya did."

Darion kept his mouth shut about forgetting it was Harvest Day when he went out hunting earlier. He dragged the animal towards the shed and hung it up inside as he had done before.

"There, now nothing will disturb my game," he said. Then, he turned to Kero.

"Thanks for helping me out today," he said.

Kero was taken aback by the compliment.

"What did I do?"

"For one, you kept quiet about the deer and kept it together during inspection. Two, you let me know that it was Harvest Day in the first place."

Mr. Daniels shook his head. "Still don't know how you

forgot." He took off his straw hat and wiped his forehead. "Yep, it was a rough Harvest Day this year." He strolled towards the barn. "I'm gonna make sure the rest of the crops are okay."

"That guy needs a break," Darion commented. He opened the front door of their house and went inside. Kero looked around the farm. Everyone needed a break, she realized. No, more than just a break; they needed another way of life.

Later that night, Kero laid on the mattress in her room, reading her book. She hadn't taken off her boots yet, so she just hung her feet off the edge of the mattress. The taste of deer meat still lingered in her mouth. She was actually full for a change, and they still had meat left over.

Kero was about to put her book back in its safe spot when the door downstairs flung open. Heavy footsteps stomped up the wooden staircase. Kero didn't have time to move the mattress to get to the floor board. She quickly shoved the thin book under the mattress.

Two Patrol officers barged into Kero's room and pulled her up to her feet. "What are you doin?" she screamed.

They dragged her down the stairs and through the front door of the farmhouse. Darion stood with his hand cuffed behind his back. A Patrol officer held his bow in front of him.

"You know hunting is forbidden!" He placed both hands on the bow, bending it down over his knee until it broke in half.

"That was my father's!" Darion yelled. The officer punched Darion in the face, leaving a bruise on his cheek. "You're coming with us!"

No!" Kero screamed. "You can't take him!" Darion watched his sister try to fight off the soldier who held her captive.

"Kero! Stop!" Darion yelled. The officer shoved Kero onto the ground and held her down. "Please, let her go," Darion begged. "She has nothing to do with this. I'm the one who chose to go hunting."

Even on the ground, Kero kept trying to fight, kicking her legs and trying to get off the ground.

"All the Empire does is take and take! I'm sick of it! The Empire killed our parents and they did nothing wrong!" Now Kero's rage began to change into tears.

The officer who held onto Darion ignored Kero and proceeded to put him in a small carrier airship. Kero cried out in mental anguish. Suddenly, she bit the hand of the Patrol officer. He cried out, then delivered a blow to the back of her head. Everything went black, but that wouldn't be the worst of it. Getting arrested was the worst thing that could happen to a person on Anu. They would be better off dead.

CHAPTER TWO

Tale of the Spirit Dragons

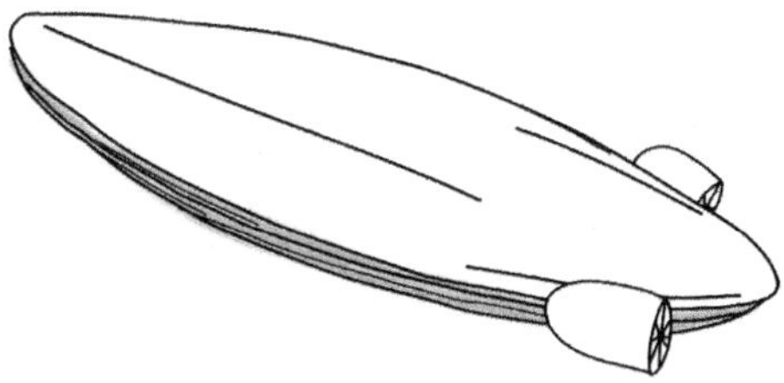

Kero slowly opened her eyes. She felt the surface under her vibrate. As she pushed herself to her knees, her eyes adjusted to the dim lighting.

Where am I? she wondered. Something in front of her came into focus. She was behind metal bars. They were all around her. The realization came to her that she was in a cage. Her mouth felt so dry that she couldn't speak. She could barely swallow. She needed water.

While she sat helplessly in this cage, half terrified and half confused, something outside the cage moved towards her. A light flickered on and Kero saw the face of a young woman with light blonde hair.

"Don't worry," she whispered. "I'll get ya outta there." Kero tried to speak, but she couldn't. She nodded instead. The blonde-haired girl took a pick from her shirt pocket and began twisting it around in the cage lock. In the next moment, she heard a click. She removed the lock and opened the cage door.

"Come on," the blonde said in a hushed voice. Kero followed. "Don't worry, I'm getting us out of here." Kero wondered how she was going to do that exactly. Kero still felt parched. She almost asked the girl for water, but she most likely didn't have any.

Suddenly, the young woman turned around "I'm Blythe, by the way"

"I'm Ker–" Kero tried to reply. She found herself in a fit of coughing. The girl took a flask from her belt and handed it to Kero. Slowly Kero opened the top of the flask and took a sip. Refreshing water poured down her throat. It wasn't really cold, but not too warm either. It tasted wonderful.

"Thank you," Kero said. Other than her brother, this girl was the nicest person she's talked to in a while.

Blythe led Kero to a strange oval door. When she saw the door, Kero understood why the floor vibrated. They were on an airship. Well, of course they were. She must have been taken by the Patrol and now she was on an airship heading towards the capital of Anu, the city of Michael. Suddenly, the memories of what happened back on the farm raced through her mind. Darion…they took him too.

"I have to find my brother!" Kero shrieked in panic. The girl put a finger to her lips.

"Shhh! The soldiers will hear you." Her face relaxed as she

addressed the more tender issue. "I'm sorry, but I haven't seen him. I only found you." Kero's heart sank.

From the door on the other side of the room, they heard someone with a strong male voice.

"Go check on the newcomers! I hear one of them has a mouth on her. Don't take any back talk from those lowlifes."

"We have to go," Blythe said strongly. She lifted the hatch and opened the door of the airship. Sunlight burst into the dark cabin. Gales of wind blew fiercely, almost pushing Kero off balance.

In the bright light of day, Kero could clearly see the girl next to her. Blythe stood a few inches taller than Kero, her long braids of her light blonde hair blew in the wind. Her outfit consisted of a violet sleeveless shirt with light blue trim, accompanied by indigo colored pants and black boots. Kero gazed downward with wide eyes. Was this girl planning on jumping out of the aircraft?

"Uh, what are you doing?" Kero asked nervously.

Blythe took a small metallic cube from the pouch around her waist. After pushing a small button on top of the cube, it transformed into a long, white board. Bythe stood on top of the board. Her feet locked into place like a magnet.

"We're using this airglider to escape. Get on," she instructed.

Kero shook her head. "There's no way I'm ridin' on that thing."

Suddenly, the door on the other side of the cabin slid open and two men in uniform walked into the room.

"Let's check on the prisoners," one of them said, brandishing a long metal pole. Electrical sparks emanated from the tip of the weapon.

Blythe tried to coax Kero into getting onto the airglider.

"Come on! You'll be fine. I promise."

Kero finally got enough nerve to step onto the strange metal board. When she did, her legs locked into place on the board. Kero didn't have a moment to complain as the board took off.

"Hey! Get back here!" They heard an officer yell at them. As the office approached, he got blown back by the exhaust coming from the pipe on the back of the board.

The girls were in the air now. Blythe seemed to know what she was doing, as she swiftly moved her body left and right to steer the board through the sky. Kero forced herself to look down to see only water underneath them.

"Where are we?" Kero yelled.

"I think we're over the Etheric Ocean," Blythe replied. The airglider rode over the giant ocean waves.

Up ahead, Kero thought she spotted some trees. Blythe saw them too.

"Oh good, we're approaching land," she said jovially. Kero noticed that they were heading towards the shoreline pretty fast.

"Uh, maybe you should slow down," Kero suggested.

Blythe was about to respond when a blast of energy hit the back of the board, causing it to flip upside down. Kero screamed and was prepared to plunge into the water below. However, her feet stayed attached to the glider. Blythe shifted her weight and turned the board upright. She twisted her head around to see a Patrol officer wearing a jetpack chasing them.

"Hang on!" Blythe yelled. "I'm goin' through the trees!" She shifted her body, maneuvering the vehicle around the tree trunks. Kero gripped onto this girl she barely knew, silently praying that they wouldn't crash. The officer was on their tail, firing more laser beams at them. The energy blast grazed the board, but Blythe moved out of the way and ducked under a tree branch. She turned her head around to see the officer catching up to them. He fired another shot, this one hit Blythe in her shoulder. She cried out, and lost her concentration. The airglider swerved and crashed into the river below. The magnetic pull of the board was broken, causing both girls to fall into the water. As Kero fell into the shallow water, her head fell back, hitting the rocky bottom of the river. Blythe fell onto her back and couldn't move for a moment. The Patrol officer took advantage, flying at full speed towards the girls. As he approached, his body was suddenly held back by an invisible force. His body hung in midair for a second before being flung into a nearby tree. The officer hit the ground. He didn't move.

Blythe slowly rolled over and pulled herself out of the water. Her gaze trailed over to a beautiful white mare with a silvery horn on her forehead. Blythe's eyes moved up the person riding the mare, a woman with long dark hair. She was just as lovely as the mare. Her hair was decorated with flowers and twine and she wore a stunning green gown. The woman hopped off the mare and raced over to where Kero lay. She gently moved Kero's head upright. Blythe exclaimed in alarm when she saw a large gash on the girl's forehead.

"Don't worry. She will be fine," the woman in green said. Reaching into her pouch, the woman pulled out a quartz crystal and an amethyst. Holding the crystals over the wound, the woman began to chant in a foreign language. The woman continued her strange prayer, placing the crystals on Kero's heart, then moved them over her wound.

After a few moments, Kero groaned and slowly opened her eyes. They focused on the face of the woman who just saved her. Kero quickly sat up, but almost fell backwards again from sudden dizziness.

"Easy. I'm A'keara. Are you alright?" she asked.

Kero realized she was sitting in the river. She quickly stood, then sloshed her way over to the river bank, stepping up into the long blades of grass. Her clothing was soaking wet and stuck to her body. She also noticed a drop in temperature. It was much cooler here than in Athena.

A'keara noticed the gash on Blythe's shoulder.

"Here, let me take care of your injury," she said. Blythe studied her shoulder. A'keara held the two crystals over Blythe's wound. She watched in amazement as the deep cut began to close up, becoming smaller until her skin was fully healed.

"How did you do that?" Blythe asked in awe. A'keara held the quartz crystal and amethyst in the palm of her hand.

"I used these crystals to heal," she answered simply. Blythe looked over at the four-legged creature beside the woman.

"That's an interesting uh–horned horse you've got."

"Aurora is a unicorn," A'keara curtly replied. "You've never seen a unicorn before?"

Kero and Blythe exchanged confused glances.

"So, all unicorns can make people float in the air and slam them into trees?" Kero asked.

A'keara chuckled a little. "Aurora used her telekinesis to stop that imperial soldier." She mounted the unicorn. "We should get away from this area."

Kero had no idea what telekinesis was. She was about to ask when something else caught her attention. Kero realized that the mare didn't have a saddle or reins.

"Yer ridin' without a saddle?" Kero asked. "Aren't ya afraid, she'll run off on ya?"

A'keara replied with a peculiar stare. "Aurora is my companion. I use my words to communicate with her." A'keara bent down to speak softly to the animal. "Let's go back home," Aurora began to move forward, happily swishing her tail. "Follow me," she said to the two girls.

"Do you live out here?" Blythe asked.

"Sort of. You'll see."

Kero and Blythe followed the woman through thick grass and patches of dirt as they ventured through the woods. A'keara helped Aurora move around some thorn bushes.

"We need to watch out for those," she said.

Kero stared ahead through the trees. A large cave came into view.

"That's home right up ahead," A'keara told them.

"You live in a cave?" Kero asked, raising an eyebrow. A'keara nodded.

As Aurora moved through the mouth of the cave, her horn lit up. Both Kero and Blythe stared in wonder at the magnificent creature.

"I wish the horses on the farm could do that," Kero said.

"It would be useful if you had to work underground too," Blythe added. She noticed tiny blue lights on the walls of the cave. "What are those?"

"Light crystals," A'keara replied.

"What an appropriate name," Blythe noted.

"So, you have a bunch of crystals and your horse is a lantern," Kero said dryly.

"Unicorn," A'keara corrected. "Yes, we depend on natural resources."

The cave grew wider and the girls saw a modest size fire. Behind the fire was an elderly woman sitting on a rug with a colorful pattern. By the right wall of the cave was a cart containing four barrels and a few clay pots.

A'keara dismounted Aurora and carried a small pouch over to the other woman.

"I got some berries and nuts," she said. "However, I didn't get the opportunity to fish. I got a little distracted." She turned to the newcomers.

"You brought some friends," the elderly woman chirped.

"Grandmother, this is Kero and Blythe. They were being chased by an imperial soldier. They were riding on some type of flying board–"

"It was an airglider," Blythe said.

"Right," A'keara agreed. "But, they fell off of it and Kero hit her head."

The old woman studied Kero for a moment, which made the teenage girl feel awkward.

"You must have healed her. She looks fine."

"Of course I healed her," A'keara abruptly replied.

The elderly woman stood. "My name is Aponi. I am one of the priestesses from Etheria."

Kero narrowed her eyes. "From where?" Aponi widened her stare and she and A'keara quickly exchanged concerned glances.

"I know it hasn't been that long since the attack on our city. How do you not know about the heart of Gaia?"

"I have no idea what yer talkin' about," Kero replied.

"Yeah, I've never heard of that place either," Blythe added. "And I travel everywhere on Anu."

"Anu," Aponi repeated. "That is what this planet is called now. It used to be called Gaia." She reached out and touched Kero's forehead. Kero quickly squirmed away.

"What are ya doin'?"

Aponi lowered her hand. "It's so strange to me when I feel someone's energy and they become afraid. I suppose I shouldn't pry into your personal matters."

"Of course not!" Kero replied crossly. "Do you just go around touchin' people?"

"Back when we lived in Etheria, everyone felt each other's energy," A'keara explained.

Kero narrowed her eyes. "Why?"

"Because, everyone knew each other. We were all friends."

"More like family," Aponi corrected.

Kero shook her head. "Sorry, but I don't understand."

Aponi's eyes saddened. "Maybe you will understand us in time."

In time? Kero wasn't planning on sticking around for too long. She had to find Darion. She had no idea of how she was going to get to Michael or even if she should try. She couldn't go back to Athena either. Would these two ladies turn her in if they found out that she was wanted by the Empire?

"So, why do you two live in a cave? Shouldn't you be part of a colony?"

"Colony?" A'keara snorted. "We won't be a part of the world that destroyed Etheria or Gaia."

"What do you mean?" Blythe asked.

A'keara turned a cautious eye to Aponi. "They have no idea what happened to Gaia," she whispered.

"I realize that," Aponi replied. She returned her attention to the two young girls. "If you need a place to stay, you are welcome here."

Kero suddenly became fearful. These two women lived out in the wilderness and didn't belong to a colony. They had to be exiles.

"Sorry, but I don't know ya," Kero said frankly. "I mean, thank you for saving me, but I–" Kero turned to Blythe, another stranger who also saved her life. How come people she barely knew were being so nice to her? Then, it occurred to her.

"Listen, I don't have any gold or nothin' I'm a poor farm girl."

"We would never ask you to give us anything," Aponi said. "However, it will be nighttime soon and trust me, you don't want to be wandering the forest at night." Kero realized she didn't have anywhere else to go. She could stay for one night, she supposed. However, she decided not to say anything about the Patrol arresting her or Darion. Even as exiles, these two women couldn't be trusted. There was no doubt a bounty on Kero's head and these women would probably love to get any money they could for her. Kero finally replied to the old woman.

"Alright. I guess I'll stay here," she said reluctantly.

Aponi turned to Blythe. "What about you?"

"I'll stay, if you'll have me," she said jovially. "But in the morning, I need to leave for Isis."

Kero returned a weary glance. "Why are you going to Isis?" Blythe tried to avoid Kero's gaze.

"Oh, I'm just meeting my friend."

"You know someone in Isis? You don't seem like the type to hang around thieves and slave owners."

"First of all, not everyone in Isis is like that," Blythe said, becoming defensive. "Second, my friend is a person of action. He single-handedly influenced many people around Anu to become part of his resistance group."

"Resistance group? I've never heard of somethin' like that," Kero admitted.

"Well its–"

Before Blythe could further explain, Kero screeched as something touched her shoulder. The girl spun around to see A'keara slowly pulling her hand away.

"I'm sorry. I didn't mean to startle you." Kero still breathed heavily. What is with these women and touching people? "It's getting late. You should probably rest. I prepared a place for you to sleep."

Kero looked over at the fire where four blue mattresses were placed in a row. Kero recognized them as bedrolls, something very easy to roll up and transport with you. Darion had a bedroll for a while. He used it to go hunting with their dad back when hunting was legal. She became sad when she thought of her brother.

"Where did you find these?" she asked, referring to the bedrolls. "They look really nice, almost brand new."

"We found them in the desert believe it or not," A'keara said. "We've found a lot of items just lying around in random places. We even found our cart there too."

"Yeah, I believe it," Blythe replied.

Kero squinted her eyes. "Really?"

"Oh yeah, there's a bunch of junk in the desert. I've seen parts of airships and other vehicles the imperial army once used."

"How wasteful," A'keara said with disdain.

Kero made her way over to the soft mattress. She welcomed the soft cotton as well as the firmness of the material supporting her body. She was so used to a broken down, dirty mattress that right now, she felt like royalty. It wasn't long before fatigue took over and Kero was fast asleep.

Several hours later, Kero awoke. For a moment, she wondered where she was. Anxiety took over and she quickly sat up. Her eyes desperately searched the area. Shadows danced on the cave walls. Her gaze went to the fire that created them. Kero also realized there was a thick blanket covering her body. She calmed down as the memories of the previous day came to her.

Blythe laid on another bedroll a few feet away. They were the only two in the cave. The other women were gone. Kero stood, then walked towards the mouth of the cave. The crystals on the cavern wall twinkled, lighting her way. They appeared magical. Kero hadn't believed in magic since she was a child.

The moon gave enough light for Kero to see two silhouettes standing outside. Kero stayed just inside the cave where she could still hear the conversation.

"So, you believe those girls can handle the power of the Spirit Dragons?" Kero recognized the voice belonging to A'keara.

"I won't be certain until I put both of them into a meditative state. If they see one of the four dragons, then it is certain that they were once bonded to that dragon in a past life." The other voice belonged to the older lady, Aponi. It was an odd time to be having a discussion out in the woods. What were they even talking about?

"Well, Blythe is pretty friendly and easy to talk to, so you might talk her into doing the meditation. However, Kero doesn't seem to trust us at all. Not that I blame her. She just met us."

"Yes, but it bothers me that many we meet are weary of us. They don't use their intuition to feel our energy," Aponi said sadly. "Well, let's give the girls some time to get used to us."

"We don't have much time," A'keara argued. "You said all four dragons need to be awakened by the next Violet Energy Moon, which is happening next week."

"A'keara, you must have faith." Aponi tried using encouraging words, but it just wasn't enough to A'keara.

"I just don't think you are being realistic," A'keara countered.

"Some people think too much," Aponi returned curtly. "A'keara, these girls didn't just show up for no reason. Yesterday, we didn't even know where we were going to find two other people. Now look! Believe me, everything will fall into place. Let our ancestors guide our path."

Kero felt her stomach tighten into a knot. Those two

women did have something planned for her. She had no idea what a 'meditation' was, but there was no way she was doing it. And what was all that nonsense about seeing dragons? Kero wished dragons were real, but they weren't. They were only in stories told mouth to mouth. Most stories about dragons made the creatures sound like monsters that just destroyed everything and ate people. The only story she knew that had nice dragons in it, was from the book she owned.

As Kero thought about her book, a feeling of terror rose from inside of her. She was reading her book when the Patrol burst into the farmhouse. She didn't have time to put the book under the floorboard. All an officer had to do was move the mattress and they'd find the book. If they found it, they'd definitely burn it.

The conversation outside continued, bringing Kero's mind back to the present.

"I'm also worried about you," A'keara said to her grandmother. "You're not as young as you once were. All of this traveling around the planet might be too much for you."

"I'm fine," Aponi insisted. "We have to do this, A'keara. Everyone we knew in Etheria is gone. We are the only two left who can bring Gaia back to her rightful form."

"I know," A'keara said in a small whisper. "I know."

Kero slipped further back into the cave. She wanted to ask questions, but also didn't want the women to know she was eavesdropping into their conversation. She heard them say the word 'Gaia.' She heard both of those women say that word before. In Kero's book, Gaia was the planet the dragons protected. It was completely asinine to believe that a silly children's book held any merit, but now Kero began to wonder.

As she turned around, she practically bumped into Blythe. Kero shuffled back a little, startled.

"Sorry, didn't mean to scare ya," Blythe said in a chipper tone. She looked past Kero to see Aponi and A'keara.

"Wonder what they're talkin' about."

Kero shrugged. "I have no idea." She continued walking towards the back of the cave.

Once Kero reached her borrowed bedroll by the fire, she laid down and pretended to sleep. A few moments later, she felt someone gently touch her shoulder. Even though she expected it, her body still winced. Kero sat up to see A'keara kneeling next to her.

"I'm sorry to wake you dear," she said kindly. "Iwondered if we could talk to you for a moment."

"Uh, sure," Kero responded.

A'keara turned to Blythe. "You too."

Blythe's mouth curved up to a smile. "Okay."

Aponi sat on the colorful rug and gestured for the others to join her.

"Please remove your boots before sitting on my rug," she said kindly.

A'keara sat next to her. Kero removed her boots before touching the soft material with her bare foot. She sat crossed legged across from the elderly lady. Blythe sat across from A'keara.

"So, you two found out that unicorns exist," Aponi said plainly. "What if I told you that dragons exist too?"

"Hey, if you could show me a dragon, that would be impressive," Blythe said. Aponi glanced at Kero.

"What about you?"

Kero already thought these two women were crazy.

"How would I know?" she asked. "I've never seen a real dragon before."

"Are dragons frightening to you?" Aponi asked further.

Kero shook her head. "Not really."

"What if I told you they were as real as Aurora?"

Neither Kero nor Blythe spoke. Aponi continued.

"In my youth, I wrote a story about dragons. I was only in my twenties, but I knew I had to write this book," she explained. "The story revolves around four dragons, one who breathes fire, one who breathes ice, another who breathes wind and the last one who breathes lightning. Each dragon represents a season. Fire is summer, ice is winter, wind is autumn and lightning is spring."

Kero knew of only onc book that was about four dragons like the ones the old lady described.

"Is your book called, 'The Spirit Dragons?'" Kero asked cautiously. Aponi's mouth curved up to a shining smile. "You've read my book?"

"Yes, many times. My mother always read to me when I was a child," Kero explained. "Is there only one copy?"

"Yes. Everyone read books in the Etherian Library. All books had to stay in the library." Aponi leaned forward. "It's amazing that you found my book."

"How did you get her book?" A'keara asked.

"My grandmother found it. My mom told me that back in my grandmother's time, the colonies didn't have walls. She and my grandfather traveled north. They made their way to the center of the planet, but the Empire was there and they told my grandparents to turn back. Before they left, however, my grandmother found the book. She gave the book to my mother and my mother gave it to me. We never knew who wrote the book because it didn't have an author."

Aponi nodded. "That is because I wrote it anonymously."

"Ya wrote it what?"

"Anonymously," A'keara said. "Which means, she didn't put her name on the book." Kero always wondered why the book never had an author.

"Why wouldn't you put your name on the book?" Kero asked.

"Because, it didn't matter who wrote the book. It's about the information in the book," Aponi replied.

"Information? It's a children's book," Kero pointed out.

Aponi nodded. "Precisely. Children have such wonderful imagination and they can believe in dragons. Adults have a harder time believing in things they don't see. But, just because they can't be seen, doesn't mean they aren't real. Dragons are real. They are no longer on this planet, but they exist in the higher realm."

Kero narrowed her eyes at the words, 'higher realm.'

"What are ya talkin' about?"

"There are realms that exist other than this one. Gaia needs to be restored. We need to awaken the Spirit Dragons and bring them back into this realm. Each of the Spirit Dragons need to be found and awakened by the next Violet Energy Moon."

"Which will happen in about a week," A'keara chimed in.

"Wait, slow down," Kero interjected. "What's a violet energy moon?"

"Oh, well violet moons appear every hundred years or so, but a Violet Energy Moon appears every one thousand years. A'keara and I were going to awaken all four dragons ourselves, but we don't know if we're allowed to bond with more than one dragon. We now found you two, so maybe you could help us make history and bring Gaia back to her great glory."

The girls stared at the old woman, speechless.

"They think you're crazy, grandmother," A'keara said.

Aponi turned to the girls. "Do I sound crazy?"

Blythe tried to be kind. "Well–I've never seen a dragon before. I just don't know if I can believe in something that's only been in make-believe stories."

Kero wasn't sure how to respond. It would be amazing if dragons were real. She never knew unicorns existed, but there was one right in front of her.

"Are dragons real? Like the ones from that story?" Kero asked.

"I can assure you, they are quite real," Aponi said. "That's why I wrote that book."

Kero suddenly pictured the Patrol finding the book and then seeing the pages being burned in a fire. Her eyes welled up with tears, but she quickly pushed them away. "I never got a chance to put that book back into my hidin' spot," she whispered.

"Hiding spot? A'keara asked. "Why are you hiding the book?" Both Kero and Blythe returned horrified stares.

"Uh, because reading books is illegal," Kero said.

The other two women matched the same horrified expressions.

"What?" A'keara gasped.

"They don't want people to read books because there's information in them that tells the truth of past events that happened on this planet," Aponi realized.

"Are there a lot of books on dragons?" Kero asked.

"There are books on all kinds of magical creatures," A'keara replied. Etheria had a grand library full of books, not just on magical creatures, but they also taught meditation and how to use your energy and help other people."

"What do you mean by 'using your energy?'" Blythe asked.

Aponi stood up. "Let me show you." She reached out and held her hand over Blythe's head. After a moment, she lowered it.

"What did you do?" Blythe asked. "I feel great!"

Kero narrowed her eyes. "She didn't do anything."

"I just cleared your energy," Aponi replied.

"Cleared her energy?" Kero questioned. "That makes no sense."

Aponi returned a kind glance. "Would you like me to do the same for you?"

"Do it, Kero! It's amazing!" Blythe squealed.

Kero shrugged her shoulders. "Fine. Whatever."

"You'll be fine," Aponi said as she raised her hand over Kero's head.

At first, she felt nothing. Then, the heaviness she felt in her head and in her body began to fade. Kero had a lot of worries, but it felt like they were all being pulled out of her. When Aponi lowered her hand, Kero felt very well rested, a feeling she hadn't ever felt in her life.

Aponi smiled at the girls. "Are you open to meditation?" Kero still didn't know what that word meant.

"What's a meditation?" she asked.

"Meditation is where you focus your thoughts and clear your mind," Aponi explained. "If there is turmoil in you, meditation will help redirect your mind and give you purpose."

Kero wasn't sure if she wanted to do the medi-whatever, but what could it hurt?

"I guess so," she finally replied.

"How about you?" Aponi asked Blythe.

Blythe returned a wide smile. "Sure. Why not?"

"Okay, I will make the preparations. Right now, you two should rest."

As Kero walked towards the bedroll she was currently using, Blythe tapped her on the shoulder. Kero once again spun around frantically.

"How do you know how to read?" she asked.

Kero did a sideways glance towards the other two women who were now talking among themselves.

"My grandmother taught my mom, and she taught me."

"Really? I wish I could read."

Kero shrugged. "I only know how to read that book. I basically memorized it."

Blythe laid down on one of the bedrolls. "Well, I guess we should get some sleep." Kero laid down on the bedroll in front of her. With her mind full of thoughts and worry, she couldn't fall asleep. However, after that weird trick Aponi did, she felt very relaxed. Her eyes closed and she drifted off into slumber.

CHAPTER 3

The Journey Begins

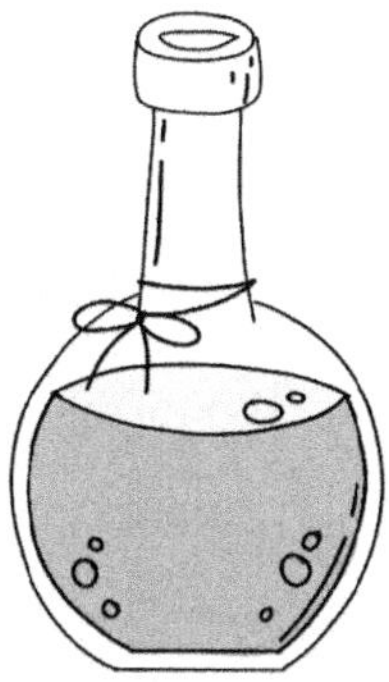

The next day, Kero awoke, feeling very refreshed. Never had she had such a good night's sleep before. As she sat up, her eyes adjusted to the environment around her. Aponi walked over and set down a bowl of berries in front of her.

"Go ahead and have some," she offered. The last time Kero ate was back in Athena when she had some of the deer meat from Darion's hunt. She scooped up a few berries and popped them into her mouth. They were very sweet. She wasn't used to that taste.

As she continued eating the berries, Aponi placed a soft, white fur rug across from her. The people from her colony never had the luxury of owning anything made of fur. They raised sheep that were sent off to other colonies, where their wool would be used to make clothing.

Aponi sat cross legged with her own bowl of berries in her lap. She studied Kero's clothing. Her white shirt was torn in multiple places and there were holes in the knees of her brown pants.

"I don't mean to pry, dear, but I noticed your clothes are in shambles. If you'd like, I have some newer clothes I could give you." Kero almost choked on the berries in her mouth. No one other than her parents ever gave her clothing. Her mother used to mend patches onto the holes of her shirts and pants. Now that Kero was grown, she knew how to do it herself. Unfortunately, she never had time during the day and was too tired in the evening to mend her clothing.

"You want to give me your clothes?" Kero asked dubiously.

"They're not mine. They were given to A'keara and I as gifts. I'll be right back."

Suddenly, Kero felt ashamed. She never cared before about how she looked because everyone on the farm looked rugged. However, as she looked over at Blythe who wore her neat looking outfit, Kero suddenly felt like an eye soar. The clothing A'keara and Aponi wore were quite fashionable as well.

Aponi returned, holding two shirts and two pairs of pants, as well as a few pairs of socks.

"Go ahead and choose an outfit," Aponi invited. *Choose an outfit?* She never heard those words before.

"I like the red shirt," Blythe said as she shoveled berries quickly into her mouth. "These are good, by the way," she said in between mouthfuls.

Kero gazed at the red shirt, then the white shirt. She was tired of wearing white. It was the color everyone wore on the farm. Colors like red, blue and purple were harder to come by because the dye was so expensive. Kero picked up the red shirt. It was simple, no elaborate designs or anything. Turning her attention to the two pairs of pants, Kero held each one up to her body. The black pants were shiny. Were these made of leather? She had never touched leather before. The other pair were just plain brown. They were nicer than the ones she had on, but Kero was more tired of the color brown, than the color white.

"I like these," Kero said, holding the red shirt and black pants.

"Ooh, that's nice," Blythe commented.

"Here, take these too," Aponi said, handing her a pair of knitted socks. Kero's eyes widened. She had never worn socks in her life.

Kero walked to the other side of the cave where she had some privacy. She practically tore her shirt apart, as she took the piece of clothing off. Aponi was correct in saying it was in shambles. She pulled the red shirt over her head. It was kind of big on her, but she liked how the material felt against her skin. Was this silk? She switched to the pair of black pants, which honestly fit her better than her old ones. She had the brown pair ever since she was fourteen. Finally, she took the pair of knitted cotton socks and pulled them over her feet before putting her boots back on.

Kero returned and Aponi nodded in approval. "Much better. How do you feel?"

Kero shrugged her shoulders. "Fine. Uh, thank you–for the clothes."

"You are very welcome," the elderly lady replied.

Aponi sat down on her white fur rug.

"I think now would be a good time to talk," Aponi said. "You two should know the truth about what happened to this planet."

Kero and Blythe did a sideways glance at each other. "We once called this planet Gaia before the visitors came," Aponi explained. "There were small villages, but Etheria was the heart of Gaia. There was a council of twelve, who consists of the wisest people on the planet." Aponi paused. "I was one of those twelve. Each council member held great knowledge. Many came in search of answers to their numerous questions. There were very few conflicts because everyone knew each other's intentions. We felt each other's energy. However, when the visitors came and tried to change our planet, the council told them to leave, but the visitors refused. Then—" Aponi took a deep breath. "They destroyed everything. Somehow, A'keara and I were able to escape on Aurora. Her ability to teleport is what saved us."

"Teleport?" Blythe asked. Aponi nodded.

"Can we actually see her teleport?" Kero asked, raising a skeptical eyebrow.

"We've been away from our home for so long. When we left, eleven years ago, the energy of Gaia began to fall. Now, the energy is a shell of its former self. So, Aurora can no longer teleport. She also lost her power to heal too."

"That's so sad," Blythe lamented.

"Well, she can still slam a human being into a tree," Kero remarked, recalling what happened to the imperial soldier.

"Yes, she can still use telekinesis, but it takes a lot out of her," Aponi replied.

Aponi stood and stretched her legs. "I believe A'keara has breakfast ready outside."

"Oh, I thought the berries were breakfast," Blythe said.

"Just an appetizer," Aponi replied. She began walking

towards the mouth of the cave. Kero leaned towards Blythe.

"What's an appetizer?" she whispered. Blythe shrugged her shoulders.

As the girls exited the cave, Kero immediately caught the aroma of something sweet. A'keara stood over a pot on a fire, stirring a reddish liquid with a wooden spoon.

"Ooh! What are you making?" Blythe asked.

"Oh, this is my berry blend. I cooked a bunch of berries, then added honey and cinnamon. It's almost ready."

Kero noticed the cart that was once in the cave was now outside. As she glanced at it in direct sunlight, the cart appeared really old. Were they all going to travel in that rickety thing?

"So, where are we going exactly?" Blythe asked. A'keara stopped stirring her pot and turned with a glare in her eye.

"The tundra," she answered flatly. "And I'm not looking forward to traveling in the icy wasteland."

"A'keara," Aponi warned. She turned a kind glance to the two young girls. "The first dragon is located on top of a mountain in the north," Aponi said.

"Wait, you already know where to find the dragons?" Kero wondered. "I thought we had to meditate first or something."

"We don't know exactly where the dragons are, but like the legend goes, the Crystal Dragon, who breathes ice, is in the north," Aponi explained.

"That makes sense," Blythe noted.

"The Golden Dragon, who breathes wind, will be found in the west," Aponi continued. "The Crimson Dragon will be in the south and finally, the Emerald Dragon will be found in the east."

"Okay, Grandmother, enough story time," A'keara said,

dipping a clay bowl into the pot. "Breakfast is served!"

Kero felt her stomach make continuous flip flops. She was way too old to believe in legends or imaginary creatures, but if what Aponi said is true, she may be able to meet a real live dragon.

"So, what happens when we find these dragons?" Blythe asked. "The world just changes? What about the Empire? They rule everything. Are they just going to leave?"

Kero wondered the same thing.

"Maybe these dragons will eat the Empress," Kero said sourly.

"Dragons are kind and gentle creatures," A'keara said. "They don't harm anyone who has no malicious intent or done anything harmful."

Kero returned a hard stare. "The Empress has hurt a lot of people. The Empire killed my parents. The Patrol came and arrested them. Then they were publicly executed." Kero's voice faded. She couldn't bring herself to speak anymore.

"Publicly executed? For what?" Blythe asked.

Kero shook her head. "I don't remember. I was only six. But, they didn't do anything! The Patrol grabbed the wrong people–"

"We are like you," Aponi said. "We lost everything because of the Empire. A'keara and I have not been able to get into any of the colonies, but we've talked to people who live like us. They said they left the safety of their colony to be free from tyranny." Kero wondered how they were able to do that. You couldn't just leave your colony. Maybe those people left when traveling outside colonies was still allowed?

Kero sat down, holding the bowl of crimson liquid A'keara gave her. She stared into the bowl. Slowly, she lifted the bowl, and took a sip. The taste of the blended berries was very sweet.

"This is good," she said.

"Thank you," A'keara replied.

Aponi lifted her bowl and drank the liquid inside. "Mmm–very good A'keara. I see you took my advice and added more honey and less cinnamon."

A'keara didn't respond. Instead, she began drinking from her own bowl.

After Aponi finished her breakfast, she handed her bowl to A'keara. Kero finished every drop of liquid in her bowl. She tasted the sweet honey, which was something she rarely got to enjoy.

"Would you like some more?" A'keara asked as Kero handed her the bowl.

More? Kero almost leapt up into the air. Asking for more food always got her dirty looks back on the farm. There was no such thing as seconds.

"Yeah! I mean, if there's enough."

"Oh, there's plenty," A'keara said. She took Kero's bowl and filled it. Kero sat down, but this time, ate a little slower.

"Oh Kero, when you are finished, do you mind bringing out that bedroll you slept on?" Aponi asked. Kero nodded as she finished drinking the liquid in her bowl. She could eat this stuff all day, but she didn't want to be rude so she returned the bowl to A'keara before heading into the cave.

A'keara began filling a couple of glass vials with the liquid before covering them with a small cork. She gave one to Blythe.

"Here you go. One for the road."

"Thanks," Blythe replied. She put the vial in her pocket.

"I have one for Kero too."

Once A'keara filled the vials, she covered up the pot and put it on the wagon.

Kero returned with the bedroll. She stared down at the cart for a moment. It wasn't that big. How would it carry all four of them, plus their supplies?

"So, can I just put it anywhere?" she asked.

A'keara took the bedroll and placed it in the front of the cart. Kero realized that one of the mattresses was unrolled, being used as a cushion against the hard wooden floor of the cart. Blythe walked up to the cart, carrying a basket of fur coats. As she tried lifting the basket, she almost lost her balance but Kero snatched and helped lower it into the cart.

"Whew! That's done," Blythe said as she wiped her brow.

Kero peered down at the coats. "Where did ya find these?" she asked.

"They were given as gifts from the same couple that gave us those clothes," Aponi replied. "In return, we gave them a few of our crystals for light and healing."

It was then that A'keara noticed Kero's new outfit.

"Oh, that looks good on you," she gushed. A'keara glanced over at Aponi who was on her way towards the cave entrance. "Grandmother, I'm going to go pick more berries," A'keara announced. Aponi waved her hand.

"That's fine." Aponi continued walking into the cave.

Kero wandered to the mouth of the cave. The twinkling lights faded one by one until she stared into a dark cave. Aponi came out, holding a bunch of light crystals in her hand.

"Where do crystals come from?" Kero asked.

"They were once part of the planet," Aponi explained. "There were much larger crystals back in Etheria. They lit up the entire city."

"So, how exactly do the crystals light stuff up?"

"Well, during the day, they gather sunlight and at night, the crystals use that light."

"I wish we had those in Athena," Kero said. "There were so many nights when it was cold and the sky was just black." Aponi gave her a sympathetic smile. "I believe this journey is the beginning of great change," she said. She climbed into the back of the cart. Blythe climbed in next. Kero wasn't sure she trusted this shaky old cart, but boarded anyway.

A'keara emerged from the woods with her basket full of berries and nuts. She strolled over to the cart and handed the basket to her grandmother.

"I gathered plenty of food for the next week," she replied.

Kero took note of the contents of the basket.

"Uh, are we just going to be eating berries and nuts?" Kero asked.

She was the last person who should complain about food variety, but on the farm, they usually had rice and corn to fill everyone's stomach.

"We still have some honey left," A'keara replied. "I'll try fishing when we get to a river. If we come across any rabbits or squirrels, I can set traps for them, but there seems to be a scarcity of animals in this area."

"That's because the Empire has either captured most of

the animals or killed them," Kero replied grimly.

"They want to control the food supply," Blythe added. Aponi smiled weakly, then turned towards A'keara

"Well, I believe it is time to leave for our journey," she said.

"Yes," A'keara agreed. "It will take us at least three to four days to reach the tundra." Her expression hardened as she added. "This is why I'm doubting that we can even come close to completing this mission in the allotted time.

"Akeara," Aponi warned. "Being negative isn't going to bring us any good fortune."

A'keara clenched her mouth shut, realizing that her words would not change the mind of her old, stubborn grandmother.

"Dragons can fly." Kero chimed in. "Just use the dragon to fly to the next place ya need to go. It won't take ya that long to awaken the rest of the dragons."

"Yes, exactly," Aponi agreed.

"What about Aurora?" A'keara asked in a haughty tone. "We can't get her onto a dragon. Also, we can't leave the cart with all of our supplies."

"Don't worry about it, A'keara. The answers will come to us. Let's be on our way."

A'keara pushed the air out through her nose with an aggravated sigh. She mounted Aurora, clicking her tongue as a signal for her to move forward. The mare trotted forward, pulling the cart with ease. The cart moved at a pretty good pace. Kero was surprised by how fast the unicorn moved. The supplies they had were not too heavy, but the cart itself had to have some weight.

"I'm surprised yer horse isn't strugglin," Kero said.

"You mean, unicorn," A'keara said while keeping her gaze

forward. "Don't you have horses to pull carts on your farm?"

"Yes, but the male horses do the work and the female horses are there for breeding."

"While it's true that male unicorns are stronger than female ones, unicorns themselves are much stronger than horses."

"Really, then we should have unicorns work on the farm."

A'keara turned her head around, giving Kero a disdainful glance.

"That would be a complete waste of their time and talent." Her head turned back around. "Unicorns are our equals. Sure, I asked Aurora to pull the cart, but she did it because we're friends, not because I am forcing her. It is sad that Aurora has lost most of her abilities. She should be able to teleport us to where we want to go."

Kero stared at the unicorn curiously, wondering what it would be like if they all teleported to the tundra. Then, she realized how cold it was going to be. Her eyes floated over to the basket of coats. She wasn't used to the cold at all. She had spent her entire life in a warm climate.

"Uh, can I put on one of those coats?" she asked.

"Of course," Aponi said as she removed the lid of the barrel. She handed Kero a brown fur coat.

Now that she was warm, Kero's thoughts drifted to everyone on the farm. She wondered if they were okay. She was sure that the Patrol announced the arrest of Darion and her to the rest of the colonists in Athena. Darion was most likely taken to the colony of Michael, where they would stick him in the giant prison under the palace. She knew there was a time limit for awaking the dragons, but maybe after they awoke the first dragon, they could go rescue Darion.

"Um–Aponi," Kero began slowly.

"Yes," the elderly woman answered sweetly.

"How long do you think it will take us to awaken all of the dragons?"

Aponi leaned back to ponder the question. "Well, I know we can do it by the next Violet Energy Moon." A'keara let out a long sigh.

"We'll see, Grandmother. We'll see."

From the conversation Kero overheard between Aponi and A'keara, they had about a week. She wasn't sure she could wait that long. Many people sent to prison don't survive for more than a few days, some even less. Aponi noticed Kero's distraught demeanor.

"Do not worry," she said. "As I told A'keara, everything will fall into place."

Kero tried to relax as she listened to the birds chirp and the clicking of Aurora's hooves on the dirt path. Only one thought repeated inside her mind.

Please let Darion be okay.

Deep within the cold and frigid tundra stood a massive structure made of steel and stone. A large iron gate kept intruders from coming inside the prison, but more importantly, it kept people from getting out. Airships flew high in the sky towards the giant prison, bringing in newcomers who would soon call this place home. Watchers circled the sky and prison guards patrolled the ground. Two guards waited at the dock on the second level of the prison. An airship flew up to the dock and lowered its gangplank.

The doors of the airship opened where two Patrol officers stood. One by one, the prisoners were corralled off the airship. There were seven males between the ages of sixteen to forty-five. Among these people was Darion. He was one of the few younger ones there. Heaven only knew why these people were here. Darion had a feeling that most of them weren't real criminals. No. The real criminals were the military, the government officials, and of course the Empress herself.

Darion felt the icy cold wind blow on the back of his neck. Then, he felt the pull on the shackles around his wrists and ankles as the prisoners in front of him walked forward. From the time of his arrest, Darion kept thinking about how the Patrol found the remains of his deer. When Darion dragged the deer back to the woods, he tried not to leave a blood trail. However, it is possible that spots of blood would lead away from his shed right to where he buried the deer. He went to get the deer after the Patrol left, but he made sure there were no Watchers around to see him go in and out of the woods. One of them had to have spotted him, but which one?

"Keep moving!" he heard one of the Patrol officers yelled out. Darion wasn't as afraid for himself as much as he was for Kero. The good news was that Kero would not be sent here. They may send her to the prison that is outside of Apollo. It would at least be warm there. However, another frightening thought came to Darion. Kero was only seventeen. They could send her to Isis to work in the taverns as a maid. Kero would hate that, especially because she would have to wear one of those big flowing dresses with a low-cut top.

The prisoners were hauled into a big room and told to sit on a wooden bench. Parts of the bench had rotted away and many pieces of the wood had broken off, leaving some very jagged edges. Darion felt a piece of jagged wood cut into his left leg. He tried to move it away, but there wasn't much space. Everyone was put right against each other. Things couldn't get much worse. That was until the head guard pointed at him.

"You're coming with us!" he spat out. Darion looked up at the man aiming his gun at him. A lower ranking officer unlocked his hands and feet and brought him forward.

Darion was cuffed once again, but this time, he had his hands bound behind his back. The officer grabbed him by the arm and escorted him through the security door. It beeped, showing a green light. After they entered a long hallway, the door shut behind them and beeped again, showing a red light. Darion was led down a long red carpet towards a podium where three men in long white robes waited. These men were judges for this prison, Darion realized.

The head judge who sat in the middle podium was the first to speak. He read off a parchment that held each crime committed by a felon.

"Prisoner 8468, Darion Embers. Arrested for hunting and abandoning his post." He lowered the parchment. "Why did you commit this disrespectful act?"

Darion wasn't prepared to speak. His mouth felt dry as he looked up at the elderly man with thinning gray hair.

"I did it because the people in my colony didn't have enough food."

"Your Empress has given you more than enough food," the councilman haughty returned. "The sentence usually is a month of confinement for hunting and another two weeks for abandoning your post," he continued. "We also have information on your sister's crime." His eyes squinted at the writing on the paper in front of him. "Refusing to yield to a Patrol officer. Also, yelling and threatening the Patrol." He gave the other two council members a bewildered stare. "Who does that? No one in their right mind, I'd assume."

Darion had to stifle a laugh. Not many were as bold as Kero. Thinking of his sister again, he nervously asked about her location.

"Um–sir, where is my sister?"

The man narrowed his eyes as he stared down at him. "Quiet!" Then, his gaze went to the prison guard. "Where is the girl?"

"She should be on her way to Apollo," he answered.

The man in the right podium whispered something to the head judge. He returned his attention to the guard.

"Are you aware that two prisoners escaped from the airship heading to Apollo?"

The eyes of the guard widened. "Uh, no sir."

"Yes, two young girls escaped. You'd better let your superior know. But not before taking Mr. Embers to his cell.

"Uh, yes sir." The guard grabbed Darion in the same manner as before and hauled him through another security door and down a spiraling staircase where he was met with another long hallway. Darion wondered if Kero was one of the girls who escaped that airship. He hoped she would escape. However, if she did, she couldn't just go back to Athena. She would be subject to anything and everything in the world outside the colonies.

Finally, the guard stopped when they reached the end of the hallway. He opened the iron door of the cell and shoved

Darion inside. Darion heard the click of the lock from the other side of the door. One month, plus two more weeks. He added the amount of time to be six weeks. He wasn't sure if he could survive there that long.

There was a raised stone surface by the back wall. Darion sat in the cold, dark cell alone. He could see his breath as he breathed in and out. They didn't give him anything like a coat or clothes that would keep him warm.. He sat there in his farm clothes, a torn t-shirt and jeans. At least he had his boots. He rubbed his arms, trying to keep them warm. He had to do everything he could to stay alive so he could see his sister again.

CHAPTER 4

Visions

Nighttime had fallen. Twinkling stars covered the sky along with a crescent moon. Kero stared upwards feeling tranquil. They had traveled all day and the sun descended beyond the horizon about an hour ago.

"I think this is a good place to set up camp," Aponi said.

"I thought we were going to travel through the night," A'keara replied swiftly.

"I think Aurora would appreciate being able to sleep for the night," Aponi retorted.

"We don't have a lot of time, Grandmother. Aurora will be fine." Aponi became quiet for a moment. After a couple seconds of thought, she spoke again.

"I think it would be a great place to meditate," she said. "The weather is fair. I don't know if we'll get a better opportunity once we go further north."

A'keara realized that her grandmother was right. She lightly pulled on Aurora's reins. "Stop please," she whispered. The mare came to a halt and waited. She dismounted and walked over to the cart.

"I'll set up the tent," A'keara said.

"Tent?" Blythe asked. "I didn't see you put a tent in the cart."

A'keara looked at the tarp underneath the girl. "You're sitting on it." Blythe got up and jumped off the cart.

"Oh, that's a tent?" she asked. A'keara nodded as she pulled out the tarp as well as four thick long sticks. She headed towards a small clearing in the woods. Kero got out of the cart and walked over to where A'keara worked.

"Ya need help?"

"Yes, if you could hold onto this end," A'keara said, handing her part of the tarp. The woman pushed one of the sticks into the dirt and pushed one of the corners of the tarp onto the sharp point of the stick. She put another stick in the ground, about a few feet away and pushed the second corner of the tarp onto the stick. Kero held out the tarp as far back as it could go. She noticed there were already holes in the fabric. A'keara came over with a third stick and secured the edge of the tarp. Then, she did the same to the last corner of the tarp. Once they were done, they had a small shelter to keep themselves covered from the wind and rain. However, from the way the night appeared, they wouldn't have to worry much about either.

"A few efforts later, the tent was set up by A'keara with some help from Kero and Blythe. Kero was used to hard labor, it's what she did every single day back in Athena.

A'keara asked the girls to look for dry twigs and leaves so she can start a fire."

Blythe walked over, holding a few dry twigs and leaves.

"Here ya go." A'keara thanked her and tossed the twigs and leaves into the middle of the triangle of logs. She smacked two pieces of flint together until the spark was great enough to ignite the fire. Kero remembered how the people in her colony made fires to keep themselves warm at night. They used hay as kindling. Sometimes the fire would go out and they had a hard time getting it going again. However, A'keara made it look so easy as the fire already had a healthy glow.

The soothing sounds of the flames crackled and popped. Kero watched Aponi set up a bedroll under the tarp.

"I brought out the other bedrolls for everyone," she said. Kero unrolled the mattress and sat down. Blythe did the same.

Aponi studied the two girls for a moment. If these two girls saw a spirit dragon, it either meant that the dragons found them worthy or they were the original ones who bonded with the dragons a thousand years ago.

"So, now that we've set up camp, let's try meditating."

Kero kept her eyes away from Aponi. She still wasn't sure if she wanted to do this. Blythe, on the other hand, turned to the woman with a smile. "I guess I can try. Are you ready, Kero?"

"I'm not sure what to do," she replied stiffly.

"It's very simple," Aponi spoke gently. "First, I need you to close your eyes and just relax."

"Does medi-whatever really do anything?" Kero asked.

"For the people who lived in Etheria, meditation was a daily practice. However, this one as I've already explained is very special."

"So, ya think I'm gonna see a dragon?"

Aponi smiled. "We won't know until we try. Go ahead and close your eyes." She looked over at Blythe. "You too."

Kero and Blythe both had their eyes closed while sitting in a cross-legged position. Aponi looked both girls over. Blythe appeared calm, but Kero scrunched up her face. Aponi could feel the tension in the girl's body. The elderly woman began chanting using a foreign language. A'keara recognized the language as an Etherian prayer.

As Kero tried to keep her body still, she felt a little silly. Was anything really going to happen? Her body felt very uncomfortable. She didn't know if she could stay in this position much longer. After what seemed like several minutes, Kero opened her eyes and lifted her head to look at Aponi. However, the elderly woman was no longer sitting across from her. She twisted her neck towards Blythe who had also disappeared. Kero was alone. Where did everyone go?

Getting tired of sitting in the same position for minutes at a time, Kero stood up and stretched her legs. The fire stayed full and healthy. The air was strangely warm. There was a gentle breeze and Kero caught the aroma of cinnamon and pine. The scent of pine had to be coming from the tree branches they burned. She wasn't sure where the smell of cinnamon came from, though.

Kero stared deeply into the fire. It was so quiet except for the crackling of the burning wood. She opened her mouth to call out to her traveling companions, but instead a deep and somewhat terrifying voice emanated from within her.

"I am the Crimson Dragon. Who comes before me?"

When Kero gained control of her mouth again, she tried to speak, but still couldn't form any words. Her eyes stayed fixed on the fire. She felt something was there with her. Suddenly, embers exploded from the fire. The flames grew brighter, spreading out around her. Kero cried out as she covered her face. She shut her eyes tightly to shield them from the smoke. She began coughing violently. Her legs buckled under her before she collapsed and passed out.

"Kero!" she heard someone yell. The voice sounded so distant, like it was miles away. "Kero!" she heard the voice again, but it was closer this time.

Kero opened her eyes to see Blythe standing over her. Kero sat up.

"What happened?"

"You just fell over," Blythe replied.

"Did you see something?" Aponi asked.

Kero blinked a few times. "I-I don't know." She turned to Blythe. "Did you see anything?"

Blythe returned a wide grin and laughed. "No."

"Me neither," Kero quickly answered.

"I'm not sure if that's true," Aponi said thoughtfully.

Kero sighed. "I think I was just dreamin,"

"It was a vision," Aponi replied. "Can you describe what you saw?"

Kero fidgeted with her fingers. "Uh, it was really weird. You all just disappeared."

Blythe squinted her eyes. "We didn't go anywhere."

Aponi kept her focus on Kero. "Anything else?"

Kero kept her head down, keeping her eyes away from Aponi.

"I heard this low voice speak. Uh–something like, 'I am the Crimson Dragon'–uh, I forgot the rest." Kero looked up at Aponi who had a big toothy grin on her face. She wrapped her arms around Kero, which shocked the teenage girl. She continued to hold onto Kero's shoulders, looking directly into the girl's eyes.

"I knew you were the one we were looking for. So, it is the Crimson Dragon that found you." She pulled her arms away, giving Kero some relief. "That is the fire element and the season of Summer. Did you get the name of the dragon?"

"No. I didn't get a name."

Aponi sighed. "Well, I'm sure we'll find out later." She clasped her hands together. "This is such wonderful news!" She made a short laugh through her nose. "And A'keara doubted me," she said sourly.

With new excitement, Aponi walked over to where her granddaughter cooked on another fire she made. Kero smelled cinnamon. A'keara was making more of that liquid stuff. Maybe that's what she smelled earlier.

"I didn't think it would work," Blythe said, shaking her head. "I can't be hypnotized."

"Hypnotized?" Kero questioned.

"Well, yeah. Aponi was doing some weird chant. I think she was trying to hypnotize us so we'd see dragons or something."

Was that what she was trying to do? Kero leaned closer to Blythe and whispered,

"Do you believe in this dragon business?"

Blythe shrugged. "I'm not really sure." Kero began to worry. She turned to see Aponi trying to tell A'keara how to stir and A'keara waving her away. They seemed to argue a lot.

"I don't know if I trust them," Kero said, suddenly.

"So, why are you sticking around here if you don't trust them?" Kero was taken aback by the question.

"Hey, I would have left by now, but I kinda wanna see if dragons really exist."

Blythe returned a hard look. "That's not why you haven't left." She kept a stern gaze on Kero. "You can't leave. You're stuck here, just like me."

It bothered Kero how she said that. Even so, Kero couldn't argue against what she said. She was right.

"So, what are we supposed to do about it?" Kero answered just as harshly.

Blythe put a finger to her chin in thought. "Oh, I almost forgot. What about your brother?"

Kero returned a cynical stare. "How did you know–?"

"You mentioned him when we were on the airship. Having a dragon would definitely help you find him."

Kero was at a loss for words. She never told Aponi or A'keara about what happened back in Athena.

"Hey, don't tell those women about my brother, okay?"

Blythe narrowed her glance. "Why not?"

Kero suddenly felt a lump in her throat. She tried swallowing.

"Look, I wasn't even gonna tell you," Kero hastily replied. She realized that it was the spur of the moment when she mentioned her brother to Blythe. "Look, I don't know Aponi or A'keara. I don't really even know you. They could turn me over to the Empire."

Blythe crossed her arms over her chest in a defiant manner.

"You really think they'd do that?" Kero wasn't sure how to answer her. "Look, we're all fugitives at this point. Both you and I got arrested and Aponi and A'keara have been living outside the colonies for years. You don't think that all four of us wouldn't be thrown into prison if we were spotted by a Watcher or a Patrol officer?" Kero stayed silent. "Listen, it's up to you. I'm not going to tell them anything, it's not my place. But honestly, you really don't have anything to worry about."

Kero headed towards the fire. As she approached the two Etherian women, A'keara turned to her.

"So, I heard you connected with the Crimson Dragon."

Kero shifted awkwardly on her feet. "I guess so. I heard a voice speak to me, but I didn't actually see a dragon."

"Really? When I did it, I actually saw the Emerald Dragon. I saw her waking up from slumber."

"She doesn't have to actually see the dragon," Aponi said. A'keara turned her attention towards the stewing pot on the fire. "And what about Blythe?"

"She didn't see anything, but that doesn't mean that she

isn't meant to bond with a dragon," Aponi replied. A'keara noticed Blythe standing behind Kero.

"So, what did you think of the meditation?"

Blythe smiled. "It was an experience."

"It is said that there are four souls that will remember their past life with their Spirit Dragon. Two women and two men. If you two are the women, that means we need to find two men who will bond with the other dragons."

"Wait, I'm confused," Blythe admitted. "Didn't you say that you and your grandmother had visions of the dragons?"

"We are not the souls who originally bonded with the Spirit Dragons," A'keara explained.

"But, the Elder Dragons gave us the visions because we prayed and asked them to," Aponi finished.

"Or who you think are the Elder Dragons," A'keara haughtily added. Both Kero and Blythe squint their eyes at her remark. "The downloads my grandmother received came from a higher source. However, we're not sure if the information is from our great ancestors, the Elder Dragons or Source itself."

"I know they are from the Elder Dragons," Aponi insisted. "Who else would have the information?" A'keara rolled her eyes. She chose to keep quiet at that point.

Kero looked down at the bubbling red water in the pot.

"Is this more of that berry stuff?" Kero asked.

"It is," A'keara replied. "But, I'm adding some rabbit meat in the pot this time."

Rabbit meat was something Kero hadn't had in a while.

"Just be careful when yer huntin'. Ya don't want a Patrol officer catching you. Also, the skies have the Watchers."

"We don't have to worry about any of that out here," Aponi assured her.

It was so strange to Kero that the Watchers stayed around the colonies. This meant that anyone who was lucky enough to escape their colony was basically free to do whatever they wanted.

Kero peered into the dark forest. She heard crickets chirping in the distance. Blythe was right. The real reason she stayed with these women was that she had nowhere else to go. She wanted to believe she would bond with a dragon, but who knows what was going to happen.

When the mixture in the pot was ready, A'keara dipped a wooden bowl into the bubbling liquid and handed it to Kero.

"Careful, it's hot." The steam rose, swirling around Kero's nose. It smelled so good, she wanted to eat it right away.

"Everything will be okay," she heard Aponi say as she dipped her bowl into the pot. Kero nodded.

Kero began to feel the heaviness of her situation. Her plan to rescue her brother made sense to her when she first thought of it, but how would the dragon feel about it? Would the dragon care enough to help her?

Returning to the bedroll, Kero sat down, holding the bowl in her hands. She placed the bowl on the ground beside her. When people were lost, they would pray, but Kero was never one to pray. She picked up the bowl and took a sip of the liquid. It tasted so sweet and the savory flavor of the rabbit was good too.

Kero was suspicious of Aponi and A'keara only because they were too nice. Not many people like them existed. She finished the liquid and saw there was a lot of meat left on the bottom of the bowl. She began scooping it up with her hand and eating it. Rabbit. It wasn't an animal she usually ate. When Darion hunted, he usually came back with something. Sometimes, he came back with a couple of coyotes or snakes. It was a treat for him to catch a deer. Suddenly, Kero felt sad. Her head dropped into her hands.

"Is this what I'm supposed to be doing?" she whispered. Tears fell from her eyes. It wasn't long before she was sobbing in her arms. What was wrong with her? She was acting like a child. She pushed her emotions down, forcing herself to stop crying.

"Are you okay?" The voice startled her. Kero looked up to see A'keara through her blurred vision. Kero quickly wiped the tears away.

"Yeah–I'm fine."

"No, you're not."

Kero just shrugged her shoulders. "I never said 'thank you' for helpin' me. Ya know, back at the river."

"It's nothing at all."

"It is," Kero insisted. "No one has ever helped me–I mean, my brother cared for me after my parents died, but–"

"You have a brother?" Kero froze.

"He's still in Athena," she lied.

"So, how did you get out of your colony?"

Kero didn't have an answer to give her. "I-uh-the Patrol just took me. I don't know why."

"Oh, that's terrible." Kero felt bad about lying. Was Blythe right? Should she just say what really happened? A'keara spoke again.

"People need to help each other," A'keara said. "That's how humanity survives. We can get downloads from the heavens above, but we need people on this planet that we can trust."

Kero narrowed her eyes. A'keara used that word before, but she didn't know what it meant.

"I'm sorry, we get what?"

"Downloads. Oh, I'm sorry, downloads are information given to us by the higher realms."

"Listen, I'm a dumb farmgirl. Yer gonna have to make things simple and don't use such strange words."

A'keara stood with her hands on her hips. "Why would you say that about yourself?" Kero squinted her eyes in confusion. All of her life, she was called dumb. Every manager on the farm called her dumb or 'no good' whenever she made a mistake.

A'keara softened her expression and knelt down beside Kero.

"You are not dumb. You can't know something you've never been taught." She smiled and Kero managed to crack a tiny grin. "This is how it works. You can receive downloads or information when you meditate. The higher realms are also referred to as the heavens. I don't believe it's only above us. Realms are other planes of existence. They could be other planets. The dragons come from another realm and when we open the gateway, they will be able to come here to Gaia." Kero supposed she would just have to see it for herself. "Even those who have passed on are now on another plane of existence."

It was strange, but Kero actually was starting to understand.

"I think I get it," she said.

Before A'keara could respond, she heard her grandmother call to her.

"A'keara, you left the pot alone. I've been stirring it for you. Are you coming back?"

A'keara let out an aggravated groan. "Yes!" She got up and headed back to the fire.

Kero sat still for several moments. Many thoughts swarmed around inside her mind. In the midst of all these thoughts were the words Blythe spoke to her about trusting Aponi and A'keara. She supposed she should tell them about what happened to her and Darion. She at least needed to see if the legend about the Spirit Dragons was true. Once she bonded with a dragon, not only would she be able to rescue her brother, but she would be able to put an end to the tyrannical empire that ran this planet.

CHAPTER 5

Mt. Sansin

Finally, Kero made her appearance out by the campfire. She sat down on one of the logs and watched A'keara stir the pot with a long stick.

"Do you want any more, Kero?" she asked. Kero nodded. After handing her a bowl, A'keara turned to Blythe. "How about you?" Blythe lifted her empty bowl with enthusiasm.

"Yes, please. I love rabbit meat. My friends and I love hunting for rabbits. Sometimes, we can only find squirrels."

"Yes, we've found them too," A'keara replied.

Kero tilted the bowl, pouring the smooth liquid into her mouth. Her eyebrows raised.

"This is better than before," Kero remarked. She chewed on some of the rabbit meat. "Hmm, the meat is really tender."

"That's good to hear. The meat has been stewing for a few hours now."

Aponi lowered the bowl from her mouth. "Yes, A'keara. It's very delicious," she complimented. "Once we are all finished eating, I will do an energy clearing for us before we go to sleep."

"Energy clearing? Is that the same thing you did to Kero and me yesterday?" Blythe asked.

"Yes. A'keara and I usually do one every night before we go to bed."

Kero nodded. Then, she took a deep breath.

"Uh, there's somethin' I need to tell you– I want to be truthful, but I also want a promise that you won't turn me in to the Empire."

Blythe looked up at Kero with a knowing grin. Aponi and A'keara looked kindly at her.

"We are all on the same side," Aponi said.

Kero took another deep breath. "My brother is not in Athena. We were both arrested by the Empire. My brother regularly hunts in the woods for deer or whatever he can find. But, like I said, huntin' is against the law. The Patrol found the deer–Darion and I were dragged out of our house and we were put into a carrier ship to go to Michael-at least I think that was where we were going." Kero went quiet.

Aponi nodded. "I felt there was something you were hiding." Kero winced from her words. "Well, thank you for being honest. And we would never turn you into the Empire. We will find a way to rescue your brother."

"Um, if I bond with a dragon, then I can go save my brother," Kero said. "Do you think the dragon will help me?"

Aponi smiled kindly. "Yes, I believe he will."

After Aponi's energy clearing, Kero felt drowsy and fatigue quickly took over her body. She made it to her bedroll, just before shutting her eyes and falling asleep.

Many hours passed, but Kero swore she just fell asleep when she heard Aponi calling to everyone.

"It's morning! Time to get up!" Kero opened her eyes and rolled over. She saw Aponi by the cart, busying herself with arranging the two barrels and sleeping mats. She turned her head around to see the others eating by the fire.

"We should get going. The sun is almost up," she called to them.

Kero still felt tired, but it wouldn't be the first time she had to wake up before dawn and drag herself out of bed.

"Would you like some, grandmother?" A'keara raised the pot up to the old lady.

"Why not?" She took a sip. "Oh, that's really good, A'keara. Your cooking is getting a lot better." She handed it to Kero. There was a little left. She felt strange about drinking from the same bowl as someone else.

"Go ahead and finish that up," A'keara said.

Kero drank the last of it, then handed the pot to A'keara.

"Thank you," Kero said.

"You are very welcome," the woman replied. She turned to Aponi. "I'll wash the pot when we find a river." Her grandmother nodded.

After breakfast, no time was wasted in getting on their way. Kero sat in the front of the cart, facing the back end. Aponi sat adjacent from her against the side of the cart, and Blythe sat on the opposite side, across from her. All of the supplies took up the rest of the space. Even so, it wasn't as cramped as Kero initially thought it would be.

"So, the first dragon is on the top of the mountain?" Kero asked.

"Yes, the tallest mountain on Gaia, Mt. Sansin." A shiver went down Kero's body. She still wore the coat that Aponi gave her.

The elderly woman opened up one of the barrels. She pulled out another fur coat.

"It's going to get cold," the elderly woman said kindly. She handed the coat to Blythe who graciously took it.

"How cold is it going to be when we get to the tundra?" Kero asked.

"At least twenty below," A'keara said.

"Twenty below what?" Kero asked innocently.

Blythe laughed. "You're not used to the cold, huh?"

"I've lived in a warm climate all my life," Kero returned in a crude voice.

"I remember when we met the couple who lived in the Northern Region," A'keara said. "We never needed coats because Etheria is in a genuinely warm climate. After we left, we headed north. That's when we met the elderly couple living in a cabin in the woods. They decided to leave their colony and live off the land. The man, in his younger years, killed a wolf and a bear and skinned the animals to make fur coats.

"Am I wearing a wolf or a bear?" Kero asked.

"Not sure," Aponi replied with a tiny laugh.

"Maybe it would have been better if Darion and I just left Athena and lived out in the wilderness," Kero said.

Aponi smiled. "How old is your brother?"

"He's twenty-two," Kero answered. "He's taken care of me since our parents were killed. I was six and he was eleven at the time."

"An eleven year old taking care of a six year old?" Aponi asked, aghast.

"I mean, we had help from others in our village. Mr. Daniels, our colony's speaker, always helped us out."

"Athena and the Salamand Islands have most of the food supply," Blythe explained.

"Yeah, we're responsible for feeding everyone on this planet," Kero spoke haughty.

"Well, you guys provide the food, but there's slaughter houses in Apollo. They put all of the food into nice aluminum cans." No one missed the sarcastic tone in Blythe's voice.

"That sounds awful!" A'keara exclaimed.

"Yes," Aponi agreed. "Maybe we should change to a more cheerful topic of conversation."

Blythe immediately began telling stories about her friend and his resistance group. Kero already heard this information. Her mind drifted off to the day she and Darion were arrested. What if they had left their colony to go live off the land? She knew deep inside that they wouldn't have made it past the wall.

Kero tried to take her mind off her brother and stared out at the thick pine trees. The yellow sun peeked through the spaces between the trees. It was bright, but Kero realized it was getting even colder. Thick clouds floated across the sky, partially blocking the sun. Tiny white crystals fell onto Kero's forehead.

"Hey, it's snowing," Blythe said.

"Snowing?" Kero asked. She shivered in the cold. "I've never seen snow before." More clusters of snow fell as they ventured further through the forest. Kero folded her arms, keeping her hands inside the coat sleeves.

"A'keara, I have a coat and gloves for you to wear," Aponi said.

"I'm fine," A'keara replied.

"It's getting really cold," Aponi pressed. "At least take the gloves."

A'keara didn't reply.

"I'll take the gloves," Kero intervened.

"A'keara. Please. The temperature is quickly dropping. It's going to be below freezing soon."

"Fine. I'll wear the gloves."

"And the coat?"

A'keara sighed. "Hault," she whispered to Aurora. The mare stopped and A'keara reached out and took the coat and gloves from her grandmother.

"Do you have another pair of gloves?" Kero asked.

"Here," Aponi handed her a pair of brown leather gloves. "I have gloves for you too," she said to Blythe.

"I have my own gloves," she said, pulling out a pair of black leather gloves from one of her many pockets. *This girl had a lot of pockets,* Kero realized.

After about a day and a half of travel, Kero noticed there was ice on the ground. The mare continued to pull the cart through the falling snow. The snow on the ground became thicker and thicker as they moved on.

Another day passed as they headed even further north where there were mounds of snow everywhere. Even with a coat and gloves, Kero was freezing. Aponi noticed the poor girl was shivering. The elderly lady pulled a thick blanket from the barrel in front of her. Kero recognized it as the same blanket used to cover her the first night she spent with these women.

"We can cover ourselves with this," Aponi said as she unfolded the large piece of soft material.

A few hours later, the woods cleared and now they headed across an open plain towards the base of the mountain.

"See A'keara, we actually made it to the tundra in three and a half days," Aponi said.

"Yeah," A'keara replied quietly.

Even though A'keara already explained how strong the unicorn was, it still astonished Kero that one lone horse-like creature with a rider could pull the cart holding three females, several barrels, firewood and a tent up the mountain.

"So, is that horse— I mean unicorn, supposed to get this cart up to the highest mountain top?" she asked.

"Yes," Akeara responded. "She can do it. Unicorns are ten times stronger than a regular horse."

Enormous sheets of snow lay before them. The white clumps packed around the tires of the cart, slowing it down. Aurora kept pulling, but the cart would not move any further. Finally, she stopped.

"What's wrong?" A'keara asked. Aurora whinnied. "It's just some snow."

“The wheels are getting caught in the snow,” Aponi said.

Akeara dismounted Aurora and checked the tires. She kicked one tire, causing a few clumps to fall off. She did the same to the other ones.

“There,” she said. And jumped back onto the mare. She clicked her

tongue, giving Aurora the signal to walk. The cart moved again, but not for long. Suddenly, Aurora had snow almost up to her belly. She looked back at A’keara.

“The snow is too deep,” Aponi said.

“Yes. I realize that,” A’keara replied sharply.

“This is no good. There has to be a better way,” Aponi said just above a whisper. “We have to reach the crystal Dragon.”

“How?” A’keara asked, her eyes moved to her grandmother as if she had an answer. However, the old woman sat in the cart and closed her eyes.

“What are you doing?” A’keara whispered loudly.

“What is she doing?” Kero asked.

“You two are making a lot of noise,” Aponi said. “If I could get some quiet, I could concentrate on the messages coming through.”

A’keara slapped her forehead, realizing what her grandmother was doing.

“She’s meditating.”

Kero studied the elderly woman. She looked so still. How was she able to do that? Kero couldn’t stop from shivering. Why didn’t they make a cover for the cart? Wouldn’t that have made sense? Blythe leaned towards Kero.

"You know, the cart probably needs some skis on it, instead of wheels," she whispered.

"What are skis?" Kero whispered back.

"They're long and thin and can glide over the snow."

"So, where would we find skis?"

Blythe looked around. "Let me see what I can find." She climbed out of the cart as quietly as she could.

Once out of the cart, Blythe hopped through the mounds of snow. Kero watched her.

"What is she doing?" A'keara asked in a half whisper.

"She's lookin' for skis," Kero replied.

"What are skis?"

Meanwhile, Blythe was about fifteen feet ahead of the cart, searching for anything that resembled skis. It may appear to be a futile effort, but she had to at least try to find something they could use. They'd never make it up the mountain with those shaky wooden wheels.

Blythe continued exploring the area, until her eyes landed on something sticking out of the snow. Trudging through the snow, she finally made her way over to the object. She brushed the snow away to reveal metal underneath. She continued moving more snow away until she saw two seats, and the propellers of the large fan sticking out of the back of this strange vehicle. Suddenly, she realized what she found. A snow glider. Swiping away more snow, she saw the Imperial insignia on the base of the vehicle. It was upside down with the skis sticking upwards. They could just take this thing up the mountain instead of the cart. Well, as long as she could get it to run.

Blythe ran back to where everyone waited.

"Hey everyone, I found a way to get to the top of the mountain. It'll be faster than this cart."

"Really?" A'keara asked skeptically. "I have to see this." She dismounted Aurora, then undid the reins attached to the cart.

"You don't need that thing weighing you down," she said to the unicorn. Aurora replied with a small whinny of thanks. A'keara looked at her grandmother.

We'll just leave her to what she's doing."

A'keara and Kero followed Blythe to the side of the mountain.

"I hope this isn't too far," Kero said.

"It's right up here," Blythe said.

Blythe showed them the snow glider. Neither Kero or A'keara ever saw anything like it before.

"That's a strange contraption," A'keara remarked. "What is it used for?"

"It's a vehicle the Patrol use when they're in the colder climates," Blythe explained.

"So, they do patrol outside the colonies," Kero concluded.

"There's a prison somewhere around here," Blythe continued. "The officers who run it, use this thing to patrol the area."

There's a prison out here? Would Darion be there? Kero wondered.

"This thing looks like it was abandoned a long time ago," A'keara said.

"Can you two help me turn it over?" Blythe asked. All three

ladies did their best to push over the vehicle. It still didn't budge.

"It's really stuck in the snow." Blythe tried brushing away some lumps of snow until she found only ice.

"I have an idea," A'keara said. She backtracked towards the cart. Aurora had her muzzle in the snow. She was probably looking for grass to eat. A'keara took some oats from a small bag hanging around her waist.

"Here ya go." She held her palm out, face up so the mare could eat. "Now, can you help us with something?"

A'keara came back with the unicorn and tied her reins to the skis of the snow glider.

"I'm going to have Aurora pull and we'll push on the vehicle from the back." The three women stood in the mound of snow behind the snow glider.

"Okay, get ready," A'keara instructed. "Pull, Aurora," A'keara requested. Aurora started walking. "Start pushing," she said to the girls. The reins became taunt and with great effort, the vehicle started moving. It slid down the small slope of snow.

"Perfect!" Blythe cried. "We just need to get it upright." Once again, the three women pushed on the side of the snow glider. This time it flipped over and landed with the skis facing down.

Kero got a good look at the vehicle. It was painted white and red with gold on the trim. The Imperial symbol of course was the usual colors of red and gold. It was just some weird design, never made any sense to her. Blythe began messing with the switches, but nothing happened.

"I guess the battery died. It's not starting."

"Can't ya just take off the ski part?" Kero asked.

"I don't have the tools to do that," Blythe said.

"Hold on," A'keara said. She brought out her crystals. "Where's the battery?" Blythe pointed at the propeller on the back of the vehicle. "The motor is under the fan. We could jump it, but we don't have jumper cables or another running vehicle for that matter."

A'keara took out two light crystals and placed them onto the battery.

"These crystals are fully charged from the sun. Just give it a minute."

Kero smirked at whatever the woman was trying to do.

"What are you doing? Are you expecting your crystals to recharge the battery?"

Just as Kero asked that question, the engine revved up. She stared with wide eyes. She couldn't even speak. Blythe was equally as speechless.

A'keara smiled proudly. "It worked. Now what?"

The three returned with Blythe driving the snow glider.

Aponi opened her eyes. "Oh, that's an interesting machine."

"We found this," A'keara said.

"Great! What are we going to do with it?" Aponi asked.

"We can take this thing up the mountain," Blythe said.

"That's a wonderful plan, but I don't think all of us could fit on that thing. Also, we can't put our supplies on it either."

"What if you used that snow glider or whatever you call it to pull the cart?" Kero asked.

"We can try it," Blythe said. "We need some rope. Or what about Aurora's reins?"

"That's a good idea," Aponi replied.

"Okay, and what about Aurora?" A'keara asked hastily. "This is the problem I told you about before, grandmother. I can't put her on the snow glider and I won't leave her behind."

"Put her in the cart," Kero said. "It looks like the snow glider fits three people. That means, three of us can ride on it and that leaves one of us to ride in the cart with Aurora."

"I guess I'm riding in the cart with Aurora," A'keara said. Kero got on the snow glider behind Blythe and Aponi sat on the back seat. It appeared that the seat was made for someone to face the opposite way of the driver.

"We'll see if it works," Aponi replied.

Blythe took out a pair of goggles from one of her many pockets. She placed the strap over her head, then lowered them over her eyes. Once all of the safety measures were met, the blonde revved up the engine of the snow glider. Carefully, she pushed the gearshift forward. The glider jerked forward and ascended up the mountain. Kero looked behind her shoulder to see that the vehicle was actually pulling the cart.

"It's working," Kero said. Blythe smiled.

Aponi was fine sitting on the back seat as she could look to make sure the cart was okay. There were a lot of bumps. The snow glider was made for the harsh environment, but the cart was not. A'keara felt all of the bumps on the trail. She turned towards Aurora, who appeared to be very distraught. She tried to reach her hand out to soothe the animal. Just as she touched Aurora's coat, the cart went over the next large bump in the snow, causing one of the back wheels to come off its axle. The cart tipped to the side, making A'keara fall backwards into one of the barrels.

"Stop!" she cried.

Aponi saw what happened. "Stop the glider," she called to Blythe. Blythe put the gear into neutral.

A'keara jumped out the cart to check the wheel. The wheel was now wedged underneath the cart.

"I knew this would happen!" she yelled.

"Really?" Aponi asked. "You knew this exact thing would happen?"

"Stop being so smug. It was stupid for us to try to go up a mountain. And why? So we can awaken a dragon? And what happens if there's no dragon?"

"You know, you waste too much energy. That energy you use to scream at me could be used to fix the problem instead."

"Actually," Blythe spoke in an upbeat tone. "I have an idea." She got off the snow glider. "We need to take all of the wheels off."

"How is this thing going to move without wheels?" A'keara asked in exasperation.

"See the wheels aren't made to go over ice and snow," Blythe explained.

"I know," A'keara said crossly.

"So, let's take them off and see if the cart will just slide across the ice." She walked to the other side and began pulling on the wheel. "You know, these are kinda loose anyways. Can someone hold the cart still for me?" Kero came over. She held the side of the cart while Blythe took off the wheel. Then the two of them lowered the cart onto the ground.

"Wow! You're really strong," Blythe commented.

Kero blushed. "Uh, I do work on a farm all day."

Blythe moved towards the back wheel.

"I'll probably need help with this one too."

A'keara looked over at her grandmother. "I hope this works."

"You hope too much," Aponi replied.

After the girls were done, they walked back to the snow glider.

"Hold on," we can't just leave the wheels behind," A'keara said. "We might need them later."

"Let's put them in the cart," Aponi said.

Once the four wheels were in the cart, Kero and Aponi returned to their original place on the snow glider. A'keara got back into the cart with Aurora, who surprisingly, was putting up with all of the chaos with no complaints. Blythe sat at the driver's seat of the glider. "I'll go slower this time," she said.

Blythe started to move the glider again. The cart slid along the ice. There were still bumps here and there, but it wasn't as bad. A'keara looked over Aurora, making sure the mare was okay.

"Well at least we're moving again," she said. "We need to at least find a cave for shelter before nightfall." She looked up to see dark clouds forming in the sky. The snowfall became heavier. Getting all the way up to the summit was going to be a challenge.

CHAPTER 6

The Crystal Dragon

A few hours had passed since the four women started their journey up the mountain. Kero still wasn't sure how opening this gateway would change everything. How would it stop the Empire from controlling everything? Just as she had these thoughts, Blythe spoke.

"You know, I honestly think we can make things better by standing up to the Empire," Blythe shouted over her shoulder. "If we continue to blindly follow a tyrannical leader, then nothing will change. Why should anyone expect things to be different if they keep doing the same things day after day?"

"I don't blindly follow the Empire. My family has always done what they had to survive," Kero curtly replied.

"It's not that you're following them willingly. But, when everyone just does what they are told, nothing changes."

"So, what have you done to change things?"

Blythe kept her glance ahead on the trail. She slowly turned the wheel to make it around the curve of the mountain trail.

"I met some people. They were a resistance group."

"Were?" Kero asked.

"Most of them were killed by Imperial soldiers. I barely escaped."

"You mentioned something about being underground," Kero said.

Blythe became strangely quiet.

"Are you from Luna?"

Kero felt Blythe's shoulders tense up. "I was born there, but after I met some new friends, I went to live in Apollo."

Kero nodded. "Ya know, it's strange, I thought the people down in those tunnels couldn't breathe normal air."

Blythe returned a cynical stare. "You really believe that? We're no different than anyone else."

"Hey, my mom told me and my brother stories about the misshapen creatures who mined for gold in Luna."

"Do I look misshapen to you?"

"Well no, but how do I know you're from there?"

"I don't think she'd lie about it," Aponi pointed out.

"Right," Blythe swiftly. "So, as I was saying, I joined this resistance group–"

"How did you meet those people?" Kero asked, but Blythe went silent.

"You don't have ta talk about it," Kero quickly followed up. Maybe she was prying too much. Blythe sighed.

"I was sold by my parents. They sold me to a slave owner in Isis. I was only eight years old at the time." Kero felt a chill go down her spine. Blythe kept her glance on the snowy trail ahead. "I was rescued along with the other children by a man named Xan. He and four others broke into the building the slave owners used."

Kero stared down at the moving ground. "I'm sorry that happened to you."

"It's fine. I went with Xan and his group and I've never looked back."

"So, what happened to Xan?"

After a few moments of silence, Blythe finally answered.

"About four months ago, Xan went on this top secret mission. Right after that, our base was found and the imperial soldiers killed everyone, except me and another member. We escaped, but he ran off somewhere and I've been trying to find him and Xan."

"So, how did you get caught by the Empire?" Kero asked.

"I was caught trying to get into Isis," she said. "It was my fault for not having a proper ID. Xan made everyone a fake ID, but the guard at the gate realized it was fake. So, when I get back to Isis, I'm not using the gate to get in."

"You're going to ride on a dragon?" Kero asked.

Blythe laughed lightly. "Sure," she said sarcastically. "I have yet to even see a dragon and bond with it, but I guess it's possible."

It took most of the day to get up the mountain. Kero huddled inside the large coat. Blythe also shivered inside her coat.

"It's getting colder," she said.

"Yeah," Kero replied. She turned to look over her shoulder.

"Hey Aponi, do you know what will happen when we get up there? I mean, is the dragon just standing up there waiting for us?"

Aponi laughed. "The Crystal Dragon went to sleep inside the ice and snow on the summit. I received the vision of her first, so most likely, I'm the one who is bonding with her."

"What about Blythe? Isn't she going to bond with one of these dragons?" Kero asked.

"Um–I'm not sure if I want to do that," Blythe said wearily. Kero turned to her surprised.

"I thought you were going to."

"I never said that. I didn't see anything during the meditation. Why do you think I'd bond with any of the dragons?"

"It's fine. I will bond with the Crystal Dragon," Aponi said.

Kero didn't speak again. This whole dragon bonding business was over her head anyways.

Back in the cart, A'keara watched after Aurora. It was much colder than she thought it would be. The fur coat kept her warm, but now she was worried about her mare friend.

"Are you doing okay?" A'keara asked. She took the blanket from the floor of the cart and placed it around the unicorn. Aurora responded with a tiny whinny.

"I can't believe we're doing this," the woman whispered to

the animal. "It's freezing and we're heading up towards the highest mountain top on the planet. All so we can awaken a dragon. I keep having fears that the dragon won't be there or we'll all freeze to death before even reaching the summit."

The mare didn't whinny this time. She turned away from A'keara.

"Oh, you don't agree? So, you think Aponi is right?" Aurora turned to her, staring silently. "Well, I guess we'll see."

The mountain trail curved to the right and everyone saw an opening to a cave. Blythe slowed the glider down. There was no way around, so they had to enter it. She searched for the switch to the glider's headlights and turned them on.

As they entered, Aurora's horn glowed blue.

"I guess it would have made more sense for Aurora to be out front," Aponi said. Kero looked back and saw the glowing horn. It was so pretty.

When the snow glider approached the center of the cave, Aponi looked over her shoulder towards Blythe.

"I think this would be a good place to rest." Blythe stopped the vehicle.

"Rest?" Kero questioned. "How long are we going to rest? Don't we have a time limit to awaken these dragons?"

"We have about five days at this point," Aponi said. "We still have time to rest for a few hours," Aponi stated firmly. "We might as well spend the night here and continue up the mountain in the morning."

A'keara walked with Aurora towards the rest of the group.

"I'm actually glad we're stopping," she said. "It's getting darker out and we shouldn't climb the mountain at night."

Kero wondered how she was going to rest when she was shivering so much from the cold. She watched as A'keara led Aurora around the cart.

"You'll feel better if you move your legs a little," she said to the mare. Aurora whinnied happily. The others smiled as they watched.

"We have logs for a fire, right?" Aponi asked.

"Yes," A'keara answered. She pulled one log out of the cart, and headed off to look for a dry enough spot to build the fire.

A'keara made the fire the same way she did before, but this time she had some dry leaves to add to the twigs she found. The twigs and leaves started smoking. She blew lightly until there was a flame. The flame grew, until there was a healthy fire.

Kero hopped off the snow glider and rushed over towards the warmth. Holding out her hands, she instantly felt the heat. As she stood there, she heard something crack under her. She turned to tell the others, but A'keara was already heading over. Kero pointed down at the thin ice on the cavern floor.

"It's okay. The ice is cracking from the fire," A'keara said. "It's solid rock underneath. It would be different if we were on a frozen lake."

Aponi and Blythe walked over with a few bedrolls.

"Go ahead and get one," Aponi said.

Kero followed A'keara back over to the cart. She grabbed one of the rolled-up mattresses and took it over to the fire.

"I'm actually really tired," Blythe said as she laid down.

Kero did the same. She didn't think she could actually fall asleep, but somehow she did.

All that was heard was the crackling of the fire. It was calm and serene. Then, the silence was broken by an ear-piercing scream. Kero awoke with a pounding heart. She turned to see Blythe cradling herself.

"What happened? Are you okay?" Kero asked frantically.

Blythe turned to her, catching her breath. "I saw her! I was riding a blue and purple dragon!"

Aponi, who had already been awake, addressed her.

"You are the one who is supposed to bond with the Crystal Dragon. Can you tell me more about your dream?"

"I stood on top of a mountain. There was snow blowing everywhere, I was in the middle of a blizzard. Then, the ice cracked open and out of it came this beautiful dragon with blue and purple scales. The scales were pure crystal. I climbed onto her back and–we we're flying."

"Did you get her name?" Aponi asked.

"No. But I–I'm not sure if I want to bond with a dragon."

A'keara rolled onto her side and glanced carefully at Blythe.

"It will be fine," Aponi said.

"Don't say that. You don't know how she feels," A'keara argued.

"Actually, it would be helpful to have a dragon. I need to get into Isis, but I'll get arrested again if I try to go through the gate. Having a dragon would help me."

Kero realized that she and Blythe needed a dragon for the same reason, to get into a place that was heavily guarded.

"Well, if you do bond with this dragon, the rest of us will know what to expect," Kero said.

"Yeah, but–I don't want to be the first one to try this – experiment."

When Blythe said the word, 'experiment', it made Kero shiver. It wasn't a shiver from the cold, but an eerie feeling that made her feel dread. Blythe had already been forced into slavery as a child. Maybe the same feelings of something being forced onto her were coming back again.

After Kero heard about Blythe's dream, she was beginning to understand that something big was about to happen. It seemed too perfect that she and Blythe met Aponi and A'keara when they did. She had the vision back when they were in the forest, and now Blythe had a dream.

"So, why didn't she have a vision when I did?" Kero asked.

"It is hard to say," Aponi replied. "Perhaps she was just not ready for it at the time."

"Maybe we should get some more sleep," A'keara suggested.

Blythe sat up straight. "I can't sleep," she protested. "After all of that? Can't we just start up the mountain now? I'm sure the sun will be up soon."

"I know you're excited," Aponi began. "However, the sun won't be up for another three hours or so."

Kero wondered how she knew when the sun would come up? They weren't in a location where they'd be able to see the sunrise. Kero tried to settle down. She laid on her back, staring up at the ceiling of the cave.

"It seems everyone is on edge," Aponi said. "I'll do another energy prayer to soothe our spirits." Aponi began chanting. It didn't take long for Kero to feel drowsy and closed her eyes.

When morning came, everyone gathered everything and headed through the rest of the cave. Blythe, Kero and A'keara ended up pushing the snowglider because there was too much concern over the vibration of the running engine causing a cave-in. Aponi sat in the cart with Aurora this time. It wasn't too long before they saw the cave exit and the rest of the trail leading up the mountain.

"Okay, we're out of the cave. Now we use the vehicle again," A'keara said.

"Yes," Aponi agreed. "Don't go too fast, Blythe. We want to avoid causing an avalanche."

This time, A'keara took the seat on the back of the snow glider. The path curved suddenly. Blythe quickly turned the glider, which jerked the cart a little. Not too much further and another cave came into view.

"Another one?" Kero asked.

"There's lots of caves in the mountains," Blythe said.

The snow glider moved on ahead, still at a slow, steady pace. The vibration of the snow glider made ice and tiny stones fall from the ceiling of the cave. A'keara turned around to face Blythe.

"You need to slow down," she said.

"What's wrong?" Blythe asked.

"The vehicle is making too much noise."

"I can't go any slower," Blythe replied. "I have it on the lowest gear."

Inside the cart, Aponi sat with Aurora, petting her so she

would remain calm. Suddenly, the unicorn sat upright, her ears twitched. She moved her head, as if searching for something.

"Something is here," Aponi realized. "Aurora, dim your light." The brilliant light of the mare's horn dimmed down. A low growl came from within the cave.

"What's in this cave?" Kero asked just above a whisper."

"I've heard stories about snow beasts in the mountains," Blythe whispered back.

"You know, I don't think we have any weapons," Kero realized. More growls erupted through the cavern. Aurora moved her head from side to side and swished her tail. A'keara noticed from the back of the vehicle.

"Something is bothering Aurora. She's pretty uneasy," she noted.

"Uh-maybe we shouldn't go through this cave," Kero suggested.

"It's the only way up to the summit," A'keara informed her.

"Actually, I'm with Kero. Do we have weapons?" Blythe asked.

A'keara stared at the cart carrying her grandmother and Aurora.

"We have torches. Stop the glider." Blythe pushed the gear into neutral.

A'keara hopped off the back of the vehicle and practically slid over to the cart. She began searching for the torches. Aurora nuzzled her face.

"Hi there," A'keara greeted.

"What are you doing?" Aponi asked.

"We still have those torches, right?"

Aponi put her head back in thought. A'keara opened one of the smaller barrels. "Here they are." She grabbed two, and handed one to her grandmother.

"Here. This will help keep any living animal away from us. She used some flint to light the torch. Aponi held the torch out over the edge of the cart. A'keara lit her torch as well. "Okay. We should be good."

Returning to the vehicle, she jumped onto the back. "Let's try to get out as fast as we can."

Just as she said that, something jumped in front of the glider. The headlights of the glider illuminated a large furry white animal standing in their path. Blythe cried out, putting the vehicle into the highest gear. The vehicle jerked forward and Blythe steered around the creature. A'keara gripped tightly onto her seat with one hand and tried to keep a hold of her torch with the other.

"Hey! Don't go so fast!"

Blythe shifted down a gear. The creature wasn't following them. The beast hurried away to the far corner of the cave.

In the cart, Aponi held up the torch while scanning the area. Five more giant furry beasts huddled together by the cave wall. She hoped that they would be out of the cave soon. Then, the cart stopped. Aponi looked ahead to see that Blythe stopped the snow glider.

A'keara turned her head around to look at Blythe.

"Why did you stop?" A'keara asked. Blythe peered downward to see a deep chasm.

"Uh–we can't go any further."

A'keara stared out at the chasm. "Oh no! How are we going to get across!"

She jumped off the glider and rushed towards the cart. "There's nowhere for us to go!"

Aponi climbed out of the cart and inspected the chasm.

"Well, we won't be going that way." She noticed the distraught expression on A'keara's face. "Oh, don't look like that. We'll find a way to cross.

Meanwhile, Kero sat on the glider looking over the chasm. She could see to the other side where the rest of the cave was. The gap was too big for any of them to jump over it. After searching with her eyes, she spotted a flat piece of rock that bridged over the chasm.

"Do you think we can make it over that?" Kero asked, pointing at the makeshift bridge. Blythe studied the slab of rock.

"I don't know. We can try."

The girls walked over to the others by the cart to report what they found. Aponi moved towards the glider, but couldn't see anything.

"Oh, I'm afraid my eyesight isn't keen like you young girls," she said.

A'keara looked over and saw the thin piece of rock.

"There is no way we're crossing on that!"

"Looks like it's our only choice," Aponi replied. "May our ancestors watch over us and guide us safely across."

Kero's heart raced. If they fell… The piece of rock appeared wide enough for them to cross by foot, but she wasn't sure if they could get the cart across or the snow glider.

"Do you want to ride Aurora over the chasm?" Aponi asked her granddaughter.

"No." She let out a long sigh. "But, I'll do it anyway."

A'keara helped Aurora get out of the cart. She mounted the mare and guided her towards the rock bridge. As Aurora approached the long piece of rock, A'keara wondered if her four-legged friend would even cross. If Aurora didn't want to go over that slab of rock, there would be nothing A'keara could do about it.

However, to A'keara's surprise, the mare stepped onto the slab of stone and continued to carry her across the chasm. Everyone watched until Aurora made it to the other side.

"I'll stay with the cart," Aponi said. "Take your time, Blythe."

Kero and Blythe climbed onto the glider and Blythe put the vehicle into gear. As the glider moved onto the stone slab, Blythe realized it was still connected to the rest of the cave floor. That meant that the so-called stone bridge couldn't collapse from underneath them. It was also wider than she first thought. They could easily get the glider and the cart across.

As they were crossing the chasm, Kero made the mistake of peeking over the side of the glider to look into it. Her head spun and she felt her stomach drop. Halfway across the stone bride, fragments of loose pebbles fell from the ceiling. Kero felt some go into her eyes. She tried to stifle a cry as she rubbed them.

"Are you okay?" Blythe asked. Just as she did, more pebbles fell onto them.

"Maybe pick up the pace," Kero said.

"We can't go too fast," Blythe responded. "These rocks are a little slippery." Kero finished rubbing her eyes and glanced ahead to the other side. Something stood there, a lot of 'somethings' that were very large.

"And what about them?" Kero asked, pointing in the direction ahead of her.

On the other side of the chasm were a band of furry white beasts. They appeared like a wall, blocking their path.

"What are those things?" Kero asked.

"Well, some call them snow beasts or Yeti," Blythe answered. One of the Yeti stepped onto the rock bridge.

"How smart are these creatures?" Kero wondered.

"Uh, I'm not sure. They've survived for thousands of years," Blythe replied. "Or so I've been told." Kero held out the lit torch in her hand. Aponi, who was still in the cart, saw the same imminent danger and held out her torch. "Where's A'keara?" she wondered as she tried to look for the woman.

On the other side of the chasm, A'keara sat on top of Aurora, several feet away from the yeti. They had moved to this corner of the cave when they saw the beasts come towards them.

"It's okay," A'keara whispered to the animal. Suddenly, Aurora's horn glowed bright. The yeti on the stone bridge took another step towards the snow glider. However, with its next step, the snow beast levitated into the air.

Kero and Blythe stared in awe from the glider while Aponi did the same from the cart. Then in the next moment, the beast was tossed into the other members of his clan. About four of them ran off into the shadows of the cave, while three of them stayed.

As the snow glider approached the other side of the chasm, the three yeti blocking the path began to back away. Kero sighed with relief as they were safe from falling into the deep hole. Blythe now put the glider into a higher gear and moved forward. As the cart passed the yeti, Aponi waved the torch around. Two creatures ran from the fire, but one beast gripped onto the side of the cart with his giant claw. Aponi looked up at the creature. She got a sense that he was the Alpha of the group and was protecting his kind.

"I'm sorry, we are in your territory," Aponi spoke calmly. "Let us by and we'll leave your cave as fast as we can." The yeti let go of the cart and backed away.

A'keara met the others by the mouth of the cave. She

petted Aurora.

"That's the second time that I've seen Aurora use her telekinesis. I'm surprised her powers are getting stronger," she said.

"I'm not," Aponi replied. "Are you getting back into the cart with Aurora?"

A'keara sighed. "I guess." She coaxed the unicorn back into the cart while Aponi sat on the back seat of the glider.

The rays from the sun pierced everyone's eyes as they continued up the snowy trail. It was astonishing how bright the sun was, yet the air was frigid. The wind blew harshly, stinging everyone's faces as they approached the summit.

"We're almost there," Aponi said with excitement. Kero took deep breaths, only feeling like she received a little air.

"Why am I having a hard time breathin'?"

"The air is thinner up here," Aponi replied.

Blythe drove the snow glider through the thick snow. They approached the middle of the summit when her ears started pounding.

"What's that?" she asked out loud.

"What's what?" Kero wondered. Blythe put a hand to her right ear. She brought the snow glider to a halt. "Why are you stopping?"

Aponi suddenly hushed her. Kero spun her head around, staring daggers at the old lady.

"I hear it too, Blythe," Aponi said.

"Hear what?" Kero asked more irate.

"I hear this heartbeat," Blythe replied. She got off the snow glider and walked a few feet.

The heartbeat became more intense. As Blythe moved forward, her boot slid on a patch of ice. She quickly put her hands out to balance herself, but she fell forward into a pillar of ice. When she looked up, she saw two ice blue eyes staring down at her. Blythe cried out, actually falling backwards into a pile of snow. Aponi carefully trudged through the snow towards Blythe. She looked up and saw what they'd been looking for.

"The Crystal Dragon! You found her!"

Kero finally made it over. Her eyes widened as she saw the giant creature with blue and purple scales.

"How do I get her out?" Blythe asked, tapping on the sheet of ice. Blythe put her hands on the glacier. "Hello?" she called. She placed her forehead on the ice. Suddenly, the dream she had the previous night flashed inside her mind. She heard a kind voice speak.

I am the Crystal Dragon, who comes before me?

Blythe moved back, shocked by the voice. She once again placed her hands on the ice glacier.

"My name is Blythe."

Right after she spoke those words, her whole body froze, becoming encased in ice. The others gassed in horror. Before anyone made another motion, the ice cracked. Shards of ice burst out in all directions. Everyone shielded themselves.

The ice fell away from Blythe. She gazed up at the magnificent dragon spreading her wings. The dragon's scales glistened in the sunlight like crystals, showing hues of blue and violet. As this happened, the others were blinded by the brilliant light.

Far away, the light could be seen by the people of Michael and Gabriel. The Empress stood at the window in her throne room, her mouth agape at the wondrous sight. No one would be able to see her expression of course due to the golden mask hiding her face. The gown she wore was, encrusted with jewels that showed her wealth. It was magnificent.

General Kain waited outside the doors of the throne room. He stared adoringly at the designs crafted in the woodwork, framed in gold and jewels. The bell rang, permitting him to enter. Kain walked into the room, with his head held high with a look of poise and dignity.

The Empress spoke while still staring outside the window. He followed her glance to the beam of light. He almost lost his professional composure.

"Do you see it?" Her voice hummed sweetly. His wide eyes locked onto the bewildering phenomenon on top of Mt. Sansin.

"What is that?" he asked in awe.

"Do you not remember the story I told you?"

"You've told me many stories," he replied.

"How about the one with the awakening of four dragons and the destruction of our world?"

General Kain stared at her with disbelief. His gaze went from her to the streams of blue and violet light.

"So, dragons do exist," he confirmed.

CHAPTER 7

The First Meeting

When the light faded, the Crystal Dragon landed on the mountaintop. Everyone turned to her in awe.

"Hello dear ones, my name is Eira," the dragon said. Her voice sounded so bold and majestic. Aponi stepped forward.

"Hello, my name is Aponi, a high priestess from the city of Etheria."

"I am very pleased to meet you," Eira replied.

"I am A'keara and this lovely unicorn is Aurora." Eira gazed kindly at the unicorn. Aurora replied with a joyful whinny. This surprised A'keara.

"Oh, do you like the dragon?" she asked. Aurora replied with a soft nicker.

Now, the dragon glanced at Kero. "And you are?"

"Kero–uh ma'am." It was strange talking to a dragon.

The ma'am part just came out. Kero wasn't sure how to properly address a dragon.

Blythe swelled with all sorts of emotions. When she first heard the tale of the Spirit Dragons, she wasn't sure how to respond. She went along with the meditation just to be polite. However, she was overjoyed now that she actually not only saw a dragon, but bonded with one as well. In all of this excitement, Blythe suddenly realized that something appeared around her wrist. She gazed down to see a bracelet with white, blue and purple crystals.

"What's this?" she asked. "I usually don't wear jewelry."

"That is my gift to you," the dragon replied. "The crystals store a wonderful power that you now possess. It signifies our bond. The two white crystals are quartz crystals, the purple crystals are called amethysts and the blue one at the top is called lapis lazuli."

"Are the rest of us getting bracelets?" Kero asked.

The dragon replied, "Each of us spirit dragons have a different gift to give to our bonded."

Aponi was happy for their victory of awakening the first dragon.

However, now that they got the introductions out of the way, they had more pressing issues to face.

"Do you know about the gateway to the realm of dragons?" Aponi asked Eira.

"Why yes. I am the first dragon you have awakened, and there are three more who need to come out of their slumber."

"Shouldn't we get going then? We're on a time limit," A'keara said hastily.

"Calm yourself," Aponi replied gently. She turned to Eira. "I'm guessing you can take us to where the Golden Dragon is sleeping."

"I–don't really know where my brothers and sister are exactly. I know that my brother, Aeolus is somewhere west of here in the desert. And he is the second youngest of us Spirit Dragons. Did one of you get the vision?"

"I did," Aponi replied. "Well, honestly, A'keara and I are not the 'original bonded.'"

Eira nodded. "I know. So, where are the original ones who bonded with those dragons?"

"Wait a minute," Kero intervened. "Are ya tellin' me that you don't remember? How come you don't know?"

"Forgive me," Eira spoke kindly. "It's been over a millennium since we went to sleep. I believe most of our memories were wiped of the humans who bonded with us back then."

"Wait, a millennium is like a thousand years, right?" Blythe asked.

"Yeah, the people who bonded with ya are dead now," Kero realized. She turned to Aponi. "So, me and Blythe are not the original people who bonded with the dragons."

Aponi sighed. "Let me explain. See, it's not 'you,' the incarnation that stands here now. It is the 'you' that was incarnated here one thousand years ago. You all should have memories of this and realize that you needed to bond with your dragons again, but–"

"You don't remember anything," A'keara finished.

Suddenly, Blythe shivered from the cold. Kero realized her feet were numb.

"Uh, maybe we can talk more after we get off this mountain?" Blythe asked.

"Yes. It is time to go," Eira agreed.

Blythe looked up at the majestic creature.

"So, how do I get up there?" Blythe grabbed Eira's horns on her back.

"Uh, maybe I can just lower my head and you can get on," Eira suggested.

"Wait, what about the cart?" A'keara asked. "And Aurora. I'm not leaving her behind!"

"Of course, she won't get left behind," Aponi said. "Can you transport a unicorn?" she asked the dragon.

A'keara rolled her eyes and groaned.

"Hey, I can still steer the cart back down the mountain," Blythe said.

"It took a day and a half to get up here," A'keara said. "We have five days, no, actually four days now to awaken three more dragons. How are we going to get the cart and Aurora across the tundra and then to the desert, then to the islands, then to–"

"A'keara," Aponi said sternly. "Don't get so excited."

"What troubles you, my dear?" Eira asked.

A'keara just wanted to scream, but she held it in. "We have to awaken all of the Spirit Dragons by the next violet Energy moon, right? There's no way we can travel that distance in such a short amount of time."

"I can get to the desert in about four hours," Eira said.

"I know you can, but this cart has all of our supplies and

I can't leave it behind and I definitely can't leave Aurora behind."

"You also need to find the one who will bond with Aeolus," Eira informed.

"Right now, it is me who will bond with him," Aponi said. "I prayed to the Elder Dragons and they gave me the vision."

"I'm not sure if it works like that," Eira said. "But, we'll see. I can take you over there. I guess your companions will just have to meet us there later."

Aponi had another idea come to mind. She turned to her granddaughter.

"A'keara, maybe you should take Kero to the islands where she will bond with the Crimson Dragon. We'll meet you there."

"She'll have to wait for us," Eira said. She can't bond with Phoenix until you bond with Aeolus." The name rang in Kero's ear.

"The dragon I saw in my vision, his name is Phoenix?"

Eira nodded. Kero suddenly realized something. When she was young, she named the dragons from her book. She gave the fire breathing dragon the name Phoenix. She shook it off as a coincidence, but something told her it was more than that.

As everyone talked about how everything would go next, Blythe recalled that she also had a mission. Shc had to go to Isis.

"Uh, Eira, actually, I wondered if we could take a slight detour first."

"We don't have time for that," A'keara said harshly. Blythe returned a look of disdain. She didn't hide the fact that what A'keara said irked her.

"Let's talk about it after we have awakened my brother," Eira replied.

"We'd better get going," Aponi replied. Kero was ready to get off the frigid mountaintop, but then she thought of something else.

"Um, so you and Blythe are going to ride on Eira?" she asked.

Aponi nodded. "So, who is driving the snow glider?"

"You can do it," Blythe said. Kero's eyes went wide. "Uh, there's no way I can drive that thing."

"Okay, I'll have to drive it down the mountain then."

"I'll go with Eira to the desert," Aponi said. "I'm the one who has to bond with the Golden Dragon, anyways." Eira lowered her head and Aponi climbed onto her.

Eira took off, her massive wings flapped, creating a chilling breeze.

"Okay, let's go already!" Kero yelled, while shivering.

Blythe climbed onto the snow glider. Kero climbed into the seat Aponi sat in previously. A'keara stayed with Aurora in the cart.

"Actually, we'll move faster down the mountain than we did climbing it," Blythe informed.

"Don't go too fast," Kero said nervously.

Blythe started the snow glider and pushed the gear forward, propelling the vehicle forward. Everything was going smoothly for a moment. Suddenly, loud roars came from the distance.

"Look over there," Blythe said. Kero turned her head around to see a swarm of yeti standing in a line across the summit.

"What are they doing?" Kero asked.

"Apparently, they're trying to block our way."

"How did they get over there? They were on the other side

earlier." Then, she saw another group of yeti make a line on the opposite side of the mountain.

A'keara saw what they were doing.

"Hey! Hey!" She waved her arms. Kero turned to Blythe.

"There's more yeti on the other side." Blythe did a quick glimpse over her shoulder. Suddenly, she pushed the gear as high as it could go. The snow glider sped off, pulling the cart with it. A'keara fell backwards onto the floor of the cart and Aurora cried as she almost fell out. A'keara rolled over to her side and grabbed her mane.

"What is Blythe doing?" A'keara asked crossly.

Blythe swerved around one of the yeti, but the cart ran right into the creature. The yeti grabbed the cart and easily pushed it over. The reins tied to the cart broke off. A'keara and Aurora fell onto the snow and rolled towards the edge of the cliff. All the stuff in the cart went flying in all different directions.

Kero saw everything. "A'keara and Aurora fell out of the cart!" Blythe finally turned around. She brought the snow glider to a stop.

A'keara helped Aurora stand and she quickly climbed onto her back. However, now they were surrounded by the yeti. A'keara desperately searched for an opening to get out of the circle of yeti. As the mammoth snow beasts closed in on them, the unicorn's horn glowed and her body flickered. The yeti backed away for a moment, not sure what the unicorn was doing. A'keara looked down at her own body becoming transparent. A'keara realized that Aurora was trying to teleport. She hadn't used that ability in over ten years.

"Aurora, try to teleport us to the other side of the mountain." Unfortunately, the teleportation didn't happen. Aurora stopped glowing. The yeti swarmed the two again. As they came closer, something flew down from the sky. Ice crystals plummeted downward, striking the yeti. A'keara looked upward to see Aponi riding on Eira. From the dragon's mouth came more blasts of ice. The yeti withdrew, moving across the summit, back towards the caves. Eira landed in the snow.

"Are you alright?" she asked.

"Yes, but Aurora and I fell out of the cart. All of our supplies are everywhere!"

"I am so sorry," Blythe said as she drove over. "I thought we could just barrel through them." Everyone was quiet for a moment.

"Don't worry about it." A'keara said, waving her hand. "Let's just put the stuff back into the cart and tie the reins back up."

Aponi smiled. She thought her granddaughter was going to explode, but maybe she was finally learning some patience.

It took four of them to turn the cart over, then everyone looked around for their supplies now half buried in the snow. Once everything was put back together, A'keara tried to get Aurora back into the cart. However, this time, the unicorn would not budge.

"Aurora, are you okay?" The unicorn looked down. A'keara understood right away. She turned to the others. "She's not getting back into the cart."

"So, what do we do?" Kero asked. A'keara untied the reins from the snow glider and put them on Aurora.

"We're going down the mountain like this," A'keara said before mounting the mare. "We'll take the cart back down the mountain."

"But, I thought you were concerned about the time limit," Aponi said.

"I'm more concerned about our safety," she replied. "Besides, you're going over to the desert on the dragon, right?"

Aponi nodded. "Glad you see you're thinking more clearly." Eira and Aponi took off once again. A'keara turned to Blythe and Kero.

"I'll meet you guys at the bottom." Blythe put the vehicle in gear and drove off.

The girls made their way down the mountainside very easily. Kero wasn't sure what they were going to do next. She couldn't bond with Phoenix until Aponi bonded with the other dragon first. She wondered how long that would take. Blythe made a hard turn suddenly, almost making Kero fall off.

"Hey! Slow down!" Kero yelled.

"Sorry." Blythe said. "I guess I'm getting excited. All of this dragon stuff is happening. I mean, if awakening these dragons means the end of the Empire, I just—" Blythe took a deep breath. "I can't wait to see it."

Kero was all for the downfall of the Empire, but she also had to find her brother. Blythe mentioned that there was a prison in the tundra. He might be there.

"Blythe, do you know much about the prison in the tundra?" Blythe was silent for a long moment. "Why do you ask?"

"Uh, just curious."

"You think that's where your brother is being held?"

Kero shrugged. "Maybe."

Blythe took another turn. Kero had to grab onto the side of the seat.

"I told you to slow down!" Kero yelled. Another turn, then another. "Blythe, are you listening?"

"Uh-oh, Kero, we have company."

Kero looked around, expecting more of those yeti, but she didn't see them. Instead, she saw something flying over them. At first, she thought it was Eira, but this creature wasn't alone. Two more showed up. They came into view and she realized they weren't dragons. Their stature was much smaller. Each one had a long body like a dragon, but the face of a bat. From their mouths came blasts of ice and wind.

"What are those things?" Kero asked, terrified.

"I don't know!" Blythe replied just as panicked. Blythe swerved, trying to avoid the attacks. The snow glider skidded down the side of the mountain, right into a large boulder. The collision caused Kero to lose her grip on the seat. She fell backwards off the glider. Blythe turned, horrified as the girl fell off the side of the mountain.

"Kero!" she screamed.

The wind blew fiercely; fragments of snow crystals twirled and spun around violently. Kero held onto the edge of the cliff several feet below from where she fell. With all of her strength, Kero pulled herself up onto a narrow ledge. She wasn't sure how far she fell. The wind picked up even more and now her fingers were numb. She sat alone on the side of the cliff on the highest mountain on the planet. It was then that she greatly regretted going on this journey.

CHAPTER 8

Holding onto Faith

In a cold dark cell, Darion sat huddled in a blanket with shackles around his wrists and ankles. Even with the blanket, his body ached from the cold. He was told that the only reason he had the blanket was that he was needed alive for questioning.

Suddenly, the door opened, bringing some light into the cell. The man who opened the door, held a lantern. His tall and muscular stature would intimidate most people, but Darion was used to dealing with people with the same appearance. There were a few men his size on the farm, the ones who did a lot of heavy lifting. The only difference of course was that the man standing in front of him wore a military uniform.

"Darion Embers," the man spoke in a gruff voice. "You're coming with me."

Two guards came into the cell and unlocked the shackles around Darion's wrists. Darion was made to stand up. When he did, he clearly saw the large man's face.

"Hold on–yer General Kain."

The man returned a stern glare. "Do not speak my name. To you, it's Sir." He turned to the guards. "Take him to the interrogation room."

High in the mountains, Kero did her best to make her way down the trail. She'd eventually reach the bottom, unless she froze to death first. Suddenly, she became angry at Blythe. She told the wench to slow down. Then again, she supposed it wasn't completely her fault. Those creatures that chased them contributed to Blythe losing control of the snow glider. Damn it! Now what was she supposed to do? Aponi went off on the dragon. A'keara was coming down with the cart and Blythe was hopefully making her way down on the snow glider. Then, something else occurred to her. It wouldn't take Blythe that long to find her. Maybe she should wait for her.

Through the harsh wind and falling snow, Kero spotted an alcove within the rockwall of the mountain. She hurried under it and sat down on a large rock. It was a little better. It was far from perfect, but at least her face didn't sting as much from the cold. However, she could barely feel her fingers and toes. She prayed silently that Blythe would find her soon.

About two hundred feet up from where Kero sat, Blythe drove around the mountainside, taking sharp turns and skidding across the ice. Her heart raced every time she took a turn. She heard Kero's words in her head. *Slow down!* Blythe pulled the gearshift down a notch. At least those bats or whatever they were flew off and left her alone. They must have entered their territory and now, she moved out of it. Maybe their home was up in those caves they passed earlier. Continuing down the slope, the glider stayed at a steady pace. Blythe breathed a sigh of relief. Hopefully, she'd find Kero. Kero had to be okay. She kept convincing herself of this.

About a hundred feet up from Blythe, A'keara stirred Aurora down the slippery slope. Without wheels, the cart kept slipping from side to side. She had to stop her companion every few feet or so to make sure the cart was okay. They weren't moving very fast at all.

"This is so stupid," A'keara said all in a huff. "Maybe we should just leave the cart." She studied it for a moment. They could replace most of the items. To be honest, they wouldn't be coming this far north ever again. She coaxed Aurora to move forward. They traveled several feet until A'keara heard wood cracking behind her. She gasped and stopped Aurora again. She dismounted the mare and hurried over to find a huge hole in the middle of the cart. The floorboards broke. All of the barrels were in the snow. There was no way to fix this right now. A'keara cried out in frustration.

"What else can go wrong?"

As if to answer her question, a shot of ice struck her in the shoulder. A'keara cried out, grabbing where she was wounded. The coat provided some protection, but her shoulder still ached. She looked up to see two creatures with the faces of bats flying towards them. A'keara tore the reins off the cart then jumped onto Aurora.

"Go!" she yelled. The unicorn took off.

Aurora did well to stay on the mountain path, however, the two bat-like creatures were attacking them relentlessly. The blasts of ice struck Aurora. She stopped in her tracks and rose herself to her hinged legs, whinnying loudly.

"Aurora! You have to keep moving!" Another blast of ice

struck A'keara in the lower area of her back, causing her to fall off the mare. She laid motionless for a moment. Aurora nuzzled her. A'keara slowly rolled over. Her eyes opened just as one of the bat-faced creatures flew towards her. Aurora's horn glowed; she twisted her neck, sending the creature into the side of the mountain. The bat fell into the snow and laid motionless.

A'keara relaxed and mounted Aurora again. As she climbed back onto the mare, more attacked. Aurora took off once again, galloping down the slope. A'keara tried to hold on as the unicorn increased her speed down the mountain path. A'keara looked up to see the two creatures stop their pursuit and fly into a nearby cave.

Grabbing Aurora's reins, A'keara pulled them back, beckoning the unicorn to stop. Aurora spun around, but her hoofs slipped on a thick patch of ice. She started to fall backwards. A'keara wrapped her arms around the mare's neck as she fell off the side of the cliff. A'keara closed her eyes, silently praying. As Aurora fell, her body became transparent, then completely disappeared.

Several feet below, the mare reappeared on the mountain path. A'keara

opened her eyes to find herself still hugging Aurora's neck. She sat upright on the mare. She pet Aurora to comfort her.

"What did you do?" A'keara wondered. Aurora, who usually was talkative, now was completely silent. A'keara looked up to see the path where they had been.

"Aurora–did you teleport?"

An excited whinny came from the mare's mouth. A'keara joined the unicorn with a cry of delight. "You teleported!" She hugged her four-legged friend. "We're almost at the base of the mountain." She pointed towards the path for them to follow. "Let's go."

As Aurora slowly walked down the path, A'keara realized they left the cart and all of their belongings behind. She didn't have a choice. She just prayed that her grandmother wouldn't be too cross with her.

Kero had been waiting for a while now. She looked up the mountain path. It was taking Blythe a while to get there. It would probably take A'keara even longer. Maybe she should just keep walking down the mountain. At least if she kept moving, she could keep somewhat warm. She stood up, brushing the snow off of her. With one foot in front of the other, she made her way down the mountain trail.

Kero didn't go too far before hearing the low roar of the snow glider coming her way. She turned around as Blythe pulled up beside her.

"Want a ride?" she asked with a smile. Kero actually smiled back.

"Sure." She jumped on the back.

"I'm so sorry. I can't believe you're okay. I thought you were d–" Blythe stopped, feeling tears whelmed up inside of her.

Blythe breathed in deeply before asking, "Are you okay?"

"I'm fine, I guess," Kero said quietly.

"Have you seen A'keara?

Kero shook her head.

"I'm not sure how long it's going to take her to get down the mountain," Blythe said.

"So, where are we going after this? Aponi left with that dragon," Kero asked.

"They're heading towards the plateaus in the Western Region," Blythe replied.

"The plateaus?" Kero questioned.

"There are plateaus in the desert. You'll see when we get there."

Suddenly, Kero felt a little dumb. "Uh, what are plateaus?"

"Oh, well a plateau is made up of rock and it's higher than flat land. It's not nearly as high as a mountain. It's hard to explain. That's why it's better just to see it for yourself."

Minutes later, they reached the bottom of the mountain. Kero was relieved, but still cold. She had no idea when they would meet up with A'keara.

"So, are we going?" Kero asked.

"I thought we were waiting for A'keara and Aurora."

"Do you think they'll take much longer? Maybe we can head towards the desert." Kero shivered.

"Oh, uh, I guess so. I just didn't want to leave her behind."

"I get it," Kero said hastily. "I just don't want to become an icicle while we wait for her."

Blythe sighed. "Okay, we can head southwest towards the desert. I mean, honestly, I can only drive a snow glider in the snow. Once we get too far south, we won't be able to use this thing."

She sped off across the snow drifts. Up and down, the snow glider took them on a vigorous ride over the snowy hills. Kero actually started having fun. She turned around to look at Blythe. She wondered how this girl was so nice. In fact, Aponi,

A'keara and Blythe were the nicest people she's ever met. She had been told as a child to be careful of people who were too nice, because it usually meant they wanted something. Kero didn't have anything though. All she had was a desire to get a dragon and then rescue her brother. After that, well, she wasn't sure yet.

Not too far away, Darion sat on the interrogation chair in the deepest level of the prison. General Kain paced back and forth in front of him, while his guard stood just staring at Darion menacingly. In his hands was a long stick with a metal tip on the end.

Darion stared at the general, wondering if the man was ever going to ask him anything. All they had done so far was prod him with an electrical stick. His body still ached.

Finally, the general stopped pacing.

"I believe I gave you enough time. Now you tell me where your sister ran off to."

Darion would have fallen out of his chair from shock if he wasn't strapped to it.

"Why are you asking me that? You arrested her when you arrested me."

Suddenly, the general smacked Darion across the face. His face stung from the blow.

"I will ask you what I wish!" he hollered. "And you will answer me!"

"I don't know where she is," he said. It was the truth, but even if he did know where Kero was, he wouldn't say a word to this man.

"Your sister somehow escaped from the airship," Kain said crossly. "Did you make plans? Where has she gone?"

Plans? Was this guy serious?

"I didn't know she escaped," Darion admitted. He wished he did know where she went. Kain slapped him again.

"I'm tellin' you the truth," Darion insisted.

General Kain nodded to the prison guard next to him. The guard raised the stick, sparks crackled from the electric tip.

Suddenly, a knock came at the door. Darion felt relief as the general pushed a button on his remote control. The door unlocked with a beep; the red light turned green. When the door opened, he saw a nervous guard standing on the other side. The general was about to strike him when the guard pleaded for forgiveness.

"I'm sorry sir! The Empress wants to speak with you."

Kain lowered his hand. He turned towards the guard inside the room. "You come with me." He turned to the nervous guard at the door.

"Guard the prisoner until I come back." The guard with the prodding stick hastily jammed the weapon into the other guard's hands while giving him a searing glare. Both men left the anxious man in the room alone with Darion.

The metalic door locked and beeped; the green light on the top of the door turned red. Darion realized that the man wasn't holding onto the prodding stick very tightly. If he wasn't tied up, Darion probably would have been able to wrestle the weapon away from the man.

Finally, the guard addressed Darion.

"All of this because you killed an animal on imperial land?"

Darion just stared at the man. "You don't look like you have any secrets." He walked over to Darion. "I mean, if you did, you would have talked, right?"

Darion shrugged his shoulders, remaining silent. The guard sat down, facing Darion.

"If you don't know anything, just make something up. It's better for you to be put into a cell and forgotten."

Darion took a deep breath. "Fine. Tell General Kain to look inside an erupting volcano."

The guard shook his head. "It's not a good idea to be a wise guy. Trust me. Just tell the general where ya think she might be. It will be enough for him to leave ya alone." Darion went silent.

In another location, General Kain walked into his private quarters and sat down in front of a large monitor. He looked up at the screen to see Empress Celise.

"Yes, your majesty?"

"Where have you been?" she asked.

"I told you I'd find out where those traitorous lowlifes were going. I have the brother of that girl, Kero Embers. My men arrested her at the same time as him and somehow she escaped while still on the airship."

"You're wasting your time. That boy doesn't know anything. Didn't you tell me that two girls escaped from that ship?"

The general recalled there was another girl.

Kain walked over to his desk where his laptop sat next to a picture of a woman with long dark hair. He checked the patrol officer's notes. Under Kero's name was another, Blythe Krystal. Kain narrowed his eyes. He peered down at the screen on his laptop. At the top of the screen in bold letters was the caption, Colonists of the Empire. Kain typed in the names of the two escapees. Kero's information came up, but Blythe's did not. The general scrunched his eyebrows.

"There's no file on this girl named Blythe," he noted. The general thought for a second. "It has to be a fake name," Kain said to himself.

Under his notes was an ID with Blythe's picture. The general showed the ID to the Empress. "This ID is fake. The guards at Isis arrested her after she tried to use it to get into the city."

"You told me that your men found a group of people with fake IDs," Celise reminded him.

"Yes. They were a group of rebels planning to overthrow you. Every one of them had a fake ID. Don't worry, I'll find both of those girls."

"You have a lot on your plate," the Empress hummed. "You have to send your men to the plateaus in the Western Region. Remember, that is where the next dragon will awaken."

"What if these two girls are behind the awakening of the dragons?" Kain asked.

"It may be possible, but you won't know until you go there, will you?" General Kain closed his laptop, then stood and bowed to the Empress.

"Thank you for sparing your time with me." He raised his head and turned off the monitor, then headed out.

A few hours passed since Kero and Blythe left the base of the mountain. The temperature grew warm enough for her to take off her gloves and remove the hood of her coat. The snow had melted enough to see blades of grass poke out.

"How close are we to the desert?" Kero asked.

"We're not even out of the Northern Region yet. But, don't worry. At least it's warmer, right?"

Kero nodded. "So, are we waiting for A'keara?"

"Do you want to wait? I'm not sure how long it will take her to get here." Just as Blythe finished her sentence, they heard a whinny coming up from behind them. Both girls turned to see Aurora trotting towards them with A'keara riding atop of her. "Never mind. That didn't take long at all."

"Yeah," Kero agreed. She looked up at A'keara as she approached them. "How did you get here so fast?"

A'keara smiled. "Aurora finally figured out how to teleport."

Blythe and Kero shared equally shocked expressions on their faces.

"She teleported? That's amazing!" Blythe squealed.

"Yes. It seems Aurora is getting more of her abilities back."

"Well, now we're all here," Blythe said.

Kero suddenly realized something was missing. "Uh, where's yer cart?"

A'keara's eyes fixed on her. She breathed in deeply before replying.

"We had to leave it behind." Both Kero and Blythe returned apologetic looks. "It's fine. That cart was just slowing us down." Her lips formed a weak smile. "Let's head towards the desert."

It felt like they'd been riding forever. Kero thought they had to be almost out of the Northern Region by now. Suddenly, Blythe stopped.

"What's going on?" Kero asked.

"Look," she said pointing out at a field. "No more snow."

"So, now what? I don't see a desert."

Blythe chuckled. "Did you actually think we were going to make it to the desert? We'll have to walk the rest of the way."

"Walk?" Kero asked. "I'm too cold to walk." A'keara and Aurora pranced up to them.

"Hey, A'keara, can Aurora carry three people?"

"Uh, I'm not sure. What happened to the snow glider?"

"No more snow," Kero replied. A'keara nodded.

"Well, we can see if Aurora can carry all of us."

Kero easily swung her leg over to get onto the unicorn, but Blythe was having trouble.

"How did you do that?" she asked Kero.

"I ride horses a lot on the farm." Blythe nodded. "Right." She finally made it onto Aurora's back.

"Okay Aurora, concentrate on the desert."

"The desert?" Kero asked.

"Yes. Aurora is going to teleport us to the desert."

"Does she know where the desert is?" Blythe asked.

"All she has to do is focus on Aponi," A'keara explained. "She's in the desert right now."

"Uh, wouldn't she be up in the air?"

"Maybe, but that won't matter."

Aurora's horn began to glow and her body became transparent. As Kero stared at the ground, everything went white. She closed her eyes, gripping tightly onto A'keara's shoulders.

"We're here!" the woman yelled. Kero opened her eyes to see the white desert sand all around them.

"I can't believe it!" Blythe exclaimed.

"But, where's Aponi?" Kero asked.

A'keara looked up to see the crystal scaled dragon fly over them with Aponi riding her.

"I can't believe that worked," Kero said.

"I'm a little surprised too," A'keara admitted. "I wonder if the dragon had something to do with it."

"What does the dragon have to do with anything?" Kero inquired.

"Dragons have a lot of energy. They are even more magical than unicorns. It's possible Aurora meeting Eira activated her power to teleport."

"Maybe Aponi and my power will come back too."

"Wait, you two have powers?" Kero asked.

"Everyone on Gaia did once. After Etheria fell, no one remembers their abilities. Connecting with our ancestors is one of our gifts as well as being intuitive."

"That's not a power. I mean, can you teleport like Aurora just did?"

"Some of the Wise Ones could. Some of them could make things materialize out of thin air. However, most people on Gaia were telepathic and they were in tune with nature. Some even had abilities to control elements like fire, water, lightning and wind."

"What about ice?" Blythe asked.

"Ice and water are the same. Ice is water when it is frozen."

"Speaking of ice and water, it would be nice to have both right now. It's really hot here," Kero said.

"You were just complaining how cold you were just a few minutes ago," Blythe replied.

A'keara started to laugh. "You don't know what you have until it's gone."

"You seem like you're in a better mood," Blythe said.

"I guess it's nice to know that our powers might be coming back to us. I was so upset with Aponi because I wasn't sure about this dragon business, but I guess what she said had merit. And what she said at the beginning of this journey holds true as well."

"What did she say?" Kero asked.

A'keara smiled. "Have faith."

CHAPTER 9

Battle in the Sky

Aponi and Eira reached the plateaus, set in the Western Region of Anu. There were five plateaus standing in a perfect semi-circle. Eira landed on the ledge on the plateau directly in the middle. The dragon and her rider stared into the dark abyss of a small cave.

"He might be in there," the crystal dragon informed her.

"The cave doesn't look big enough for me to go inside," Aponi replied.

The elderly lady dismounted Eira and moved a few steps towards the cave. She bent down, almost crawling inside the hole in the side of the giant rock formation. Aponi took out a few of the light crystals from her pouch. With the crystals in her hand, she was able to clearly make out a thin path between the rock walls. She continued about a quarter of a mile in before reaching a dead end.

"This can't be the right place," she said to herself. She suddenly realized that she couldn't turn around. "I guess I have to walk out the same way I walked in." She began moving her legs backwards in her hunched over position. "I feel like a crab." She laughed lightly to herself.

Once she made it back outside, she addressed Eira about the situation.

"I didn't find him," she said.

"It's possible that he's in a different cave," Eira said. "There are many caves in these plateaus. We'll keep looking." The dragon lowered her head, so Aponi could climb onto her back, then she took off to the other side of the plateaus.

Down below them was a cave. Eira flew towards the entrance.

"I might be able to fit inside that one," she said. As the crystal dragon neared the cave, something shot at her. She hovered for a moment in the air, looking around. A large shadow loomed over them, covering the sun. The two looked up to see a large airship.

"What is that?" Eira wondered. Aponi squinted her eyes. It took her a moment before she realized what it was.

"That's one of the Empire's warships," Aponi replied. "Let's get inside the cave, quick!"

Eira flew downwards, barely missing another shot. She landed on the cliff outside the cave. Now that she looked at it, she realized she was too large to go inside.

"Go inside," she said. "I'll take care of that ship."

"By yourself?" Aponi asked, concerned.

Eira returned a genuine smile. "Don't worry. It doesn't appear to be moving that fast. I can easily move around it." Aponi jumped off the dragon and ran inside the cave. Eira took off into the sky. Hopefully, this was the right cave. If Aponi found the

Golden Dragon here, he would be able to help Eira.

The crystal dragon flew towards the contraption in the sky. She breathed some snow flurries and ice. The ship was barely fazed by her attacks. Suddenly, a beam of energy shot her in the chest.

Aurora carried her companions through the desert until the plateaus came into view. Blythe suddenly winced from pain as she touched her chest.

"Ow!" she exclaimed.

"Are you alright?" A'keara asked.

"I just felt a sharp pain in my chest," she replied.

Kero turned to look at her. "Maybe it's somethin' ya ate."

Blythe shook her head. "That would be my stomach. I felt a pain in my chest." She thought for a moment. "Something's wrong. She looked down, a light blue aura glowed around her bracelet.

"I need to find Eira!" she cried frantically.

"Aurora, try to teleport to Aponi again," A'keara instructed.

Aurora's body flickered and then faded. When she reappeared, everyone looked around to find themselves in a cave. Aponi was only a few feet away from them facing the cave wall. She turned her body, then stumbled backwards from shock.

"How in the world did all of you get here?" she asked. A'keara returned a wide smile.

"Grandmother, it was amazing! Aurora regained her ability to teleport."

Aponi gazed at the unicorn with admiration. "So, she just started teleporting again?"

"This happened after she met the dragon."

"By the way, where's Eira?" Blythe asked.

Aponi pointed upwards. "She's taking care of that Imperial ship."

"An Imperial airship?" Kero questioned. "Why are they out here?"

There were sounds of explosions from outside. Blythe's bracelet glowed again and she felt a tiny pain in her right leg. Without a word, she ran towards the cave's exit.

"Wait! Where are you going?" Kero called to her. She chased after Blythe until she came out of the cave into the light of day. Blythe stared up at the sky at Eira swooping around and spitting out ice crystals at the airship. Laser beams jetted from the guns around the ship. Every time Eira was struck by a laser beam, the bracelet glowed and Blythe felt pain somewhere on her body.

"She can't fight that airship on her own," Blythe said.

"What are we supposed to do?" Kero asked. "I mean, once Aponi wakes up the other dragon, it can go help Eira." Blythe nodded.

The girls ran back inside the cave to where Aponi and A'keara stood by the back wall of the cave.

"There's no way this is the dragon," A'keara said.

"I know it sounds strange, but I just have the feeling that it is," Aponi told her.

"Did you find the dragon?" Blythe asked. The women turned around, a little startled.

"Yes, I believe I found Aeolus," Aponi said. Kero and Blythe gazed at the wall for a moment.

"I don't see a dragon," Kero said.

"That's what I said," A'keara confirmed.

Aponi regarded everyone with a knowing smile. "Like I said to A'keara. I can feel Aeolus is here in this cave." She turned towards the cavern wall. "See this spot right here?" Everyone's eyes saw a large indentation in the rockwall. The section of the rock was a different color; it looked like sand instead of stone.

Aponi held out her light crystal, creating a nice bit of light so everyone could see a curious outline. One end looked like a head and the other a tail. There was a small brownish colored stone in the patch of sand. Aponi backed up a little, keeping her eyes on it.

"I can see it," she said. "Look, it's the dragon."

The other three stared at the patch of sand for a moment.

"Well, if it's the dragon, go ahead and wake him up," A'keara prompted.

Taking a step forward, Aponi kept her gaze on the wall for a moment before putting her hand onto the sand. Suddenly, she heard a voice speak inside her head.

"I am the Golden Dragon, who comes before me?"

Aponi's eyes widened. She wasn't expecting this.

"Hello, my name is Aponi, one of the last survivors of Etheria. I had the vision of you. I am not your intended bonded, but the Elder Dragons gave me the vision."

"I accept you as my bonded until I find the true soul I am meant to bond with."

A small squall whirled around Aponi. For a moment, she couldn't move or breathe. Then the wind died down. She turned back to see the sand within the rockwall spilling onto the ground.

Aponi backed away.

"What's going on?" A'keara asked. Aponi turned to her just as stunned, shaking her head.

"I thought the sand was the dragon. Where is he?"

Suddenly, a loud cry was heard outside. Everyone rushed out of the cave and looked up at the sky.

A moment ago, there wasn't a cloud in the sky, but now, a large, fluffy cloud floated towards the plateaus. The cloud changed color from white to gold. For a moment, it looked like there were two suns in the sky. Finally, the Golden Dragon fully appeared. The golden scales glistened in the sunlight, practically blinding everyone.

On the airship, the captain had to shield his eyes from the bright light. He looked over the control panel. A red light came on signifying that one of the engines broke down. The aircraft shook violently.

"Sir! The dragon just froze one of the engines!" one of the fighter pilots called to him. Before the captain could respond, General Kain threw open the door.

"Why is that dragon still in the sky! Blast it down already!"

The captain turned towards the general. "We're trying sir, it's just–" Suddenly, Kain grabbed the man by the throat. "Don't try! Do it!" He tossed him into the steering wheel. Comparing the two men, the general was not only a half a foot taller, he outweighed the captain too.

The captain fumbled as he pulled himself to his feet. He looked through the window to see the Golden Dragon flying towards them. He released a gust of wind that stopped the airship in mid-flight.

"Another dragon?" the captain exclaimed.

"Shoot it down!" Kain yelled. "Shoot down any dragon you see!"

One of the gunmen turned to his partner. "Geez! Never knew the General hated dragons so much.

"What? Ya didn't know? His own mother was eaten by a dragon," the other said.

Suddenly, General Kain grabbed the man by his collar. "Ya hear me talkin' to others about your business?" The gunman fearfully shook his head.

"S-sorry s-sir! I-I hate dragons too! I-I'll shoot every dragon I see!"

The General dropped him and the man scrambled to his seat.

From the side of the cliff, the four women watched Eira and Aeolus fly around the airship. Eira attacked with ice, and Aeolus attacked with wind.

"Those two could start a blizzard," Aponi remarked.

"Grandmother, what's that on your robe?" A'keara asked. Aponi looked down at a golden broach.

"Oh, now I have a little trinket. It's a gift from Aeolus. Now that I am his bonded, this broach signifies our bond."

"So each one of us will get some piece of jewelry?" Kero asked.

"Maybe," Aponi replied. "Remember, this is new to me too. I don't know everything."

Kero wondered what she would get when she bonded to a dragon. She looked up at the sky, watching the two dragons fly around the airship. If those two can take down an airship, what would four dragons do?

Eira and Aeolus attacked relentlessly. A few times, the laser hit one of their wings or feet or tail. It was a tiny sting, nothing too serious. Eira flew to Aeolus, trying to get his attention.

"Brother! Let me use your wind."

Aeolus turned to her as if her presence was unexpected.

"Eira? Is that you? I didn't notice you were here!"

"Yes brother, it's me! I'm so glad you're awake. The humans in this aircraft mean to harm our bonded."

"I know," he replied. Suddenly, a laser beam hit Aeolus on his right side. He cried out and returned large gusts of wind at the airship. Eira spit out sharp balls of ice. The wind carried the ice with faster speed at the ship. Another engine came to a halt, the blades were frozen in place.

Back at the plateaus, Aponi felt pain in her side.

"That's strange," she said.

"What?" A'keara asked.

"I don't know. It felt like I just got bit by something."

"Well, there are probably bugs in these caverns. Also, watch out for scorpions."

Aponi looked on the ground, but then realized the pain was on her side. She touched the spot where it hurt a moment ago. Her broach glowed, and a golden shield appeared around her. Then, she noticed something similar happening to Blythe, only the shield around her was light blue.

Inside the airship, the captain began to panic. *At this rate, those beasts would take out the other two engines and they would crash.* Aeolus and Eira flew under the airship as another beam nearly missed them. They used the same strategy as before to take out the third engine.

Once the third engine froze, the airship stopped moving forward. It hovered in the sky, and smoke burst out from the three failed engines.

"Sir, we need to evacuate!" the captain yelled to General Kain. The general met him with a scowl on his face. Many of the other crew members ran towards an escape vessel. The captain ran towards the one set aside for him, but General Kain beat him there.

"Where are you going?" he asked, raising an eyebrow. "The captain goes down with the ship." The General swung his fist, connecting with the captain's jaw. A loud crack erupted as the man's jaw bone cracked. He let out a loud wail while holding the right side of his face. The general walked to the escape vessel as fire burst all around the aircraft. Those lucky enough to escape, got away before the aircraft plummeted to the ground.

Eira and Aeolus hurried back to the cliff. Once the dragons landed, they embraced, twirling their necks around each other.

"Aeolus, my brother, I am so glad we're awake again," Eira said.

"Me too," Aeolus replied. They looked at the humans. "Hello," the golden scaled dragon spoke kindly. He turned to Aponi. "I accept you as my bonded. However, I need to know where my true bonded is and why he couldn't be here. Has he passed on?"

Aponi realized that the dragon asked if his true bonded had died.

"Unfortunately, I cannot answer that question. See, my granddaughter, A'keara and I were going to bond with all four Spirit Dragons. Both her and I would be bonded with two dragons.

"The Elder Dragons would never allow such a thing," Aeolus stated. "Only a bond between one human and one dragon can happen."

"It's true," Eira said. "The Elder Dragons made sure one human could not possess the power of more than one dragon. It would be too much power."

"Well, I guess it's a good thing Kero and I came along," Blythe said cheerfully.

"Yes, there are four of us now," A'keara said.

"We'll see if it works," Aeolus said. "For now, we need to awaken our brother, Phoenix. Who is his bonded?" Kero stepped forward.

"I'm bondin' to him," she said.

"Wonderful!" Eira exclaimed. "Aeolus and I can easily take you four to the next destination."

"Oh yes," Aponi hummed. She turned to Kero. "Where's our next location?"

Kero returned a bewildered stare. "Uh, I have no idea. I heard the voice of the dragon and I saw all this fire, but I don't know where he is exactly."

"Phoenix will be somewhere in the Southern Region," Aeolus said.

Kero realized they would be headed towards Athena. She silently prayed that she wouldn't have to go anywhere near the farm.

"Hopefully, you will remember more as we go farther

south," Aponi said.

"We really should be going," Eira said.

Just then, Blythe realized that they were very close to Isis. Xan was supposed to be there.

"Hey Eira, remember back on the mountain when I told you I needed to make a slight detour? Well, I have a friend waiting for me in one of the cities near here. You just need to fly me over the wall into the city. I'll find him and then we can leave."

"Are we bringing this friend with us?" Eira asked.

"I don't think so. I just need to get some information from him."

A'keara let out an aggravated sigh. "Listen Blythe, I understand that you want to find this friend of yours, but we can't waste any more time. Once we awaken all four dragons, the Empire will be finished. Then, you can go find your friend."

Blythe turned away from everyone.

"He might be dead by then," she spoke softly. She slowly turned to face the others. Her eyes were mournful. It appeared as if she was trying to hold back her tears.

"We were all part of a resistance group. The imperial army found our base and now, they're hunting us down. I was caught when I first tried to enter Isis because I had a fake ID. I'm sure the military has that ID and they're probably looking for me. They also know what my friend looks like. If they find him, they'll kill him. I'm sure he's doing a good job hiding, but–"

Everyone was silent. Then Eira spoke.

"I can feel your emotion," she said. "And I understand what is at stake. I'll take you to this Isis city."

"What should the rest of us do?" Aeolus asked. "Should I take the others to awaken Phoenix?"

"That will be fine," Eira replied. She looked at the human women. "Blythe and I will meet you later."

As they parted ways, Kero had a lot on her mind. It was going to be interesting when she meets her dragon. She mounted Aeolus, sitting behind Aponi. She wasn't sure what to hold onto, so she grabbed two small horns poking out the golden scales. The dragon took off and Kero tightened her grip. Her eyes peered downward to see A'keara riding Aurora at an incredibly fast speed. Kero was hopeful, but also fearful at the same time. A thought forced its way into her head. What if she couldn't find the Crimson Dragon?

CHAPTER 10

The City of Sand

Blythe stared down at the desert plains from on top of Eira. It was so exciting to be riding a dragon for the first time. Blythe looked ahead to see the colony of Isis. The tiny city had many buildings made of sand and concrete. Around this city was a gigantic border wall.

"See that wall circling around the city?" Blythe yelled over the racing wind. "That's where we need to go."

"Strange. Are all of the cities locked behind a wall like this one?" Blythe turned her eyes downward. "Most of them, yes. Except for Luna, which is underground, and the Salamand Islands, which are of course surrounded by water." She took a small breath. "I grew up in Luna, the one underground."

"You must've had some sad memories from that place," Eira noted.

Blythe tried to shake herself out of her gloom. "It doesn't matter. I don't live there anymore."

"Listen Blythe, keeping emotions locked up inside will only hurt you. You don't have to act happy when you're sad."

"It's okay. Really. We just need to find my friend."

"How many of these cities are there?"

"Well, for one, they're called colonies. There are seven colonies," Blythe explained. "Michael and Gabriel are at the top, the two brother colonies that rule over everyone else. Then, we have the five 'lesser' colonies, Apollo, Isis, Athena, Salamand Islands and Luna."

"So, the Empress is the one behind this planet's disruption?"

Blythe wasn't sure what the dragon meant by 'disruption.'

"I guess so?"

Eira laughed lightly. "I mean, is she the one responsible for making the planet the way it is now?"

"Yes," Blythe answered strongly.

"So, we will ask her to stand down," Eira decided.

Blythe laughed. "You think she would just stop being the Empress by choice? Sorry, yer gonna have to just put her down."

"By 'put down,' do you mean kill?"

Blythe winced as she heard that word. "Probably."

"That will be our last resort," Eira replied."

Eira neared the wall of the city when something shot one of her wings. She cried out and circled back. Once she was far enough away she turned back around to see the threat. Blythe saw what it was.

"The laser is coming from one of the towers," she explained. "They're programmed to shoot anything that comes by the wall."

"Oh, I see," Eira replied. She charged at the tower, spitting out ice crystals. The laser on the tower exploded, sending pieces of metal everywhere.

Eira flew over the wall and landed just inside the city border. Blythe hopped off her back.

"Finally I'm here!" She turned to Eira, but she was gone. Where the dragon stood was a stream of blue energy. The energy flowed into the lapis lazuli stone on top of her bracelet. "What's going on?" Suddenly, Blythe heard Eira's voice.

"Don't worry. I'm still here." The lapis glowed while the dragon spoke.

"What did you do?" Blythe wondered. She eyed the blue crystal. "Are you inside the stone?"

"Yes. We can become energy and keep ourselves in our bonded crystal. It's just a way for us to regenerate and it's a nice way of staying out of sight."

"Oh."

"So, where is your friend?"

Blythe looked around. They were in a back alley. No one was around, which was good. Blythe walked out of the alley to see some shacks where people were living. Most of the wood was rotting away. As she passed a clothes line, she grabbed a piece of cloth that was hanging there. It was barely anything. Quickly, she wrapped up her hair and kept some of the cloth hanging over her face.

"That probably belongs to someone," she heard Eira speak. How did the dragon see her when she was in the crystal?

"Uh, I'll return it. I just don't want the guards seeing me."

Blythe made her way into the heart of the city where many

merchants were busy selling their goods. It was hard to know where to start looking. Most likely, her friend would stay hidden in a place away from the crowds.

"This city is so big. I'm not sure where to start looking," she admitted.

The crowds thinned as Blythe walked away from the Marketplace. From the corner of her eye, she caught an old man with a long beard running towards an alleyway. She hurried after him. The man crawled through a small hole in one of the buildings.

"Was that him?" Eira asked.

"Can you see from inside that piece of rock?"

"Of course. I can see everything you can. I'm using your eyes."

That sounded a little creepy to Blythe, but she turned her focus back to the matter at hand.

"I'm not sure who that was," Blythe admitted. She hurried over to the hole and bent down. The stones had begun to erode away. The building itself didn't appear very sturdy.

"Be careful," Eira warned. Blythe crawled through the hole and came out into an empty room. The place had long been abandoned as there were numerous cracks in the walls, and many holes in the roof. It would have been pitch black in this room if it wasn't because of the sunlight coming through those holes.

"I sense someone is here," Eira said. "Over in that corner."

Blythe slowly approached the far corner where she saw someone crouched on the floor. The lapis lazuli on Blythe's bracelet lit up, shining a bluish glow in the darkness. Blythe saw the man's face.

"Ramon?" she asked.

The man jumped to his feet.

"Who are you?" he demanded.

Blythe rolled her eyes and removed the cloth from her head. His eyes widened.

"Blythe? How the hell did you get here?"

"Never mind that," she hastily answered. "Where's Xan?"

Ramon let out a long sigh. "A lot has happened in the last week or so. Xan isn't here anymore. He left."

"But we were supposed to all meet here. That was the plan."

He looked away. "Well the plan changed. "What do you mean, the plan changed?"

He didn't answer. "Ramon," she tried.

"The last time I talked to him, he was heading northeast, towards Gabriel."

Blythe's head dropped and she sighed. "I was hoping to talk to him before he went on his mission. I don't know how long this whole plan of his is going to take. I don't know if I can wait until he comes back."

"If he comes back."

Blythe's eyes hardened. "Of course he'll come back!" Ramon didn't say a word as he looked away.

"So, are you sticking around?" he asked.

"Uh, I'm kinda working on my own plan." Ramon turned to her with bewilderment. "Your own plan?"

"Don't worry about it," Blythe replied quickly. Ramon shrugged his shoulders. "Whatever. Ya probably don't want to stay here too long anyways. Now that Xan is gone, I need to find a way out of here."

"You got in with the fake ID, right?" Blythe asked.

A smirk formed on Ramon's mouth. "I didn't use no ID. I told Xan that the guards would spot it was a fake. No, I found my own way in."

Now Blythe was interested. "How?"

"I snuck inside a cart of cabbages."

"Oh."

"Did you actually use that ID?" he asked further.

A flush of pink formed on Blythe's checks. "Uh, don't worry about it."

"So, how did you get in?"

"Uh, not by using the ID, that's for sure." Blythe answered nervously.

"Good. It was a stupid idea," he said crossly. "Oh, hey, do you have any food?" the man asked.

Blythe usually had something like dried fruit or canned beans or rice. However, since she had a run-in with the Patrol, she lost all of her rations. Then, she remembered that weird blend of berries A'keara gave her. Taking it out of her vest pocket, she handed it to Ramon. He eyed it for a moment.

"What's this? A magic potion?"

"It's really good. It's a mixture of wild berries and cinnamon."

"I'll take what I can get," he said.

"Hey, Ramon, I uh–have a way for you to leave. I had

some help in getting into the city." Blythe looked down at the bracelet. "Uh, Eira, can you come out?" Ramon squinted his eyes at Blythe. "Who are ya talkin' to?"

"I think we should wait until we're by the border wall," Eira replied. Ramon jumped at the disembodied voice.

"Who said that?"

Blythe looked kindly at her friend. "We need to get to the wall, then my friend can help us leave."

"What friend?"

"Ya gonna think I'm crazy, but I bonded with a dragon."

Ramon narrowed his eyes, then let out a boisterous laugh.

"I know it sounds ludicrous, but it's true." Blythe quickly gave Ramon a watered-down version of the story she heard from Aponi about the awakening of the Spirit Dragons. Ramon still stared at her in disbelief. She couldn't blame him.

"So, you want to go to the border wall? We have to go to a spot where there aren't any guards."

"I figured that. Come on. I'll show you where we came in."

Blythe led Ramon towards the spot where she and Eira flew over the wall.

They approached the clothes line they found earlier. Blythe took off the piece of cloth from her head and hung it back on the line.

Blythe let out a long sigh. "So Xan is in Gabriel. I don't know how I'm getting into Gabriel though. Even with a dragon, it's going to be hard. Gabriel is one of the Brother colonies." Blythe looked at the lapis lazuli stone on her bracelet.

"We're at the wall," she said.

"I know," Eira said. A long stream of blue energy rose from the stone. Ramon's eyes grew really wide. His heart almost stopped when the giant blue dragon appeared in front of him. Blythe jumped onto Eira's back.

"Don't tell me I have to ride that thing. How am I supposed to get up there?"

"I'll help you," Eira said as she gently picked the man up by his shirt. Ramon started screaming. Blythe hushed him.

"It's fine Ramon. Be quiet or the guards will hear you."

Eira placed Ramon behind Blythe just as two guards ran towards them.

"What the hell is that?" One guard yelled.

"I don't know. Just shoot it!" the other replied. Eira took off before any laser beams hit her or her riders.

Blythe looked down at the city as it grew smaller and smaller. Eira headed south through the desert.

"Let me off this thing!" Ramon cried. He wasn't sure what to hold onto as Eira's scales were pure crystal and very smooth. He ended up just holding onto Blythe.

"Where are you going to go?" Blythe asked. "You should just come with us."

"Just drop me in the woods somewhere."

"I'm afraid the woods are several miles north," Eira said. "And I have to fly south."

Just tell this thing to land!" Ramon yelled at Blythe.

"But we're in the middle of the desert." Blythe replied.

"I can drop him off in the savannah," Eira suggested.

"Yeah, do that," Ramon agreed.

Once Eira reached the savannah, she landed by some brush. Ramon jumped off the dragon's back. As he landed, his legs buckled underneath him and he fell onto his back. Blythe hopped off the dragon to help the man to his feet.

"Are you okay?" she asked.

"Oh, I'm doing great!" he replied sarcastically.

"Listen, we're on our way to the Southern Region. You can come with us. We'll eventually be in the east and we can go see Xan in Gabriel."

"I'm not getting back onto that creature," he said pointing at Eira. "I don't want to go into Gabriel, anyways. I'm fine out in nature away from any government run colonies." Blythe gaze saddened. "Don't look at me like that," Ramon said feeling guilty. "How about I meet you in the Eastern Region outside Gabriel, okay? What are ya doin' anyways?"

"Remember, I said we're going to wake up the other dragons?"

"So, what are these dragons going to do?"

"I already explained that," Blythe said a bit irate.

"Yeah, ya did, but it didn't make any sense."

"Okay fine. We'll meet outside of Gabriel in–" She looked up at Eira. "How long do you think it will take to awaken Phoenix and the other dragon?"

"We need to finish our mission within the next three days."

Blythe turned to face Ramon. "Meet us in three days."

"Fine."

Ramon walked over to a tree stump and sat down.

"I'm gonna rest here for a moment," he said.

Blythe wondered if Ramon was going to be okay. She wished he would just come with them. Eira whispered in her ear.

"He'll be okay. Have faith," the dragon said. Blythe breathed in deeply and prepared for their flight towards the islands in the Southern Region.

"See ya soon," she said to her longtime friend.

Eira took off. Blythe turned her head to see Ramon becoming further and further away. Her eyes began to tear up. *Xan,* she thought to herself. *You'd better be in Gabriel. All of this chaos you caused, better be worth it.*

CHAPTER 11

The Crimson Dragon

Kero sat on top of Aeolus behind Aponi. She was about to go meet the dragon she would bond with. Once she had a dragon, she would go rescue her brother. Then, she may have the dragon roast every one of the Imperial soldiers and burn down the palace with the Empress inside.

Aeolus landed by a river in the thick jungle of the Southern Region. Kero felt strange being back in the Southern Region. They were in Athena and her farm was only about two hundred miles away. She wasn't too far away from home.

While they waited, Aurora and A'keara materialized in front of them.

"Wow, that is strange to see on this side," Kero commented.

A'keara steadied Aurora. "We'll we're here."

"So, can Aurora just teleport to Aponi?" Kero asked.

"She can teleport to anyone she has a strong bond with.

It could be me or Aponi. She can do basic teleportation too. She teleported me and herself from a mountain ledge down to the base of the mountain."

"You might have to wait for me to get to the right location on the island," Aponi said. "Otherwise, Aurora won't know where to teleport herself."

"Actually, I wondered if I could just wait here. Aurora and I don't have to go to the island, right?"

"I suppose not, but don't you want to see the next dragon awaken?"

A'keara shrugged. "I mean, I'm just trying to make it easy for Aurora."

Kero looked at the cool water in the river. "Hey, does anyone mind if I wash myself off? I'm just really hot from the desert."

"Actually, it would be a good idea for all of us to quickly bathe," Aponi replied.

Kero took off her boots and socks. It's amazing how they went from cold and numb to hot and sweaty in the timespan of a day. She dipped her feet into the cool water. "Oh, that's nice." Suddenly, she stripped off her clothing and jumped right in.

A'keara turned with her mouth agape. "Not shy are you?" Kero, now with the water up to her neck, blushed a little.

"Sorry, this is kind of a treat. I'm used to having a bucket of ice cold water dumped over my head." A'keara and Aponi returned a bewildered glance.

"That's how we get our baths back on the farm. We get one twice a month."

After the three women bathed, Aponi and Kero climbed

back onto Aeolus, who was keeping himself busy by watching the trees and birds flying by as the women washed themselves. Kero thought this was odd.

"Are dragons modest too?" she asked.

"Of course. We have a code of decency. We understand that privacy is important to every creature."

Kero thought for a moment about how the colonists of the Salamand Islands were going to respond to seeing a dragon.

"I wonder how the people there will react to a dragon just showing up?" Kero pondered.

"Has it been that long since humans have seen dragons?" Aeolus asked.

"You've been asleep for a long time," Aponi answered. "Well, let's go to the Salamand Islands.

"Aponi, I still don't know where to go exactly," Kero reminded her.

"Just let your intuition lead you."

Of course she'd say something like that. Kero thought to herself.

A'keara watched the dragon fly away over the glistening water. Maybe she could relax for a little while in the sunshine. She sat against the nearby palm tree. Aurora sniffed the water. The unicorn lowered her head and graciously lapped up the cool water with her tongue.

"We lost our jugs of water while on the mountain," A'keara noted. "I wish I could take some of this fresh water with us." A'keara watched the mare. It was interesting to see how the simplest things made her happy. A'keara looked up at the sky.

"That's it. I've decided to come back as a unicorn in my next life." Her eyes fell onto the mare again. "You want to know something?" Aurora stopped drinking and looked up at her. "I have no idea if I'm supposed to bond with the Emerald Dragon. Aponi hopes I will, but I'm still not sure. Besides, the Golden Dragon and the Emerald Dragon were bonded with males originally." Aurora whinnied. "I know. Just have faith."

From high above, they heard the sound of giant flapping wings. A'keara looked up to see the Crystal Dragon descending to the ground. Blythe waved.

"Hey! Where is everyone?" she wondered.

"They're on their way to the islands," A'keara answered.

Blythe raised an eyebrow. "Uh, just the islands? I mean, there's like five of them."

"Well, hopefully Kero figures out which one she should go to."

"Yeah, so, I was able to meet one of the resistance members in Isis, but the guy I'm looking for wasn't there. Turns out I have to go to Gabriel."

"I'm sorry. I don't know much about these cities," A'keara admitted.

"Well, Gabriel is one of the biggest colonies. It's not as big as Michael, but it's close. Both colonies have the best technology and the richest people live there."

"I see. What makes these people rich?"

"They have a lot of gold."

"Everyone has gold. It's all over the planet."

"No no. Uh-the gold was made into coins. Or people just wear it with jewels."

"Wait, you mean they took the gold out of the planet?"

"Out of the planet? What are you talking about?"

A'keara stood in quiet thought. "Aponi said that resources were being stolen from the planet." Blythe stared back at A'keara unable to form a response. A'keara looked up at Eira.

"Did you know that the gold was taken out of the planet?"

Eira seemed to be preoccupied. "Oh sorry. I was having a conversation with my brother. He said they're approaching one of the islands. Kero isn't sure which island Phoenix is on."

"It was easier finding you and Aeolus," A'keara said. "You were on top of a mountain and your brother just appeared in the sky."

"True, but Aponi had to find the right cavern where he slept."

"Well, it's Aponi. She's good at solving riddles."

"As for your question about the gold, it's obvious that the powers that run this planet are responsible."

"Actually, the people who live underground are the ones who mine the gold," Blythe replied.

The peacefulness of the jungle was interrupted by a large airship flying over the trees. Everyone watched the ship as it headed towards the islands.

"It's the Imperial army!" Blythe exclaimed.

"Didn't we destroy their floating device?" Eira wondered.

"The Empire has a lot of airships. This one actually looks bigger than the other one."

"So, what are we supposed to do?" A'keara asked.

Blythe looked up at the airship in the sky. "I don't suppose you can take that one down too?" she asked Eira.

"I had help from Aeolus last time. And even that was a chore."

"Maybe you can find out from your brother where they are," A'keara suggested. Eira nodded.

Aeolus flew towards the spot of land in the distance. It was the first island they came across and Aponi said they would check each one if they had to. However, the inhabitants certainly did not expect to see a dragon flying to their island. The people stood in awe, unable to speak as Aeolus landed by the shore.

"Good Day," Aponi greeted.

"Hello, Dear Ones," Aeolus spoke kindly. Murmurs rose from the crowd.

"Is that a dragon?"

"It can speak."

"Should someone call the Patrol?"

Finally, a man pushing fifty stepped forward.

"My name is Caymon. I'm an ex-soldier, and the speaker for this colony. We don't want any trouble. Please leave."

"You don't understand," Aeolus said. "I am a Spirit Dragon. We wondered if anyone knew of the location of the Crimson Dragon."

Another man stepped forward.

"We don't know anything about no dragons, now get on outta here!" Other islanders chimed in. "Yeah, get outta here!"

"Listen, we mean you no harm," Aeolus tried. "It is time

for the dragons to return to Gaia. We must awaken my brother."

"You want to bring more of your kind here?" Someone else in the crowd

shouted. "We won't allow it!" Others followed with their own shouts of protest.

"You don't understand," Aponi said strongly. "The dragons are good and

gentle creatures." She sighed. "Maybe they need to read my book," she said quietly.

"Aponi, these people probably can't read," Kero informed her.

"They can't?"

Kero shook her head. "Most people on Anu can't read. Remember, I told you that the Empire doesn't allow it.

"Yes, I remember. That's sad."

"We know these beasts are just as terrible as the ones who destroyed Anu a thousand years ago," Caymon said.

"Whoever told you that the dragons are bad, are liars," Aponi retorted.

"Yes," Aeolus agreed. "And if dragons were as bad as you believe they are, I would have blown away your homes and eaten everyone."

No one spoke.

Just then, Aeolus heard his sister's voice. *"Have you reached the island yet?"*

"We have. We're dealing with the locals." Then out loud he spoke, "Please listen, something very bad has happened to this planet. Humans and dragons have been friends for eons. Just let

us show you that we can be trusted."

Just then, the imperial airship appeared in the sky. Many of the islanders ran off into their huts. Caymon stared up at the ship.

"Thank our Imperial Highness!" he cried out. He turned to the newcomers. "Now you'll have to deal with the Empress' army." He ran off towards what appeared to be a tower, but it looked very worn out and rickety. Pieces of wood broke away from the ladder as the man climbed quickly into the lookout post.

"What are we gonna do?" Kero asked.

"We need to get away from here," Aponi said.

Aeolus took off into the sky.

"I'll contact my sister," he said.

Back on the mainland, Eira heard her brother's voice again.

"We're being pursued by an Imperial airship. We're still looking for Phoenix."

Eira repeated what Aeolus said.

"Shouldn't we go help them?" Blythe asked. "Most definitely." She looked at A'keara. "Are you coming?"

"I'm not leaving Aurora alone," A'keara stated.

Eira took off. A'keara sighed and looked at Aurora. "This is becoming too much."

Aeolus flew over the glistening water of the Etheric Ocean. He flapped his wings as fast as he could with the imperial ship on his tail. Kero could barely think. Everything was happening so fast.

"I see the next island," Aeolus said.

"Let's land there." Aponi pointed down at the treetops. "Go into the jungle. The airship won't be able to land."

Aeolus complied, heading straight towards the canopy below. Once Aeolus reached the ground, he headed towards a cave.

"Wait, yer just goin' in?" Kero questioned.

Aeolus stopped just inside the cave. The airship hovered over the treetops. Several ropes appeared from the airship. The soldiers slid with ease down into the jungle.

"Now what?" Kero asked. "They're going to find us here."

Aeolus thought for a moment. "That's fine. Let them find us." Kero returned a peculiar glance.

The imperial soldiers spread out around the area. A few came their way.

"Look, a cave," one said to the other.

"You wanna go in there?" Another asked.

"Stop stalling!" the third one yelled.

The soldiers made their way towards the cave. Kero and Aponi sat perfectly still on top of Aeolus. Kero pictured the dragon eating the soldiers. However, as the loud footsteps approached, Aeolus released a huge gust of wind from his mouth. All three soldiers shouted in protest as they flew out of the cave and into the trunk of a palm tree. Aeolus stomped towards the soldiers. They screamed in terror and fled through the brush.

"Well, you took care of them," Aponi stated. "Kero, we're not going to have a lot of peace and quiet for you to meditate. You're going to have to just feel it."

How was she supposed to just *feel it?* This was insane! There were soldiers everywhere. The airship was right over them.

They were trapped!

"I have an idea," Aeolus said. "I shouldn't fly because the airship will spot us, but even if I stay on the ground, I can take care of any soldier that comes near us."

"Alright then," Aponi said in agreement. "We still don't know which way to

go though."

"Let me see if I can contact my brother. Even in slumber, he may still be

able to hear me."

Aeolus trotted towards some tall bushes and laid low. "Uh, you think no one is going to see you?" Kero asked.

"I just need a moment," the dragon replied. Closing his eyes, Aeolus focused his energy and thoughts.

Phoenix, it's me, Aeolus. We are looking for you. Please guide us to you. From the distance, Kero heard shouts come from a few imperial soldiers. They were coming this way. She tapped Aponi on the shoulder.

"We need to get outta here!" she harshly whispered. She looked down at the dragon's scales and noticed they were glowing. Aeolus opened his eyes. Just before he spoke, Kero suddenly had her own revelation. She saw the deep jungle and a volcano clearly in her mind. Smoke swirled upwards from the volcano's mouth. Then, she saw the magma deep within it. Both she and Aeolus spoke at the same time.

"I know where he is."

Eira approached the small island where she was called by her brother. He was in trouble. She could feel it. Blythe looked down over the treetop of the dense jungle.

"I don't think anyone lives on this island," she said.

"It would be a perfect place for Phoenix to rest."

"So, I'm noticing a trend here with where each of you went to sleep.

They're in places humans don't normally travel to. Is there a reason for that?"

"We needed to be kept somewhere safe. If the wrong type of humans found us, they could destroy our resting place. Or put an enchantment on it so we would not be able to be awakened."

"I don't think people do magic stuff like that," Blythe said.

"As far as you know. I already sensed dark magic the moment I awakened."

Blythe still didn't buy the whole magic bit, but it was possible that some kind of technology could be used.

"Eira, people don't use magic. They use technology."

"What is technology?"

"Technology is–" Blythe tried to put it into words. "Science, I guess."

"I'm sorry, but I don't understand that word you used."

Blythe racked her brain, trying to find a way to explain. "Uh, science is how things work. Scientists study and experiment with stuff. So, it's different from magic."

"But there is a reason behind the working of magic," Eira said.

"I don't know," Blythe said. "It really doesn't matter to me anyways. I wouldn't mind a world of magic. It sounds more exciting."

Eira hovered just over a palm tree. Blythe looked around, but couldn't see much of anything. She looked up at Eira who seemed preoccupied.

"I don't see Aeolus anywhere," she said. "I feel that he's here somewhere near." She flew off in one direction. Up ahead was a volcano.

"That's mount Alinta," she said.

"Mount what?" Blythe asked.

"It's the oldest volcano on Gaia," Eira explained.

Eira flew up towards the mouth of Mount Alinta.

"Be careful! Don't get too close." Blythe said as Eira flew over it.

"Don't worry. This volcano is dormant at the moment," Eira said.

"What does that mean?" Blythe asked.

"When volcanoes are dormant, they have been active in the past, meaning they have erupted. This volcano hasn't erupted in a thousand years."

"How do you know?"

"I asked the volcano."

Blythe laughed. "Is it normal for dragons to talk to volcanos?"

"We talk to everything, mountains, trees, forest, deserts, the oceans– We talk to the whole planet."

"Wow! That's impressive." Before Eira could reply,

someone called to her.

"Eira!" She turned to see Aeolus flying towards her.

"Blythe!" Aponi called. "I didn't expect to see you here."

Aeolus eyed his younger sister. "You didn't have to come all the way here."

She pushed out a few puffs of air through her nostrils. "You think I couldn't feel the danger you were in?"

Kero looked down at the volcano. Suddenly, she covered her ears.

"What's that ringing ?" she asked. "Ringing?" Eira asked.

"It's really loud," Kero added.

"Do you hear a voice speaking to you? Listen to the words?" Aponi said.

Words? Kero thought to herself. What a ridiculous question. How could she hear anything with the high-pitched ringing? From the piercing ringing and pounding, a faint voice came through inside her mind.

I am the Crimson Dragon. Who comes before me?

My name is Kero.

I am inside the volcano. You must jump into its mouth. Do not fear, I will catch you.

Kero opened her eyes. She peered down to see molten rock down in the depths of the volcano.

"I need to go inside the volcano," she said this as if it were a regular thing to say.

Aponi studied her for a moment. She looked up at Aeolus. "I believe she found your brother."

Aeolus nodded and landed on the edge of the volcano's mouth. Kero hopped off and she tiptoed up to the edge of the mouth. Blythe had been watching her the whole time.

"What are you doing?" she asked, voice trembling. "Be careful or you'll fall in!" Kero looked down into the depths of the volcano. Before everyone's eyes, she jumped in.

CHAPTER 12

Reuniting Allies

Blythe gasped. "We have to catch her!"

Before anyone could take a step, a fiery blast came out of the mouth of the volcano. Strange enough, the blast of lava didn't hurt anyone. Blythe turned, astonished to see Kero riding atop a blazing red dragon.

"All we need to do is awaken the Emerald Dragon," Aponi said. "Our journey is almost at its end."

Kero held on tightly to her bonded dragon. At that moment, all of her feelings of fear and anger disappeared. All she felt was peace.

Moments later, the three dragons and their riders tore through the sky. Kero sat atop the Crimson Dragon, her eyes wild with excitement. She never in her life felt such a rush of energy. Even the dragon's eyes were balls of fire.

"My name is Phoenix," he said. "Do you remember the first time we met in the astral realm?"

"Are you talking about the vision I had?"

"It was more than a vision. You came into my dimension; the dimension of dragons."

"I did?" Kero asked in astonishment. "How did I do that?"

"You must have put your mind in a state of consciousness that allowed you to cross dimensions."

"A state of what now?"

The dragon released a low chuckle from his throat. "In simpler terms, it means you put your mind in a state that had connected you to a higher source of energy."

"That's simple?"

"Oh dear. It seems dragons have been gone for far too long. Humans don't know anything about connection to source energy?"

Kero recalled that Aponi used the words, 'source energy' when explaining the meditation process to her.

"Hey, I was told that the dragons went to sleep a thousand years ago. Why did they leave? Was it because the humans were destroying the planet?" Kero recalled that bit of information from her book.

"After the Elder Dragons requested all dragon-kind to leave Gaia, we all returned to the realm we came from. My siblings and I went to sleep and waited to be awakened again."

"Why did the Elder Dragons tell all of the other dragons to leave? This world has been enslaved since you've been gone."

"I don't have the answer to that question. You'll have to ask the Elder Dragons themselves."

"So, you didn't question why you had to leave? You just

blindly obeyed them?"

"There wasn't any other choice. They told us that humans had to live without dragons."

Kero noticed she was wearing a gold chain necklace connected to a red stone.

"What's this?" she asked.

"That is your energy stone. It connects us in our bond." Kero recalled that Blythe had the bracelet with the lapis lazuli and Aponi had the broach with the citrine.

"Is there a name for this kinda stone?"

"It's a carnelian. It restores vitality to its user and dispels apathy."

"So this stone has magic?"

"What you call 'magic,' the ancients call spiritual abilities and gifts."

General Kain stood aboard the airship, staring out of the window when one of his soldiers approached him.

"Sir! The dragons are heading back to the mainland."

"Keep on them!" he commanded.

"Yes sir!" He ran back towards the bridge.

The airship roared through the sky. Phoenix was the first to see it coming their way.

"I'm sensing some dark energy coming from that ship," he announced.

Kero turned to see the airship. "Oh great! It's an imperial

airship," she explained. "Hey, can you just shoot them out of the sky?"

"Why? Do they mean you harm?"

"Uh yeah. A lot of harm."

Let me talk to my siblings."

"Aeolus, Eira, we need to take care of the airship," Phoenix spoke inside his mind.

"Phoenix!" Aeolus exclaimed. *"It's so good to hear your voice. My bonded, Aponi needs to get back to the mainland. Her granddaughter is there. She's the one who will bond with Eden."*

"Oh, I see," Phoenix replied. "I think it's best we regroup on the mainland."

"But, the airship is right behind us!" Kero protested.

Phoenix huffed. "We can move much faster than the airship."

The dragon spotted land straight ahead. Eira led the way back to where A'keara and Aurora waited. A'keara stared up at the fiery dragon Kero rode. *She did it,* the woman realized. She was elated for a few moments, but then anxiety swept over her. If Kero bonded with the Crimson Dragon, that meant it was her turn. However, she still didn't know where to find the Emerald Dragon.

The three dragons and their riders landed. Eira and Aeolus returned joyful eyes with Phoenix.

"Phoenix!" Eira exclaimed. She rushed to her older brother. The two twirled their necks in a loving embrace. Aeolus did the same.

"We just have to awaken Eden and the four of us will be together again."

Aponi dismounted Aeolus and sauntered over to her granddaughter.

"Well, looks like we just have one dragon left."

A'keara returned with a sorrowful glance. "Grandmother, I–"She let out an aggravated sigh. "I don't know where she is!"

"Which is why we're going to do a meditation," Aponi replied.

"Uh, we're being chased by an airship," Kero said. "Probably not the best time for meditation."

"May I suggest something?" Blythe asked. Everyone turned to her. "Isn't there something in the legend about where to find the dragons? I mean, we found the Crystal Dragon in the north, the Golden Dragon in the west and we just found the Crimson Dragon in the south. Isn't the Emerald Dragon supposed to be in the East?"

"Yes, the four directions of the planet coincide with the four elements and the four seasons," Aponi stated.

"Right," Blythe agreed. "So, maybe we need to head east towards Apollo. And Gabriel is to the east too."

"Oh, you said something about your friend being in Gabriel," A'keara noted. Blythe nodded.

"Don't the dragons know where to find her?" A'keara asked, exasperated.

"The human who is to bond with the dragon is supposed to have a vision," Phoenix replied.

A'keara groaned. "I know!"

"A'keara, calm down," Aponi said gently. "We'll figure it out."

Just as she spoke those words, laser beams blasted through

the trees. Everyone looked up to see the airship.

"We need to get out of here!" Blythe shouted.

"Wait!" Phoenix's voice boomed. He looked at his siblings. "We can take care of that sky machine, right?"

"Aeolus and I already took down one," Eira said.

"So, these humans have a lot of those things?" he asked further.

"That one is bigger than the last one," Aeolus said.

"It doesn't matter," Phoenix said. A few more shots came, slicing off parts of tree limbs. Blythe quickly dogged a falling branch.

"Kero, go join your friends. You need to find shelter. Kero suddenly felt like she was abandoning Phoenix. It was strange, even though she just met him, she felt like she's known this dragon for centuries. Still, she listened and dismounted Phoenix.

"Let's move into the jungle," Aponi said. As the humans ran to safety, the three dragons took off towards the sky.

CHAPTER 13

Spiritual Gifts

General Kain stood next to the new captain of the ship.

"Sir! Those dragons we saw before are back and now there's a third one!"

The general scoffed. "Fire until all of them lay lifeless under the sea."

Phoenix led the attack, delivering fireballs at the airship cannons. Eira and Aeolus followed suit, taking out the other cannons.

"Don't let them damage the ship! You only need to hit them once!" Kain commanded.

"That's the problem sir!" one of the gunmen replied. "They're really fast!"

General Kain stomped over to the man and grabbed him by his uniform.

"Then be faster!" he bellowed.

"Y-yes sir!" Kain dropped him and the man continued to work the cannon. In the next moment, the whole airship shook. Lights flickered and the engine began to struggle.

"I got one of them in my sights," another gunman shouted. The general saw the blue and purple dragon through the scope. The man fired.

Eira was busy blasting one of the cannons when a ray beam struck her in her stomach. She cried out and plummeted down into the water. Aeolus saw this and yelled out, "Eira!"

Meanwhile, A'keara found a small cave everyone could hide out in. Kero was still hesitant to leave the dragons to fight alone.

"Are you sure they'll be okay?" she asked.

"They're dragons. They'll be fine," A'keara said.

"I think it's best we wait here," Aponi said.

Blythe chimed in. "Yeah, I mean, what are we going to do to an airsh–" Suddenly, she grabbed her stomach and cried out in pain. A bright blue aura shimmered around her body.

"Blythe?" Aponi asked.

Blythe breathed heavily for a moment. Her eyes stared genuinely at the others.

"I'm fine, but something just attacked Eira."

"How do you know?" Kero asked.

Blythe wasn't sure how to explain what just occurred. "I felt a sharp pain right here," she pointed to her abdomen. A'keara turned to her grandmother as if the old woman had an answer.

"I'm not sure what just happened, Blythe," Aponi said.

"I felt a sharp pain before when Aurora teleported us to the desert."

"Yes, I remember that," A'keara said.

"Let us know if it happens again, Blythe," Aponi told her.

Everyone continued deeper within the cave.

Up in the sky, Phoenix took out another canon when Aeolus called to him.

"Eira got hit!" he yelled.

Phoenix barely dodged another attack. "We have to bring this thing down!" he yelled back. Eira will be okay. She landed in the water."

Aeolus looked down at the water where his sister fell. As he did, a laser beam shot him in the leg. He quickly moved out of the way of the next attack.

Back in the cave, Aponi felt a sharp pain in her right leg. A golden aura glowed around her body. She uttered a small cry as she grabbed it.

"Maybe there's a scorpion in here," A'keara said.

"I wonder what that glow was," Aponi questioned. She studied her leg, but she didn't see a bruise of any kind.

"Did you say glow?" Blythe asked. Aponi acknowledged her.

"Yes, I saw a golden glow around my leg." She thought for a moment. "Wait, you had a glow around your stomach. There was something in the legend about those who bond with dragons have a force field to protect themselves from harm. Dragons themselves have the same forefield. When a dragon and human are bonded, they feel each other's pain."

"Wait, if we're seeing these weird force fields, that means the dragons are being attacked!" Kero exclaimed. "I told you we shouldn't have left them!" Kero turned to run back towards the cave entrance.

"And what are you going to do once you go back out there?" A'keara ridiculed her. "They're fighting an imperial airship. Just let them do what they do."

Aponi grinned at her granddaughter. "Now that is the most sensible thing you've said this entire journey." A'keara rolled her eyes. Kero just stewed in her thoughts. She knew she couldn't do anything alone. That was the problem.

In the sky, Phoenix fought with his fire breath, destroying the underside of the ship. Aeolus blew a whirlwind, ripping off the metal exterior. Two cannons remained intact, but they couldn't shoot the dragons if they were underneath the airship.

"What now?" Aeolus asked. Suddenly, Eira burst out of the water. She flew at the ship, covering the last two cannons with a thick sheet of ice.

Inside the airship, the gunmen reported the bad news. "Sir! We 've lost all of the cannons!" The airship shook more as the three dragons pelted them with fire, ice and wind.

"I need to land, sir!" the captain shouted to General Kain.

"You will do no such thing! Just ram into those beasts!"

"They're too fast! I can't turn the ship fast enough to keep up with them." The captain turned to the wheel. "I'm sorry Sir," he said genuinely.

Outside the airship, Phoenix, Eira and Aeolus continued attacking even as the craft headed to the shoreline. It crashed, sending out billowing clouds of sand. The three dragons flew over the ship and continued into the jungle.

"Where did our human friends go?" Eira asked.

"They're probably hiding," Aeolus replied. "I feel their energy in this direction."

They came to the cave. "They're in there," Phoenix said. "We need to catch up with them."

Kero still felt like she was betraying her new dragon ally. She continuously argued with herself that she just met the creature and not to get too attached. And yet, there was another internal voice that told her that she and Phoenix have been allies for longer than her natural life.

"Hello?" came a booming voice. Kero stopped.

"Phoenix?" she replied. "We're in the back of the cave!"

In the darkness appeared two fireballs for eyes. They moved closer until Phoenix came into view. Behind him were Eira and Aeolus.

"What happened to the airship?" Kero asked.

"Taken care of," Aeolus said.

Blythe rushed towards Eira. As she approached the dragon, she felt embarrassed. What was she doing running up to this creature like it was her mother? She regained her composure.

"Are you alright?" she asked.

"Yes," Eira replied. "I did get hit by the beam or whatever from the airship, but luckily I fell into the water, which healed me right away."

"Ya know, it was the strangest thing," Blythe said. "I was just standing here with the others and then I felt pain in my stomach."

"That happened the same time I was hit by the airship's weapon," Eira realized.

"So, I remembered correctly," Phoenix said. "Dragons and their bonded can experience the same pain."

"That's stupid," Kero said saltily. "Why would a person and a dragon want to bond if they will feel each other's pain?"

"Humans and dragons can become more powerful together," Phoenix explained. However, once you bond with a dragon, your life is intertwined with theirs. There's never really a time when the two of you should be apart."

"Okay. But, what happens if a dragon dies? Does that mean that their bonded—" Kero went quiet.

"Yes," Phoenix replied sadly.

"Maybe we should turn our attention to other matters," Aponi intervened.

"Agreed," Phoenix replied. "We still need to find our sister and we know she's somewhere in the East."

After a while, they came to a couple of smaller caves. Judging the height of the two tunnels, it was obvious that a dragon could not fit through them.

"Hmm, it looks like my siblings and I won't be able to continue this way," Phoenix said.

"How are you going to get to the other side of the cave then?" Kero asked.

"Yes, assuming there is an end to this tunnel," A'keara relented.

"We can fly over the trees and meet them on the other side," Eira suggested.

"We don't know where this cave goes," Phoenix replied.

"Maybe it's best if we all turn back," Aponi said.

As they left the cave, they were met by imperial soldiers. General Kain stood at the head, staring down the traitors to the Empire.

"This is as far as you go," he spoke crossly. "I know the legend. If you fail to awaken the Emerald Dragon before the next Violet Moon, the other dragons will go back to sleep and it will be another thousand years before they can be awakened again."

"We have three dragons already awake," Blythe spoke haughtily. "And it's called an Energy Violet Moon."

"Like I care!" General Kain snapped back. "Take them out!" he ordered.

Kero laughed. "Just eat them!" she said to Phoenix. However, in the next moment, she felt a sharp cut across her chest. She stared down, confused at the spot where she felt pain. Phoenix groaned. Her eyes went to his chest where there was a giant gash in his skin. He had been shot! The red dragon fell, and Kero followed after. Laying on the ground, Kero slowly realized that she could still move. She glanced down at her chest to see a reddish glow. Suddenly, Phoenix let out vicious flames that engulfed six soldiers. More shots blasted towards everyone. Blythe, who was in the direction of the shots ducked behind a large boulder.

Eira blew her ice breath, freezing the soldiers in front of the line. Aeolus blew the rest backwards into the trees and ground. General Kain aimed his weapon, but it was suddenly pulled from his grip. His body levitated off the ground. He looked down to see a horse with a horn on its head, and it's glowing bright. The soldiers returned fire, one laser struck Aurora. Her horn stopped glowing. A whimper escaped from her muzzle as she backed into the cave. Eira flew into the air and pelted all the soldiers with ice. Aeolus blew wind, mixed with the ice, creating an ice storm, immobilizing many soldiers. General Kain, realizing he was untouched by the storm, raced towards the cave.

"Kero, go join the others in the cave," Phoenix spoke with an authoritative voice.

"But, you're hurt," she protested.

"I'm fine," he insisted. "Now go!" Kero ran towards the cave entrance. Kain was practically on her heels as she ran. Eira noticed and spit out pellets of ice at the general's back. The force alone knocked him down. He groaned, unable to move.

Kero joined the others in the cave, their eyes showed relief when they saw her.

"You're okay?" Blythe asked.

Kero nodded. "Yeah, I thought that laser would hurt more."

"I believe that the power of our dragons have made us more resilient," Aponi noted.

"Enough talking!" A'keara shouted. "Where are we going?"

"We'll head for those tunnels we found earlier," Aponi replied. "Hopefully, one leads us out."

Outside the cave, the three dragons stood, watching the entrance. The general hadn't moved yet, and the few soldiers still left standing were hiding behind some trees.

"What do we do now?" Aeolus asked his siblings.

"I think we should follow what Kero said and eat all of them," Eira replied.

"You know we can't do that!" Phoenix reprimanded. "Not while they are unconscious and can't defend themselves. We should go see if there is another exit to this cave." He spread his wings, taking off towards the treetops. Aeolus followed, but Eira stood still for a moment. A low groan came from the general.

"He's going to go after them if nothing is done," she whispered to herself. Eira blew out a thick sheet of ice, covering the cave entrance. Once that was done, she joined her brothers in the sky.

Moments after the dragons left, General Kain found enough strength to push himself to his knees, a rare position for someone like him. His eyes focused on the thick sheet of ice covering the mouth of the cave.

"What in her goddess' name did that?" He thought for a moment as he climbed to his feet. "Where did the dragons go?" He looked around. "Where are my men?" his voicc boomed. A few soldiers came out from behind the bamboo trees.

"We're here, Sir!" they called.

Kain walked a few steps, then saw the bodies of many soldiers spread among the jungle floor. Rage boiled from deep inside of him.

"Those horrid creatures will pay for this! And those delinquents–no, traitors to the Empire are–"

"They went inside the cave, Sir!" one soldier informed. "I know!" Kain hollered back. "We're going in after them!"

The two soldiers stared at the ice wall blocking their way into the cave.

"How do we get past the ice?" the other soldier asked. Kain stared hard at the ice wall. He drew his gun and fired. The laser beam hit the ice, cracking part of the ice.

"Shoot the wall!" he commanded. Both soldiers obeyed and in no time, the ice broke away enough for them to pass.

The trio bolted through the cave until they came to two tunnels.

"You two go down that one," he pointed towards the right. I'll go this one," while pointing to the one on the left.

Deep inside the right tunnel were four tired, yet relentless humans and one persistent unicorn. A'keara helped stir Aurora down the tunnel. Blythe glanced towards Kero who was actually doing well despite getting beamed by a laser.

"So, did that laser even hurt you?"

"I felt it hit me–" Kero thought for a moment. "Ya know, when I was a kid, all of us on the farm used to play tag and we'd actually tackle each other. I guess it felt like that." Blythe returned a look of admiration.

"Let's quicken the pace," A'keara said. Kero already felt they were moving pretty fast.

"We don't even know where this leads," she protested.

"There's no going back now," Aponi said.

Kero groaned. "We've been walking for a while. I think it's safe to rest."

As she said that, two laser beams flew past her. She turned to look behind her shoulder to see the cause. The two imperial soldiers continued shooting, hitting Aurora in her hind leg and the other barely grazing Aponi. The unicorn screeched in pain.

Another beam headed towards Blythe. She turned with

her hands out as if they would stop the laser from hitting her. In a strange phenomenon, ice flew from her hands, hitting one of the soldiers. As he fell, his comrade looked over at him, shocked, then turned to look at Blythe. In the girl's hand was a round disk made of ice, the middle was hollow.

"What just happened?" she asked. "What's this?"

Aponi was about to answer, but was interrupted by the attacking soldiers. Blythe instinctively threw the disk at one of the soldiers. It ricocheted off his guns, turning it to a block of ice. The firearm fell from his hands. His comrade looked over at him.

"What are you doing?" he chastised.

"That girl–s-she–look what she did!"

While the two bickered, their assailants ran off down the tunnel.

"They're getting away! If we fail to catch them, the General will make sure neither of us would walk again!" He hurried after them.

Meanwhile, General Kain raced down the tunnel. It appeared as if he were already coming to the end, but instead, he found another connecting tunnel. He stood at the crossway for a moment. Suddenly, he heard something, the clicking of hooves. They were heading straight towards him. He drew his gun.

Aurora's horn glowed brightly, lighting the path for the others. Blythe still tried to figure out what happened.

"That was weird–ya know, with the round ice thingy?"

"I'm not sure of that weapon's name," Aponi admitted. "There are legends that those who bond with dragons can use spirit weapons that match their dragon's element."

"I can't make that disk appear again," she said sadly.

"Don't worry about it. You used it when it was needed, so I'm sure you'll be able to use it again." Aponi replied.

The group made their way further down the tunnel. Blythe looked ahead and noticed a change in the cave wall. The color appeared lighter.

"I think I see the end of the tunnel," Blythe said.

"It's not the end," A'keara replied. "It's another connecting tunnel. Where's the light coming from?"

Suddenly, a laser beam shot through the air. It almost hit A'keara square in the forehead, but something blocked the beam. Aurora whinnied and A'keara looked to see a stream of energy connected from her horn to the shield placed in front of her.

"She can create shields?" Blythe wondered in awe.

"She can when she wants to," A'keara replied dryly. "Why didn't you do that before?"

Another beam flew through the air only to have the same result.

"Who is shooting at us?"

General Kain stood, flabbergasted, wondering why his targets weren't falling. He noticed the unicorn's horn. Was that creature protecting the others? He took aim at a different target and fired. Aurora took only a few steps before a laser cut through her fur and skin. She cried out, jumping to her hind legs. A'keara gasped as she watched her four-legged friend collapse onto the ground. Everyone turned to see the general sneering at them.

"It looks like you're all out of magic tricks," he said haughtily. Blythe tried to create the ice disk like she did before, but nothing happened. The two soldiers finally caught up. One of them aimed his guns at the group, the other stood there, unarmed.

"Where's your gun?" the general fumed.

"Uh- sir! I-uh, the girl," he pointed at Blythe. "She froze my gun."

"What?" Kain spat back.

"It's true, sir," the other spoke.

Kain studied the three women who were still standing. His gaze went to Blythe.

"What sort of sorcery did you do?" Blythe just shook her head. She couldn't have explained what she did even if she wanted to.

"We use our gifts that were given to us by our bonded," Aponi replied.

Kain turned his gaze to the old woman.

"You use magic. That's all I care to know about. Magic is against the law."

"Magic is not against our law," Aponi tossed out.

Kain looked at the soldiers.

"Arrest the women and put a muzzle on the horse!"

"She's a unicorn," A'keara corrected him.

He stared daggers at her. "I don't care." A'keara knelt down by Aurora. Her eyes widened at the animal's gaping wound.

"We need to get her into the sunlight."

"Sunlight?" Blythe asked.

"Unicorns can be healed by sunlight," Aponi explained.

"Shut up!" Kain hollered. "None of you are seeing sunlight ever again!"

Aeolus reached the other side of the cave. The entrance into the cave was way too small for him to fit. He poked his head into the cave entrance. It was very cramped. He stood there for a moment. They would hopefully be coming out soon. Phoenix and Eira joined him. Phoenix kept an eye on his wound. Luckily, it wasn't too serious.

"I think this is the other side of the cave," Aeolus said.

"Great! We'll just wait here. I need to rest anyways," Phoenix replied.

"At least it's daytime. The sun will heal you in no time," Eira said. Phoenix nodded.

General Kain herded his prisoners through the tunnel. Their hands and feet were chained together. Blythe wanted to make that ice disk appear again, but no matter what, it wouldn't come to her. The soldier who lost his gun made himself useful by carrying Kero. Aurora winced as she hobbled forward. The chain around her neck cut through her fur and into her skin every time she tried to pull away. Her powers wouldn't work either. She let out a tiny whinny.

"Don't bother trying to use that horn of yours," Kain scowled. "That cuff around your neck suppresses any supernatural power. And it's the same with the cuffs on the rest of you."

"How did you make such things?" Aponi asked.

"Oh, we've had a lot of research done on suppressing magic."

"It's not magic," Aponi protested. "The abilities our unicorn has come from the higher realms and the power you saw our friend use came from her bond with her dragon."

"That's blasphemy!" the general shouted. "It won't matter. As soon as I turn you over to the Empress, she will no doubt order your execution."

Kero sat next to Blythe, and she was next to A'keara, then Aponi. The general paced back and forth with a hand on his earpiece. He furrowed his brow as only static erupted from the tiny speaker.

"I thought these things could still receive transmission even when in a cave," he fumed. "Note to self, tell that scientist to work on improving reception on the communicators."

He turned to his captives. "Well, it appears we're walking to the cave exit. Get up!"

As Kero stood with the others, she mumbled. "What else did he expect us to do?"

The general turned to her. "Do you have something you'd wish to say to me?" he bellowed.

Kero stared at the tall, burly man. There was a lot she wanted to say, but maybe for once, she should mind her words.

"Not really," she said as she gritted her teeth.

"Then move it!"

The group of prisoners were forced to walk again. A'keara turned sadly towards Aurora who was injured and being hauled by a chain. *How dare they treat such a wonderful being of light like this!*

Finally, the speck of daylight crept into the cave. The general stood at the lead with his soldiers bringing in up the rear.

"Halt!" Kain shouted. He turned towards his men. "I'm going to survey the area outside the cave. Keep an eye on the prisoners. There'd better not be any more shenanigans!"

Once he departed from everyone, the armed soldiers moved around the group with his gun pointed at his captives. The other one just stood there, looking as intimidating as possible with a scowl on his face.

Kero looked over at Aponi again. The elderly woman's eyes stared downward, deep in thought. Kero glanced over at Blythe who had a similar expression. A'keara however, had her full attention on Aurora. Even with her hands cuffed, A'keara managed to reach into her pouch by her side and grab her crystals. She held them over the mare's wound. One of the soldiers noticed right away.

"What are you doing?" he demanded. Blythe and Aponi looked up from their daze.

"I'm healing my friend," A'keara said plainly. The armed soldier rushed at A'keara, hitting her square in the head with the butt of his gun. Aponi gasped as her granddaughter fell to the ground.

"You ape!" she screeched. "You won't even let us heal our animal companion? She is the last of her kind!"

The soldier aimed his gun at the old lady.

"Shut your mouth!" he cried out. He proceeded to assault Aponi by smacking her on the back of her head. Aponi fell unconscious.

"Stop it!" Blythe screamed. The man with the gun turned, now aiming his gun at her.

"I don't want to hear another word," he spoke slowly. He looked down at her cuffed hands. "Besides, you can't do any more magic tricks now, can you?"

Kero watched the entire time, thinking of a way she could get her friends out of this, but nothing came to her. As she stood there, she noticed the carnelian on her necklace began to glow.

General Kain searched around the thick vines and plants for a trail. The jungle was thicker on this side of the cave. Maybe he should take the prisoners back the other way. He pushed on the side of his ear, where he wore his communication device.

"Hello?" he called. There was some crackling on the other side.

"We're still with the prisoners, sir!" he heard one soldier.

"I know that! Keep an eye on them while I radio for another ship." He switched frequencies to the military base.

"This is General Kain requesting a carrier ship to transport four prisoners." He thought about the unicorn. "Five, I guess. Bring a muzzle too!"

Up above, he heard the sound of large wings flapping in the sky. He looked up to see a golden dragon circling the area. He wasn't sure if he alone could take out a dragon. Instead, he made his way back towards the cave.

Aeolus ascended to the top of the hill just in time to see Phoenix and Eira heading towards him.

"Did you find another entrance to the cave?" Phoenix asked.

"I did. Down there," he pointed his nose down through the trees.

"Okay, before we go, please be careful. We cannot just barrel our way into danger. We are still vulnerable to the attacks made by these humans, and our bonded are even more susceptible than we are. From now on, we must not part from them." He shook his head. "I guess the years asleep have made my head dull."

"Don't blame yourself," Aeolus replied.

"We need to get to our bonded," Eira said. The three flew

over the canopy of trees, keeping an eye out for any sudden attacks.

General Kain already returned to the cave to address the two soldiers he had left. Nothing much had changed.

"We'll wait here for the carrier ship," he announced.

"Yes sir!" the soldiers replied in unison.

A'keara opened her eyes and quickly sat up. Looking around, she saw her grandmother laying on the ground. Aurora still laid on her side with a pained expression. The general stood at the cave entrance looking out while his two men stood on either side of him with their backs against the wall of the cave. She began searching for her crystals on the ground. One she found by Aurora's hoof. She picked it up, while kindly looking at the mare.

"Don't worry, I'm going to heal you." She only held a quartz crystal, but she had to find her amethyst and her yellow tiger eye. The clear quartz crystal wouldn't be enough to heal Aurora. She searched the ground and saw her amethyst by Blythe's foot.

"Blythe," she whispered. The girl had her eyes half closed. A'keara looked over at the two soldiers. She was afraid to move because if they knew she was awake, they might knock her out again or do something else. Slowly, she crawled towards Blythe. Just as she approached her, she heard one of the soldiers shout.

"What do you think yer doin?" She turned to see the one soldier aim his gun at her.

"I'm getting my crystals," she answered. He marched over to her.

"Again with the crystals? Do those things give you inhuman power?"

"No, I use them to heal," A'keara curtly replied. The man smirked.

"What ridiculous beliefs," he scoffed.

A'keara kept her gaze steady on him. "I can show you right now that they can heal."

She grabbed the tiger eye. As she turned away, Blythe tapped her on the shoulder.

"Here's your purple stone," she said. She handed A'keara the amethyst.

"Thank you."

A'keara walked over to Aurora and held the crystals over her wound. The soldier watched as the skin began to close. It wasn't instant, but after a few minutes, the bleeding stopped. The soldier tried to form words.

"H-how did ya do that?"

General Kain turned around. His eyes narrowed.

"What is going on over here?" He stomped over. A'keara felt herself being pulled to her feet. She wasn't quite done, but at least now Aurora wouldn't bleed to death.

"She healed the horse," the soldier said.

A'keara didn't even bother correcting him. Before the general could respond, a distant voice spoke into his earpiece.

"Sir, we're here in the jungle, but we can't land. The trees are too dense."

"Meet us on the other side of the hill. There's a clearing where you can land," he instructed. He turned his attention to the prisoners. "Let's move! We're going back to the other side."

Kero wished she could just run out of the cave, but her hands were still bound. With great irritation, she yanked hard on the chains. To her surprise, they broke. The broken ends were both really hot, she could see the red embers. How? She had no time to figure it out. This might be her only chance.

All at once, she got up and raced towards the cave exit. Phoenix was out there. She knew it! She just had to get to him. General Kain stood in her path. He was about to tackle the girl when something sharp cut through his armor. He felt his skin burn. He cried out as he grabbed his side and collapsed on the ground.

At this point, Aponi had awakened and saw the whole thing. Her mouth curved up into a smile as she saw Kero standing with a long shaft with two blades on either side. Flames burst out from the blades. Kero looked down at the double-bladed flame sword.

"What the–?" She stared at it in awe.

"You called your spirit weapon," Aponi said.

"Don't just stand there, stop her!" Kain ordered.

The armed soldier prepared to fire his gun, but Kero already reached the cave exit. The other soldier, who was unarmed, ran after her. He rushed outside only to be confronted by three huge dragons. He screamed and ran back into the cave.

Kero jumped onto Phoenix's back. "The others are still in there."

"How many soldiers?" Phoenix asked.

"There's three of them, the general and two of his men."

"I'll take care of them," Aeolus said. He poked his head into the cave and started blowing a huge tornado wind into the tunnel.

"Stop! You could hurt our friends," Phoenix said.

Inside, everyone felt the strong wind blow all around. As the wind blew, Kero realized that the shackles around her wrists broke. The same happened for the others. The wind picked up General Kain, hurling him into the wall. The other two soldiers were flung about in the wind. Unfortunately, the wind didn't just affect the soldiers. Blythe lost her footing and hit her head when her body flung into the wall.

Eira was small enough to actually move halfway into the tunnel.

"Blythe, are you okay? I felt something hit me in the head–" She saw the girl laying by the wall, holding her head. She turned to look at Aeolus.

"You oaf! You hurt Blythe!" she chastised the golden dragon.

"Eira, take care of the soldiers," Phoenix said. Eira looked over at the two terrified soldiers. "I don't think I have to do much." She tossed out a blizzard, freezing their feet into place. The two men cried out and tried to move their feet, but were unsuccessful. "Come on, hurry!"

Aponi helped Blythe stand and A'keara guided Aurora to the cave exit.

Blythe mounted Eira, her head still ached. After a moment, the pain began to subside.

"Are you alright?" Eira asked. "The sunlight should be healing your wound."

"How can sunlight heal me?" Blythe asked.

"Since you are bonded to me, you share my ability to heal with sunlight. You can also heal with ice and water too. Just as Kero shares Phoenix's ability to heal with fire."

"I can be healed with fire?" Kero questioned.

"Somewhat," Phoenix replied. "It has to be actual flames and not an explosion." Kero just nodded. Her brain was too overloaded to ask any more questions.

"We have to wait for Aurora to fully heal," A'keara said. Aponi pulled herself up onto Aeolus.

"She looks fine to me."

A'keara looked for Aurora's wound. It was gone. She hugged the mare.

"Thank you, Mother Gaia," she whispered.

She hopped onto the mare's back. Everyone took off towards the east.

CHAPTER 14

The Fallen Colony

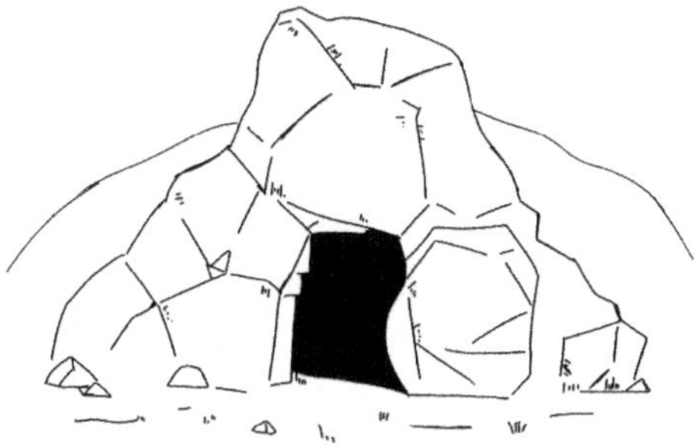

In the deep blue sky, Kero felt the agility as she rode atop the Crimson Dragon. On the left side of her was Eira and Blythe. On the right side of her was Aeolus who carried Aponi. Down below, A'keara rode on Aurora. It amazed Kero that the unicorn was so active and healthy after getting shot.

"I can't believe those people were so afraid of us," Eira said suddenly to Phoenix. "Everything has changed so much since we've been asleep."

"This is not something we should be concerned about right now," Phoenix replied. "We need to find Eden and awaken her. Then, we can open the portal and let the other dragons into this world."

"I'm sorry, I don't get it," Kero admitted. "All the dragons are going to come out and make everything better? You know what would make things better? Killing the Empress."

"Listen Kero, we can't just start taking lives. Besides, there will be retaliation from the people if we just kill their queen."

"No there won't!" Kero protested. "She's a tyrant! I know everyone in my colony will be glad she's gone."

"From what I've seen so far, all of the humans are dependent on the Empire. And they are afraid of dragons. You asked me earlier why the dragons left Gaia. Maybe it was so that the humans would learn how to stand up for themselves. Humans, as I remember them, were always so needy. They were weak and frail and depended heavily on the dragons to protect them. Maybe they needed to be more grateful to the dragons."

"The humans were ungrateful?" Kero asked.

"Some were. Let's not worry about all that now. All we need to focus on is finding Eden. The Elder Dragons are waiting for us to open the gateway."

Blythe was the first to recognize the great city of Gabriel. The tall glass buildings in the city shine brilliantly in the sunlight. As soon as the dragons landed, Blythe turned to address everyone.

"You know that all of Michael and Gabriel is run by solar power?"

"Yes," Kero answered through gritted teeth. They got all the great technological equipment and places like Athena had to use candle light.

"I was told Xan was in either Gabriel or Apollo. Hopefully he's here, because I don't want to deal with the sand storms around Apollo."

"How are you going to contact him?" Eira asked.

Blythe thought for a moment. "I dunno."

Kero rolled her eyes. She supposed she was in the same boat as she didn't know exactly which prison her brother was sent to.

"Is something troubling you, Kero?" Phoenix asked.

"No," she lied.

"You know, I can sense your emotions. I can tell something is bothering you."

Kero was about to speak, but Phoenix continued. "Of course, it's none of my business."

Thoughts about her and Darion's arrest flooded her mind suddenly.

"Phoenix? My brother and I were arrested by the Empire, but I escaped from the airship with Blythe. My brother was taken to a prison somewhere. Maybe he's in the prison inside Apollo or Michael. I guess there's a prison in the frozen tundra. She shivered, hoping it wasn't that one. Those prisoners barely got any heat. She heard it was the worst prison on Anu. It was well known that many prisoners died because they froze to death.

"Do you know how we can find out?" he asked. Kero forced back any coming tears and shook her head. "Hmm, we'll find out one way or another."

Kero dismounted Phoenix and joined with the others. She joined just in time to catch the argument between Aponi and A'keara.

"Do not be afraid," Aponi said to her granddaughter.

"I'm not afraid," she objected. "I just don't know where she is." Aponi

narrowed her brow at her granddaughter. "You told me that you stood in a jungle and you saw a temple."

A'keara closed her eyes and shook her head. Tears formed

in her eyes, and she breathed in heavily. "It looked like the temple where we used to pray, back in Etheria."

"Etheria?" Eira asked in awe. "I haven't seen that sacred place in ages."

"Unfortunately, you're never going to see it," A'keara said scornfully. "The Empire destroyed it!"

Kero felt a little uneasy by A'keara's sudden rage, but understood. Everyone had suffered in some way because of the Empire. This is why it was such a punch in the face to the dragons when those islanders acted the way they did. Kero admitted that before this adventure began, she never knew much of what was outside of Athena. She didn't know anything about the people other than the rich people in Michael and the smart people in Gabriel. Everyone else just existed.

"Listen," Aponi said to A'keara. "We have to wake up the Emerald Dragon. It doesn't matter where we have to go."

"But, it doesn't make sense. The Emerald Dragon is supposed to be in the east. Etheria is in the middle of the planet."

Aponi leaned towards A'keara. "You're thinking about the city. I'm talking about the continent."

"What do you mean?" Blythe asked.

"There's the city of Etheria. And there is the continent of Etheria."

Kero and Blythe stared blankly at the woman.

"Oh yes. I remember," Aeolus said. "The city is a small island, but there were bridges connecting it to bigger landmasses."

"I keep feeling that the Emerald Dragon is in the temple where we keep the ashes of the departed. It makes me sad to think of that place. We couldn't return to Etheria to cremate the ones who died. I wanted to cremate my mother and put her ashes in the eastern temple. And my poor daughter–she was obliterated by one of the Empire's weapons–" A'keara's voice faded. She found herself unable to speak.

Everyone turned to A'keara. "Your daughter?" Kero asked.

A'keara nodded.

"My daughter was pregnant at the time of her death. So, I lost her and my granddaughter that day."

Kero lost her words and Blythe was equally shocked.

"I'm sorry? Your daughter and granddaughter? Aren't ya in yer twenties or something? I mean, you and my brother look about the same age."

A'keara looked up at Kero and narrowed her eyes. "Oh no. I'm fifty-five years old."

The two girls tried to comprehend what the woman just said. They turned to Aponi.

"Then, how old are you?" Kero asked.

"Oh my," she hummed. "Kind of a personal question. If you must know, I'm one-hundred and eleven."

Kero's mouth dropped open. "How are you still alive? And yer riding dragons and runnin' around and doin' stuff-"

"I might be older than most, but I'm nowhere near the end of my life."

"How old do people from Etheria live till?" Blythe asked.

"We had a few older Etherians on the council. The oldest was a man named Artus. He was one hundred and fifty years old."

Kero shook her head. "I can't believe it," she said. "Why can your people live so long?"

"It's simple," A'keara replied. "We didn't have the pollution and poor food that people now have to deal with."

"We also had the power from Gaia to keep us young," Aponi explained. "Maybe we should go to the temple, A'keara."

"Fine. We'll go there, but do you even know how to get there?" A'keara asked.

"I remember well enough. It's close to the Cleo Sea."

"Cleo Sea?" Blythe asked. She turned away. "Luna is on the other side of the Cleo sea."

"Luna," Kero thought to herself. "That's where you're from, right? It's south of here."

"Southeast actually. Be careful if you go that way. The air is toxic because of all the bombs the empire tested in the area."

"How can anyone live there?" Eira wondered.

"It's underground," Kero explained. "As I was told Luna was above ground before all of that happened."

"Yeah, that's right," Blythe said, turning to her. "Luna was a bunch of tiny villages at one time. One in particular was bigger than the others and there were rivers and waterfalls. It was a beautiful place."

"Wait a minute," Aponi said. "What if–" She came out of her thoughts to address the others. "I need to pray. I'm going to find some shelter." She walked towards some open caves.

"Be careful!" A'keara yelled after her. "You don't know what's in there!" She chased after her.

Aponi ducked into a small cave. A'keara followed, using her crystal for light. The old lady sat down and closed her eyes. A'keara sat next to her grandmother. She focused her eyes on her crystal for a few long moments. Her eyes closed naturally.

A'keara opened her eyes and found herself deep within the jungle. In front of her was a strange rock formation. It appeared like a doorway made of stone. As she walked through the door, she saw urns on pedestals and hieroglyphics carved into the walls. She couldn't read any of them. She continued on down deeper into a tunnel. At the end of the tunnel was a large room with a beautiful fountain. Two statues of goddesses held vases that poured clear blue water into the basin. Then, she saw a tree grow right in front of her. It began with a trunk that twirled around itself. The swirling branches grew up around the top of the cave. Flowers bloomed from the tree.

"Have I been here before?" she wondered. The voice spoke again, but the words were inaudible. As A'keara stared at the water falling into the basin, she saw cracks form in the statues of the two goddesses. The basin cracked too. The water leaked out and began to fill the temple. A'keara wanted to leave, but her feet wouldn't move. The water moved faster now, filling up the entire room. She was drowning. She opened her mouth to scream, but no sound came out. Something shook her body. She couldn't get away!

A'keara opened her eyes for real and saw her grandmother's face in the pale light.

"Wake up!" Aponi yelled.

"What happened?" A'keara asked.

"You were yelling 'help.' What did you see?"

"I–" A'keara took a moment to collect her thoughts. "I was in the temple, the one where the ashes of the departed are kept."

Aponi put a comforting hand on her granddaughter's shoulder. "There was a tree that grew in front of me and water poured out of a fountain–I almost drowned–"

"We should go back to the others."

"Were you able to do what you needed?" A'keara asked. Her grandmother smiled. "Yes, it seems you had the vision we needed."

A'keara stared blankly at Aponi, but then realized what she meant.

"You didn't need to meditate. You were just trying to get me to sit and focus for a moment, weren't you?"

"Yes, and it worked. So, now you know where to go."

"Well, I know sort of where to go, but I'm still not sure of the exact location."

"Don't worry about it. East is where the last dragon is located, so that is where we're going."

When the two women returned, everyone still waited quietly. Aponi was the first to address everyone.

"We will head east towards Luna. Blythe, would it be alright if you helped us navigate the area?" Blythe stiffened up.

"I–" The last time she was in Luna, she was put into a cage with all the other experiments.' "I should go to Gabriel. I–uh need to find my friend, remember?" She looked at Kero. "And my friend can help Kero find her brother." Kero turned to her, surprised.

"He can?"

"We understand," Aponi said. "Only A'keara needs to be present to awaken Eden."

"Don't we have to be there?" Eira asked her siblings.

"We will be there," Phoenix said. "You will see Eden awaken even if you are not there physically." The other two dragons nodded as they understood his words. "Eira, you and I can stay with Kero and Blythe. Aeolus, please go with the other two." The gold scaled dragon suddenly appeared uneasy.

"I'm not sure I can leave you and Eira. What if something happens–?"

"Nothing will happen," Phoenix assured him. "Go with Aponi and A'keara."

Aeolus didn't say much else. Aponi climbed onto his back. A'keara was already on Aurora.

"Time to go," she said. The Golden Dragon took off into the sky.

"I hope you know what you're doing," he said to the woman.

"You should know. Don't dragons and their bonded use telepathy? He nodded.

"Really. I never thought I'd have to encourage a dragon," Aponi said.

Aeolus sighed. "There are times when dragons also feel afraid."

Hours later, the sun hung a little lower in the sky than before. It was past noon. A'keara sat atop Aurora staring at the reddish tint of the sky. Her eyes moved upwards to her grandmother riding Aeolus. In this particular temple, a stream flowed down into the temple and into a marble basin. There were trees and plants inside the temple too.

Aurora stopped abruptly, causing A'keara to pop out of

her thoughts. She looked down at a pool of mud. It was the size of a large pond.

"What's wrong?" she asked her mare.

The unicorn backed up a little and shook her mane. A'keara focused on the mud and realized it was quicksand. Good thing Aurora was more in tune with nature than she was at the moment. A'keara wasn't usually this careless. What was wrong with her?

Across from the mud pool was some grass and solid dirt.

"Aurora, try teleporting to the other side." A'keara felt her mare's hesitancy. "It's not that far. You can do it!"

The unicorn focused her eyes on the grass. Her horn glowed like before, then her body started to fade. A'keara noticed her body fading too. It was hard to describe what A'keara saw when this happened. Her vision blurred to the point that all she saw were colors. As Aurora appeared, she did too and her vision went back to normal.

A'keara was thrilled, but Aurora wasn't moving forward.

"Come on. You made it across." However, her companion returned a strained cry. A'keara glanced down to see the unicorn's back hooves stuck in quicksand. A'keara jumped off the mare and grabbed her mane. "Come on Aurora, push your weight forward." A'keara hopped off the unicorn then pulled on her reins. Finally, Aurora freed herself.

"Come on, we have to catch up with Aponi."

Once they caught up with Aponi and Aeolus, A'keara went back to focusing on the vision she had. The temple that held the ashes of her loved ones was in the middle of a beautiful valley. Yes, it would be nice to see again. There were lovely waterfalls that spilled into streams of clear water. The grass was so green and vibrant and the wind was nice and warm…

Suddenly, a big cloud of smog engulfed her and Aurora. A'keara started coughing violently. Aurora coughed too. A'keara looked forward, seeing billows of brown smoke swirling around her. Her eyes burned. She did her best to look up at her grandmother in the sky, but she couldn't see her through the smoke.

In the sky, Aeolus slowed down and hovered above the clouds of smoke.

"Where did all this smog come from?" he choked. Aponi coughed as well. She looked down towards the ground. "We need to get to A'keara."

They landed and in a moment, Aponi saw her granddaughter and her mare.

"A'keara!" she yelled. A'keara saw her grandmother and began racing towards her.

"You'll have to ride on Aeolus with me," Aponi said.

"What about Aurora?"

"I might be able to transport the unicorn too," Aeolus said. The two women looked at him. Then they coaxed the animal to climb onto the dragon's back. Aurora straddled the dragon with two hooves on each side and her stomach touching the dragon's rubbery skin. Aurora looked up at A'keara a little worried.

"It will be okay." A'keara jumped on behind the mare. Aponi got in front of her.

Aeolus took off, flying as high as he could over the clouds of smoke.

A'keara looked down. She wasn't able to see the ground.

"Wow! Blythe wasn't joking," she said. "This is horrible."

"There's something ahead, maybe a tall hill," Aeolus said. Aponi stared out through the heavy smog. "I'm feeling some strong energy. Maybe we should check."

Aponi nodded and the dragon continued until they saw the top of the hill.

A'keara looked down at what appeared to be a dried-up stream. The water would have gone over the hillside and into another stream below.

"Grandmother, this used to be a waterfall." Aponi stared down at the crevice.

"I think you're right. I believe we found the area Blythe talked to us about. I wonder where this colony called Luna is located?"

"She said it was underground."

"Excuse me?" Aeolus intervened. "I'm feeling the energy under us. Maybe there's a cave on the side of the hill?"

"Well, let's see," Aponi replied.

Aeolus flew down to look, but there wasn't a cave. A'keara groaned.

"I can't believe this! How are we supposed to find anything!"

"Calm down, we'll find–"

"No! I'm so tired. This is not the planet where we grew up. Everything changed. I mean look at this place! What kind of people do this to a beautiful planet?"

Aponi turned and put a gentle hand onto A'keara's shoulder. "We'll find the dragon, okay."

"Grandmother, what if we don't?"

Aponi never entertained the idea that they wouldn't succeed.

"We're so close," Aponi assured her.

A'keara shook her head. "It's just frustrating that we had to do all of this in the first place. I mean, if we can get visions or downloads that tell us to awaken dragons, why couldn't we get a warning about the Empire coming to attack Etheria in the first place?" Aponi opened her mouth to answer, but she realized she didn't have one.

"I prayed to our ancestors for help," A'keara continued. " I asked for everyone in Etheria to be safe during the attack. Instead, I saw everyone I knew crushed to death or struck down. My parents, my childhood friends, the elders–and even my own daughter. Everyone was killed." With all the pent up emotion, A'keara broke down into tears. "I'm sorry," she sobbed.

"Don't be sorry," Aponi kindly replied.. "I should be the one to apologize. I didn't realize how much of a burden this has been on you."

Suddenly A'keara covered her mouth. "Oh gosh! It's probably been a burden on Kero and Blythe too."

"Don't say that," her grandmother said gently. "Honestly, I don't think anything could ever bother Blythe," Aponi said. "And Kero– She has a heart of a hero. There's something about that girl. She didn't think twice about going to look for her brother even if it meant going against dozens of soldiers or savage beasts."

"We can rest for a little while before continuing the search," Aeolus suggested. "You both seem very tired."

"No, I'm okay," A'keara insisted. "We only have two days before the Energy Violet Moon. We have to find the Emerald Dragon."

"It will be fine," Aponi told her. "I think we need to rest."

"Where are we going to rest? We can't breathe in this place."

"Let's go to the top of the hill," Aponi answered simply.

Dusk approached, the sun peeked from behind the hilltops. The sky showed hues of red and purple. Aponi sat on a log, watching A'keara. Aeolus laid around the two, protecting them from the harsh wind and any wild animals that may come by. A'keara had new hope that she would find the last dragon and then all of this uncertainty would be over.

By the time A'keara was done with making the fire, the sun had fully descended and stars could be seen twinkling in the night sky. The moon gave off a violet tint. She sighed as the Violet Energy moon was almost here. Her gaze shifted to Aponi who was busy in her meditation. How was she so calm? This was it. She had to awaken the Emerald dragon tonight. All of these emotions welled up inside of her. Hopefully, she could find the dragon in time. She closed her eyes, trying to focus her thoughts.

"Are you okay?" asked a voice.

A'keara looked around. It sounded as if someone spoke to her. Someone with a soft male voice. Her eyes went to her grandmother again. Her eyes were closed, her body so still.

"Hello?" she called out. A'keara walked down the path of the desert road. Looking up into the sky, she saw millions of stars. Maybe some planets too. As she walked a little further, she noticed that the sky changed colors. It changed from a black void into a bright violet. She glanced straight ahead to see a man about the age of her grandmother sitting in the dirt. His legs crossed and his eyes were closed.

"Who are you?" she asked.

"Hold on," he spoke softly. "I'm speaking to your grandmother right

now. Yes. I know. The dragon isn't too far away."

"The dragon?" A'keara almost screamed. Then, a little quieter. "Do

you know where the Emerald Dragon is?"

"Yes. But, I wonder, why don't you know?"

A'keara shook her head. Frustration set in again. "I've tried looking for her."

"You are looking with your eyes and thinking with your brain. These are good things, but not when looking for a dragon. You must open your mind's eye. –oh, what is it you're saying?"

"I didn't say anyth–"

"Not you," he said. "Yes, she is with me. I will tell her." His eyes opened and bright white light came out of them, engulfing A'keara. "Your grandmother says to stop looking so hard. Maybe take a break."

"We don't have time! If we don't find her tonight, we won't ever open up the gateway!"

"So what if you don't." A'keara tried to find the man, but the light blocked her vision. "So, what if you don't open the portal? What will happen?" A'keara thought for a moment. She felt the planet's pain right now. People living on this planet weren't happy, but yet they did nothing about it. She and Aponi would be fine, but–

"The people living on this planet are slaves," she said finally. "It isn't right."

"Are those people upset about living as slaves?" A'keara thought about the people she and her grandmother have met through the last eleven years. Many of the people on Anu just lived their daily lives. It was just a small few who are upset about how things are.

"I don't know," she finally answered. "I just want to–" She stopped. Her eyes teared up. "I want to go home!" she wailed. "I want to go back to Etheria. I want Etheria to be alright and be standing and all of my friends and family to be alive again!"

She collapsed as she let out all of the tears she had been holding onto. And at that moment, she saw a temple. She saw roots coming through the caked dirt on the ceiling. The temple was underground. Directly in the middle of the temple, was a large tree, the one she saw from her vision earlier.

The light faded. She looked up. The man was gone. She slowly made her way to her grandmother who had completed her meditation.

"A'keara, wake up." What was she talking about?

"I am awake." Then, A'keara turned to see her body sitting on the ground. She was having an out of body experience. An internal voice responded, *"You are in the astral realm. It's time to wake up."*

A'keara awoke. She turned to Aponi who smiled at her.

"Grandmother, who was that guy?"

"That was your great grandfather. I finally made contact with him and I see you did too."

"Grandmother, I know where to find the Emerald dragon. I saw this temple. I think it's east of here.

"Okay. Good," Aponi breathed out. "Let's go."

Aeolus carried the women and the unicorn off into the night sky. The smog covered the whole valley. Aeolus flew for a while until he started coughing.

"The smog is getting worse," Aponi noted.

"There!" A'keara yelled. "See that tunnel. Go in there."

The golden scaled dragon flew into the tunnel and landed. A'keara climbed off of Aeolus and looked around.

"This is the entrance to the temple." Aponi's mouth turned up as she smiled with delight.

"I knew we could find it. It was just that all of the statues and archways are gone. I couldn't see the tunnel."

"So, this is what happened to the eastern temple," Aponi said sadly.

Aeolus tried to walk further into the tunnel, but it was too narrow.

"I'll be waiting here," he said.

As the two women went on to explore the tunnel, they heard footsteps slowly approaching them. A man who looked to be in his late thirties slowly put one foot in front of the other. His face was deathly pale, his eyes were sunken in. He appeared to be on his last breath. Suddenly, he collapsed. A'keara grabbed her crystals and rushed over. She held the crystals over the man and moved her arm up and down the length of his body. After a moment, the man opened his eyes.

"Are you okay?" she asked. He took a deep breath.

"I'm fine." he said these words without emotion. Then suddenly. "I'm fine. I'm alive–" He got up onto his feet. He turned to A'keara. "What did you do to me?"

Before A'keara could answer, he screamed. "What did you do? I wanted to die! Get away from me!" He ran back down the tunnel.

A'keara couldn't speak and Aponi was equally shocked.

"What in all that is good in Gaia–?"

"His mind is broken," Aeolus said. "He felt death was his only escape." The two women turned to see the dragon standing at the tunnel entrance.

"That man didn't even notice there was a dragon a few feet away from him," A'keara said.

"He is partially blind," Aeolus said.

A'keara suddenly felt horrible. "We should go help him," A'keara spoke with urgency.

Aponi put a hand on her granddaughter's shoulder. "I'm not sure he wants our help. Besides, we can't get distracted from our mission."

"Where are we anyways?" A'keara asked.

"I wonder," Aponi began. "Could it be possible we're in the colony Blythe is from?"

A'keara understood. This was Luna, the underground colony where everyone was forced to mine for gold.

"It's so sad how afraid these people are," A'keara said.

"Everything will change once we awaken the Emerald Dragon," Aponi said. "Where do we go from here?"

A'keara turned left, looking down another long tunnel. "This way."

The two women walked down the tunnel. As they continued, the ground sloped downwards. It wasn't too long before they walked into the temple. They walked past decorated columns and urns on pedestals that was covered in dirt and dust.

There was a feeling of nostalgia as they women looked from urn to urn.

"I have to admit, this is one temple I seldom visited," Aponi said.

"I remember coming here with my mother once," A'keara said. Memories flooded Aponi's mind of her daughter and she felt sorrowful all over again. "Ashena–she loved visiting the temples. We would have been able to visit her if she was properly cremated." Aponi sighed. At least her remains are part of the planet now."

They continued into the large open room where clear, clean water poured from above ground down into a basin.

"There's still water here?" Aponi asked.

"I remember my mother telling me there's a river near here that runs down under the ground and into this temple. Unfortunately, I don't see a dragon anywhere."

"Is that a tree?" her grandmother asked.

"Oh yes. Mother said that tree was made by a goddess and it represents life, fertility and the element of Earth and the season of Spring."

"Earth and Spring?" Aponi inquired.

A'keara began to get frustrated. She closed her eyes. "Help me, please? All my beloved, please help me find her." She opened her eyes and saw the tree.

This tree was the same one she saw many times when she came here in the past. It had a sturdy trunk even though it was curved in some spots. The branches rose up and curled along the ceiling of the temple. Two branches, she noticed, were thicker than the others. In some way, they appeared like two arms reaching upwards. Part of the trunk of the tree curved at the bottom. It strangely reminded her of a tail. Something occurred to her. The Crystal Dragon was encased in the ice. The Crimson Dragon came from the magma inside a volcano. The Golden Dragon appeared in the sky. What if…? She stared at the tree. She slowly walked up to it and touched the tree trunk.

A'keara placed her hand on the tree and waited. To her disappointment, nothing happened. She sighed deeply.

"I don't understand," she wailed. Aponi noticed there was a hole in the base of the tree trunk. She could see through the hole into the hollow tree.

"I feel like something was here, but it's gone now. We should talk to Aeolus about this."

Both women turned back to meet the golden dragon waiting for them outside the temple.

"Where's Eden?" he asked.

The two looked uneasy. "We need you to look at something," Aponi said. "Can you come with us into the temple?" The golden scaled dragon shook his head. I can't fit through the tunnel."

A'keara slapped her forehead, forgetting about that.

"However, I already know what you saw." He focused on Aponi until he connected with her thoughts. "You found an odd tree."

"Do you feel anything from this tree?" she asked. Aeolus focused on the memory of the tree. Inside his mind, he put a claw onto the tree trunk. "Eden," he said.

"Is it the Emerald Dragon?" A'keara asked.

"It–was." He took a deep breath before he continued. "She's already been awakened."

CHAPTER 15

A New Ally

After Aponi and A'keara left the group, Kero felt she could breathe a little easier. Those two always argued. A'keara had to bond with the Emerald Dragon and then they could open the portal and be done with everything. Why was A'keara making everything so complicated? Just go wake up the dragon. Was that so hard? Kero supposed it wasn't fair to beat up on the woman. However, she had her own problems. She wondered how this friend of Blythe's would help them. Would he really know her brother's location?

Kero looked up the sky to where Phoenix and Eira flew around. They said they were circling the area, making sure she and Blythe didn't get attacked.

Phoenix… Her thoughts stayed on the fiery dr\agon. He was so kind and she couldn't explain how she felt like they've known each other for many millennia.

"Kero, are you okay?" she heard Phoenix speak. Kero looked around. Her eyes scanned the area, then turned upwards. He was

still in the sky. How then, did she just hear him as if he were right next to her?

"Do not be concerned, Kero. You must have more faith." She heard the wise dragon speak.

Kero narrowed her eyes. That was odd.

"Phoenix? Is that you? How are you talking to me like this?" She heard him chuckle again.

"You still have a lot to learn about telepathy."

Kero sighed. *"It's hard to have faith sometimes,"* Kero admitted. *"I guess I'm scared that–"* She didn't want to entertain the horrible thought of her brother already being dead.

"He's still alive," Phoenix assured her.

"How do you know?"

"I feel his energy."

"What? How?"

"Everything is energy," Phoenix explained. *"Everything on this planet is connected."*

"You sound like Aponi," Kero replied.

"Aponi. The old woman is very wise. In our realm, she is known to be a Wise One."

"A Wise One?"

"Wise Ones are souls who have been around the longest. They've been to all the different realms. They communicate with souls who have passed on and higher beings like dragons."

"I guess I wouldn't understand since I'm not a Wise One," Kero said solemnly.

"Oh, and what makes you think you're not a Wise One?" Phoenix asked.

"Wait! Are you saying I am one?"

"Hey Kero!" Blythe's chipper voice made Kero jump a mile high. She turned to the blonde.

"What?" she asked, sort of irate.

"I've just been talking to Eira. Apparently we can speak telepathically to our dragons."

"Yeah, I kinda found that out myself," Kero replied.

"Oh, so you've been talking to Phoenix?" Kero nodded. "Okay, so we're going to have to come up with a plan to get into Gabriel."

"Yeah, this should be fun. We're criminals," Kero said with a salty voice.

"Well, I got into Isis while riding Eira. I'm thinking of doing the same thing to get into Gabriel."

Kero shook her head. "Gabriel is more heavily guarded than Isis."

"I wish I had a way to contact Xan," Blythe said.

"Didn't you guys plan on where to meet up?" Kero asked.

"We never actually made a plan to meet." Blythe turned away. "Actually, he doesn't know I'm coming to meet him."

"What? Then why are you–?"

Blythe whipped her head around to face Kero. "Because he just disappeared. After he, Ramon and I got away from the Imperial soldiers that attacked our base, he decided to leave us and go undercover as a scientist. I haven't heard from him in three months. I– I just need to make sure he's okay."

"So, he's in Gabriel?"

"That's what Ramon said. Besides, if he's acting as a scientist, he's most likely in Gabriel. He gave me a code to use so I can find him."

"A code? What's that?"

Blythe appeared hesitant to answer. "It's just something our group made up so we can know who we're talking to."

Blythe's explanation made absolutely no sense to Kero. "Sorry, don't get it."

"You'll see when we get there, I suppose."

"If we can figure out a way in. I mean, we have two dragons, they can just freeze or burn any of the guards in our way."

Blythe turned to Kero, alarmed by her suggestion.

"The last thing we want to do is start another battle. This is a covert operation."

"A what?"

Suddenly, Blythe let out a long groan. "Why don't you know anything!"

Kero was taken aback from the girl's outburst. Blythe's face softened.

"I'm sorry. I didn't mean that. Look, just trust me okay? We don't want to call attention to ourselves."

Phoenix and Eira glided down to the ground to meet their bonded.

"Do you have plans on how we're getting into the city?" Eira asked Blythe.

Blythe stood still for a moment, pondering the answer to that question. Suddenly, something came to her.

"Wait, Xan said that one of the cameras on Gabriel's border wall has a blind spot. You can technically go over the wall without being seen."

"A blind spot?" Kero questioned. "Why would the border wall for one of Anu's most powerful colonies have a blind spot?"

"I'm sure it wasn't intentional," Blythe said. "Some time in the morning, the sun hits the highest building in a way that blocks one of the cameras on the border wall. The camera can't fully see this area because there's a glare from the sunlight."

Kero looked up into the sky. The sun wasn't directly overhead yet. It was more in the east, between sunrise and noon.

"Do you know where this spot is?" Kero asked.

"The building that has the blind spot is Crystalline Inc., the tallest building in Gabriel. When the sun hits the glass building at noon, the sun beams bounce off the camera, creating a big glare. At that moment, the camera can't pick up anything, but a big ray of light."

"It sounds like this attempt to get into the city has a time limit," Phoenix said.

"So, did Xan tell you all of this before he left to go on this mission?" Kero asked.

Blythe nodded. "He knows what he's talking about. Trust me."

"We should go now. From where the sun is, it may be hitting that building at the right moment now."

"Can you tell the time by the sun?" Blythe wondered.

"Well, it would be easier if I could use the sundial we have on the farm, but I know the position of the sun at sunrise and sunset, and it's directly overhead at noon."

"Okay, Crystalline Inc. is actually in the back of the city. Let's head over there now."

"If I may make a suggestion," Eira intervened. "I can get inside Blythe's spirit stone and she can ride with Kero on Phoenix."

"Oh I get it. We'd be less likely to be spotted if we were only on one dragon," Blythe realized.

"I'll get inside your spirit stone," Eira said to Blythe. Her body became pure energy. The stream of blue energy flowed into the lapis lazuli on Blythe's bracelet.

The girls climbed onto Phoenix and took off towards the city.

Sunlight gleamed down onto the glass building of Crystal Inc. Many civilians walking by the company building had to shield their eyes from the irritating glare. Phoenix flew through the glare. Luckily, dragons didn't have to worry about being blinded by the sunlight.

"I hope this works," Blythe said. "Just be ready in case the cameras spot us. The guns will go off and we'll be shot by lasers."

Kero closed her eyes, silently praying they would not be seen. The next time she opened them, Phoenix had already landed on the ground inside the city.

The girls hopped off the dragon. Phoenix became a stream of red energy and flowed into the carnelian on her necklace.

"The entrance to Crystalline Inc. is on the other side," Blythe said.

"So, we just walk right in? I feel underdressed," Kero replied, looking down at her tarnished shirt and pants. While it was nice that Aponi gave her new clothes, she had been wearing the same outfit for a week. That was a new record. It was common for people on the farm to change clothing every few days.

"Oh, that reminds me," Blythe began. "We need something to cover ourselves in." She looked around, but there weren't any clothes line like she found in Isis. Then, she saw a blanket sticking out of a dumpster. She quickly grabbed it. "We can use these to cover up. I just need to cut the blanket.

"You want to use that? People in Gabriel have money. We're going to stick out even more if we use that thing."

"I'd rather risk having a few snobs stare at us than have the Patrol recognize us."

Kero sighed. "Fine."

After Blythe ripped the blanket in half, Kero took part of the cloth.

"This thing smells like the stuff we feed the pigs on the farm," she commented.

"Really? What stuff do you feed pigs?" Blythe wondered.

"Oh pigs will eat anything you put in front of them."

Kero wrapped the blank around her, covering herself from head to toe. Blythe did the same.

"Alright, I think we're ready."

Once the girls made it to the front of the building, Blythe studied the names next to the numbers of each individual business.

"Here it is. Dr. Julius Hawthorne.

"I thought his name was Xan."

Blythe leaned close to Kero. "It's a fake name of course.

That's the name he said he was going to use."

Kero shook her head. "Whatever."

After ringing the buzzer, the two girls waited only a few seconds before a voice came out of the speaker.

"Hello?" Blythe smiled as she recognized the sound of her friend's voice.

"Hello, this is Krystal. I'm here for our meeting."

"Are you one of the mice?" came the voice.

"No mice here. Just a hawk."

Kero narrowed her eyes. Blythe turned and whispered. "That's our code," she said.

"I'll be right there," the voice replied.

"So, your group is called Hawks?" Kero asked.

"The Hawks," Blythe said proudly.

"So, that whole mice, hawk thing–is there a meaning behind it?"

Blythe turned to her with a wide eared grin. "Of course. Hawks eat mice and other small animals. It's kind of our way of looking at the Imperial army. They may seem strong together, but individually they are weak. We look at ourselves as hawks and the soldiers as mice scurrying away as we "hawks" fly in to eat them." Kero returned an odd stare to Blythe's analogy. Her mouth curved upwards and the most boisterous laugh poured from her. "Wow! You and your group have a really crazy imagination."

The door opened, showing a man who looked to be in his thirties. His sandy blonde hair laid neatly on top of his head. His emerald green eyes stared at Blythe.

"Come in. Hurry."

The two girls walked into a luxurious foyer complete with a crystal chandelier hanging from the ceilings and a beautiful marble fountain spraying clear water into a pool with aqua and blue tiles.

"My office is on the 33rd floor. We'll take the elevator."

As they walked towards a glass elevator in the middle of the foyer, Kero looked around in wonder. Never did she expect to be surrounded by this much wealth. The building was breathtakingly beautiful and the people wore suits. She gazed at the clean white walls decorated with gold trimming and a large marble fountain in the center of the entranceway. As they approached the elevator, Xan placed his ID on a scanner. Once they heard a loud *beep*, the elevator made its way down to the main floor where they stood. When the doors opened, a group of men wearing white uniforms walked out. They were a contrast to the green sweater Xan wore. His forest green pants and black shoes completed his fancy ensemble.

"Hello Doctor," they greeted Xan.

"Good afternoon gentlemen," he replied. The three of them walked into the elevator. Blythe and Kero received some strange looks, but the men walked on without saying anything.

There was a light jolt as the elevator rose upwards. Kero watched through the glass as the people under them became smaller and smaller. The elevator rose to a point where the glass was covered by a black wall. Then, the doors opened into an office. Once, the three walked into the office, Blythe tossed down the blanket. Right after, she threw her arms around Xan. He returned the embrace.

"I've been looking everywhere for you! I went to Isis and found Ramon. Why didn't you come find me?"

"I'm sorry, but I told you what my plan was. Besides, the last time I was in Isis was about four months ago."

"I'm just glad we got into the city."

"Well, that's what the fake ID was for," he whispered. Blythe almost mentioned that the Patrol caught her in Isis and they took her ID. Instead, she just smiled.

Xan looked over at Kero. "How did you get in?"

Before Kero could answer, Blythe cut in. "She lives here. She–uh–wants to become a member of our group."

Xan looked the girl up and down. "Oh, I see. Well, right now we barely have a group," Xan said gravely.

"We can still get more people," Blythe countered.

Xan didn't reply. Instead, he walked over and sat down in a designer leather chair behind a red cedar desk. Blythe looked up at the plaque on the wall behind him.

"Wow! You have a plaque with your name on it? 'Dr. Julius Hawthorne,' she read. "So, everything must be going well?"

He nodded and smiled.

"How did you get this position in such a short amount of time?"

"Because of my inventions. I invented a way for people to teleport anywhere on the planet. And I made a few other inventions that gained the trust of the Empress herself."

"Wait a minute, so yer helpin' the Empire?" Kero asked.

The man turned to her. "I don't believe I got a name yet, Ms–"

"Her name is Kora." Blythe said. Kero raised an eyebrow

to how Blythe pronounced her name.

"Nice to meet you. Listen, there's more to the plan, but I shouldn't talk about that here, though. Too many ears in the walls."

Ears in the walls?" Kero asked.

"The place is most likely bugged," Blythe whispered.

"Uh, why are we here then? Won't they know anyways? We've been talking about yer plans already."

"Don't know what yer talkin' about Kora," Blythe said loudly. "We're just discussing business with Dr. Hawthorne." She began pushing Kero towards the door. "And now we're leaving."

"I'll meet you out back," Xan whispered.

Kero and Blythe stood in a small alley behind Crystalline Inc. Kero glanced over at Blythe who was nervously biting her fingernail. Kero hoped that after all of this was done, they would meet Aponi and A'keara and the last dragon would be awake. Then, she could finally go and free her brother. It took a few moments, but Xan finally came out with a large trash bag. He tossed it into the dumpster.

"Let's get going?"

"Where are we going now?" Kero asked, sounding a bit tired.

"I don't trust anyone." He pointed up at a Watcher floating by. "Here, these will be better than those blankets." He handed the two girls a couple of jackets with hoods on them. "I know you two are wanted."

"How did you know–?" He hushed Blythe. The girls put on the jackets and covered their heads. Kero felt kind of warm. The weather didn't call for jackets. Wouldn't they look more suspicious with these on?

“We need to leave the city,” Xan said. “Just follow my lead. Keep some distance between us. Let me go on ahead, then follow. Don’t walk together.” Blythe nodded. She knew exactly what Xan was doing. They actually had done this before when sneaking around other colonies. Kero responded with apprehension, but nodded. Xan casually walked through the alley and out into the crowds of people. Blythe turned to Kero. “Go ahead and follow him, I’ll be right behind you.”

Kero hurried down the alley and into the crowded street. She kept her eyes on the man. He wasn’t walking very fast, so that was good. Following Xan was easy so far. He walked down the main road towards the gate. Then he stopped and waited next to the guard. Kero stopped a few feet away.

“I have some business to attend to,” Xan said to the men guarding the gate. He turned to Kero. “Those two are with me.” Blythe caught up and was confused as Kero.

One of the guards looked Kero up and down.

“What are you doing with these two women?” he asked. He reached his hand out towards Kero, “Remove your hoods,” he demanded. Xan stopped him.

“You don’t want to do that. You see these two women are undergoing treatment for a rare disease. We are keeping distance from others so we do not affect them. That’s why they are wearing the hooded jackets. Now, please, let us pass.”

The guards stood aside, letting the three pass through the gate. Kero couldn’t believe that worked. Then again, it seemed like Xan had a lot of influence over the people here.

Once outside Gabriel, Kero breathed a little easier.

“So, now what?” she asked.

"Oh yeah," Blythe said spontaneously. "I think it's the appropriate time for us to show Xan our new companions." Kero wondered how this man would respond to meeting two dragons.

"I hope he doesn't freak out," Kero whispered to Blythe.

"Oh really? Who are these companions of yours?" Xan asked.

Blythe whispered into the jewel on top of her bracelet.

"You can come out now." The piece of jewelry glowed blue. A stream of energy flowed from the sapphire towards the sand where the dragon took its shape. Xan quickly backed away, almost tripping over his own feet.

"Are you going to bring out Phoenix?" Blythe asked.

"Uh, he's already freaked out over one dragon."

Before everyone's eyes, Phoenix came out on his own from the carnelian on Kero's necklace. Xan stared wide eyed at the two dragons.

Xan gasped. "How did you–?"

"So, this is your friend, Blythe?" Eira asked.

Xan fixed his eyes on the two dragons.

"Here, sit down." Blythe helped him to sit down on a large rock.

"I'm okay. I-uh- didn't think you'd be one to bond with a dragon."

Both Kero and Blythe returned equally shocked faces.

"Wait, you know that people can bond with dragons?"

Xan dipped his hand into his shirt pocket and pulled out a ring with a green stone. The stone glowed, and a steam of green energy emerged from within the ring. The others watch the energy form into the Emerald Dragon.

"Eden?" Phoenix asked. "How are you–?"

"My dear brother and sister, it has been so long since I've seen you. Where is Aeolus?"

"He's uh-with his bonded. They were going to your resting place to awaken you."

"That would be hard since I'm here. Who was going to awaken me?"

Kero teetered back and forth on her feet. "Uh, well, we kinda had this plan for this woman to awaken you because we didn't know who your original bonded was."

Eden looked at her siblings. "I'm sorry, but I'm confused."

"Just let me explain," Phoenix said. "This is what happened."

After one long explanation, Xan looked at the others thoughtfully. Finally, he spoke.

"Well it sounds like you've all been on quite a journey. Eden and I just bonded today." He looked over at the green scaled dragon.

"Wait a minute," Blythe replied. "You just bonded today?"

Xan quietly collected his thoughts. "A few nights ago, I had a strange dream. I left Gabriel and headed towards the ocean-I was floating by the way. I floated south towards Luna. Then, I was in a cave where I found an odd-looking tree."

Xan told his story of how he dreamed about finding the Emerald Dragon. He stood before a strange tree with a tangled trunk. The branches twirled up and around the ceiling of the cave. Water poured from above ground into a basin behind the tree.

"What is this place? Why am I here?"

He stared up at the tree. He felt instantly connected with the tree. Trees were sacred to him. Xan felt in-tune with nature when standing in a forest. Even though the woods had predatory animals, he felt safer in them than behind the border walls the Empire built.

Xan reached out his arm, lightly touching the tree trunk with the tips of his fingers. A strong power flowed from within this tree, he could feel it. The tree was more than just a tree.

"Hello?"

"I am the Emerald Dragon, who comes before me?"

Xan gazed up at the flowers on the branches. "I am Alexander. You can call me Xan."

Light illuminated from within the tree. The bottom of the tree trunk cracked open and a stream of green energy flowed out. Xan followed the stream of energy outside where he saw a beautiful emerald green dragon flying above him.

Now in the present, Xan stood silently for a moment, waiting for his audience to take everything in. Blythe smiled.

"So, what happened after the dream? How did you get to the place where you had to wake up your dragon?"

"Well, I–" Xan went into his jacket and pulled out a strange looking gun. "I used this."

"What's that thing?" Kero asked.

"Remember I said I invented a way to teleport to anywhere on the planet? This is my teleportation gun. I shoot whoever or whatever I want to teleport somewhere and then, I put in the coordinates of where to send them. I can also transport myself anywhere on the planet."

"So, you teleported yourself to the place where you found your dragon?" Blythe asked. "How did you know where to send yourself?"

"I–just knew," Xan replied. He placed the gun back into the inside pocket of his jacket.

Kero didn't didn't care how this man found the Emerald Dragon. Now that all four dragons were awakened, they could finally open up the portal.

"Um, do you know that this planet used to be called Gaia?" Kero asked.

Xan nodded. "Yes. I actually knew that before I bonded with Eden."

"You never said anything to me about it," Blythe said salty.

"That's because I wasn't sure where the information was coming from." he looked over at Eden. "Now I do."

"Do you remember a place called Etheria?" Kero asked.

Xan smiled. "Yes, it was once a giant landmass."

"I thought Aponi said it was a city," Blythe chimed in.

"It's both, actually," Xan said.

"So, you also know about the Empire destroying Etheria?" Kero asked crossly.

Xan's eyes saddened. "Yes, Kora."

"It's Kero, actually."

Xan did a sideways glance towards Blythe.

"Uh–sorry, I had to quickly think of a fake name so no one would know who she was."

"I see," he hummed. "So, do you two remember your past lives?"

Kero and Blythe turned to each other. “Not really,” Kero responded.

“Oh. I asked because after I bonded with Eden, I saw my past self from one thousand years ago. I was a man named Talon. Eden and I protected the plants, forests and jungles. Each dragon protects their domain.”

“Every dragon protects the planet,” Eden clarified. “Each spirit dragon has a specific location that they tend to stick with.”

“Right,” Xan agreed. Hopefully you both will remember your past lives too,” he said to the girls.

Kero recalled how Aponi explained that the four people who would bond with the Spirit Dragons were the same people who bonded with them one thousand years ago.

“If you remember your past life, do you remember what this planet was like one thousand years ago?” Kero asked.

Xan smiled and nodded. “Yes. Something that you might find interesting is that the population of this planet was a bit over ten thousand people.”

“Ten thousand people live on this planet?” Kero asked. “That’s more than I thought.”

“It’s actually not that many,” Xan said sadly. This planet once had millions of humans living on it. Anyways, maybe we should go find your friends?”

Kero turned to address.

“Hey, how long until the Energy violet moon is full?”

“It’s actually happening tonight. We need to regroup with Aeoulus and go to the middle of the planet.” She hopped onto

Phoenix. "Alright. Let's go! After we open that portal, I can go break my brother out of prison."

"I appreciate your enthusiasm, Kero," Phoenix replied. "However, we should wait here for the others."

"Hold on," Blythe intervened. "Maybe you should go get your brother now." Blythe turned to Xan. "Would you happen to know which prison her brother was taken to?" Xan was taken aback by the request.

"What are you planning to do? Prisoners are extremely hard to break into, and even harder to break someone out of."

Kero took a deep breath. "I know. But–I have to try. Who knows what horrible things are happening to him."

"What is his name?" Xan asked.

"It's Darion."

"Oh, nice name," Blythe replied. She switched her glance back to Xan. "You can find out where they took him, right?

Xan rolled up his sleeve to reveal a tiny version of a computer attached to a wristband.

"I can look him up. You said his name is Darion? You got a last name to go with that?"

"Embers," Kero replied. "Same as mine."

Xan punched in the name on the screen.

"What's that wrist thingy?" Blythe asked.

"This little gadget is called a Wristcomp. Everyone in Gabriel has one, it's the latest graze."

"So, can anyone just look up information on fugitives?" Kero asked rather coldly.

He gave her an earnest glance. "Anyone with a computer has all of the information about Anu at their fingertips. Once you get arrested by the Empire, all of the facts about your arrest go public."

After typing in the full name of the prisoner, Xan lifted his eyebrows.

"Wow! He was put into a special unit in the Sansin Mountain Prison. Name: Darion Embers. Incarcerated for conspiring against the Empire."

"Conspiring against the Empire? He just killed a deer," Kero said crossly.

"Doesn't say anything about him killing a deer," Xan replied. He looked gravely at the others. The prison is set right in the middle of a frozen wasteland. They put the worst criminals on the planet in there." Kero felt her chest tighten.

"I have to get him out!" Kero shouted.

"We will get him out," Phoenix said firmly.

Xan pulled out the teleportation gun from his jacket.

"Listen, I can teleport you into the prison, Kero. That is, if you are really willing to go through with rescuing your brother."

"Me? Alone?" Kero asked.

"You're not alone. You have Phoenix," Blythe reminded her.

Since the start of all of this, Kero had continuously thought about breaking into the prison and getting her brother out. Now that she had the opportunity to carry out this plan, she suddenly felt very nervous.

"Don't be afraid, Kero. I'll be with you. We'll find your brother together." Kero realized that Phoenix was speaking to her inside

her mind.

"The prison is a big place. How am I going to find him?" Kero wondered.

"According to his file, he was put into cell block C. He's in solitary confinement." Xan took out a mini speaker out of his pocket. "Put this in your ear. I'll be able to communicate with you while you're there."

Kero wasn't sure if she was ready for this. She tried to speak. "I–"

"We're ready," Phoenix said suddenly.

Kero turned to him, her eyes pleading with him. "We'll do this together," the dragon said.

"Okay," Kero replied. Phoenix became a fiery stream of energy and disappeared into Kero's necklace. Xan set the coordinates on his invention, then shot a beam at Kero. Before everyone's eyes, she vanished.

Kero materialized in a dark corridor inside the prison. It was freezing and she couldn't see anything. She almost started to panic.

"I'm here, Kero," Phoenix said from inside her necklace. "Let's find your brother."

"I thought it would be colder here."

"My fire is keeping you warm," Phoenix explained.

Kero breathed a sigh of relief and began moving down the corridor. However, she didn't make it far before a shot was fired at her.

CHAPTER 16

The Ice Prison

Darkness engulfed Kero as she looked for the source of gunfire. She wasn't expecting to be shot at so soon. She ran and ducked around the corner. Looking back down the corridor, Kero spotted a red light hanging from the ceiling.

"It appears to be a weapon that shoots at anything walking around it," Phoenix said. "I'll take care of it. Flames shot out from the carnelian necklace, striking the weapon hanging from the ceiling. The mechanical firing arm exploded sending pieces of metal scraps everywhere.

"We'll have to work quickly. Look inside the cells to see if your brother is inside." Kero peeked through the bars on each iron door

"I don't see him," she said. She moved to the next one. "It's so dark in there. I can't see anyone."

"Hold on," Phoenix interjected. More flames came from

the necklace, taking out the laser cannon just a few feet away. Kero never noticed, despite the danger being so close.

"Those things are everywhere, it seems," Phoenix noted.

"We just need to find Darion," Kero said. Her voice came out a little panicked. Phoenix noticed and tried to calm her down. "We will succeed, Kero. Believe that."

Kero was about to respond when she heard some voices from down the hall. Kero rushed back the way she came and ducked behind the corner. She got out of sight just as two guards came in her direction. In between the two guards was her brother. They practically dragged him into one of the cells. After a moment, they both returned to the hallway. One guard locked the cell and began walking down the corridor while the other stood watch.

Kero wasn't sure what to do. She found her brother at least. She considered using the fire sword, but she was still very inexperienced with the weapon.

"Phoenix, " she whispered. "Can you set that guard on fire?"

"I don't think that would be a good idea," phoenix replied. Kero rolled her eyes. "I can, however, create a diversion." Fireballs flew out from the necklace and hit a trash can on the other side of the corridor. All of the paper inside the metal can caught on fire. Smoke rose up and filled the hallway. It didn't take long for the guard to notice and rushed towards the trash bin. He called out to someone further down the hallway. In the next moment, the sprinkler system was initiated. Water sprayed everywhere. His superior rushed over.

"What did you do?" the higher-ranking officer shouted.

"N-nothing s-sir! The trash can just caught on fire!"

"Well, the fire is out now! Go reset the sprinkler system!"

"Y-yes sir!"

The two guards ran down the hallway and out of sight.

"Go now!" Phoenix yelled. Kero couldn't move. Her feet felt frozen in place. "Come on! Darion needs you!" Kero finally moved her feet and rushed towards the now unguarded cell.

"How do I get him out?" Kero asked, panic stricken.

"I'm curious. Can you summon your spirit weapon again?" Phoenix asked.

"The flame sword? I can try."

Kero knew she was going to have to use the weapon sooner or later.

"Just imagine the sword in your hands," Phoenix instructed. Kero did so. A long stream of red energy appeared in her hands, materializing into a metal shaft. Flames ignited out of either end of the shaft. She swung at the iron door, actually cutting into it. The iron melted, and part of the door caved in. Kero stood, wide eyed, trying to comprehend the power of this great sword. Suddenly, the weapon disappeared.

"Hey! Where'd the sword go?"

"You can bring it back later," Phoenix said.

Slowly, Kero stepped over the bottom part of the door into complete darkness.

"Darion?" she called. It was quiet for a long moment. "Kero?" she heard a hoarse voice. It was him. Was he sick?

"Where are you?" The gem on her necklace lit up. Her brother sat by the far wall. He lifted his head. Kero gasped at his withered appearance. His face was so pale. He held a blanket around himself. At least they gave him something to keep warm.

"How did you get here?" he asked surprised to see his sister at the place.

Kero didn't answer his question. "Come on, we're leaving." She helped him up and led him to the door as if he were a child.

"Kero," his voice came out a little stronger. "I can walk on my own."

Just as the two exited the cell, someone grabbed Kero and tossed her to the ground. Kero looked up to see one of the guards standing over her.

"Well, well, where did you come from?" Kero was at a loss for words, then suddenly, Darion tackled the guard. "Get away from her!" he yelled as he tried to keep the muscular man on the ground. The guard easily got out of Darion's grip and grabbed him, tossing him into the wall. Unfortunately, in his weakened state, Darion wasn't much of a threat.

"What's going on?" The other guard came running around the corner. He pointed at Kero. "She's the one General Kain wanted."

"Don't move!" the first guard yelled at her. The other guard snatched her by the wrists and pulled Kero to her feet. As he pushed her into the wall, her body glowed. A red aura appeared around her body. The man cried out and let go of her. He looked down at his hands, which were now badly burnt.

"What happened?" the first man asked. The guard who had been burned, rushed at Kero again. Kero instinctively pushed him away, but as she did, his body turned to ash. Even Darion stared aghast at his sister's actions. He did his best to speak.

"What did you do?" he cried out.

Kero looked down to see the sword in her hands again. The guard who still held Darion against the wall, looked fearfully at Kero.

"Y-you! Don't make any sudden movements." Kero didn't move, but fire emerged from her necklace, shooting at the man's feet. He jumped. He let go of Darion and drew his gun. Phoenix let loose more fireballs, melting the guard's firearm. The laser gun became too hot to touch. The guard was forced to drop the useless piece of metal. It landed with a clatter onto the concrete floor

"We need to get out of here!" Darion said as he pulled Kero down the hallway. Kero suddenly heard Xan's voice in her ear.

"Are you okay? What's going on?"

"We're trying to get out of here!" she called back.

"What?" Darion asked, not realizing Kero was talking to someone else. Then, she heard Phoenix's voice inside her head.

"Kero, get to the roof of the prison so I can fly us out of here."

"Okay," she replied.

"We need to get to the roof of this place," Kero said to her brother.

Darion glanced awkwardly at her. "The roof?"

Lasers shot from the ceiling. Phoenix delivered more fireballs, destroying the devices.

"I think I know where to go," Darion said. They reached another iron door. "Can you use that sword again?" Before she did anything, the door opened and two more guards stood on the other side.

"Hey! Who let those prisoners out?" One asked.

"I didn't, but whoever messed up is getting executed,"

the other said. They raised their guns at the siblings. "Get back in your cells." Kero wished for the sword to return, but instead Phoenix came to the rescue, breathing fire onto the two guards.

They ran outside into the chilling air. Up a flight of stairs, they continued running towards one of the lookout towers, while being covered in a blizzard. It was at this time that Kero realized that she didn't have a coat. However, she wasn't as cold as she thought she'd be. Phoenix said he was using his fire to keep her warm.

Darion, who left the only warmth he had back in that cell, now stood wearing jeans and a tee-shirt in eight inches of snow. Darion was thankful he was wearing his leather working boots.

"W-we need to get s-someplace warm," he said through chattering teeth.

"Phoenix, can you come out now?" Kero called to the dragon. Phoenix came out of the carnelian in a reddish glow. Darion squinted his eyes, trying to comprehend what he saw. As Phoenix materialized right before their eyes, Darion stared in wonder. He certainly wasn't expecting this. "W-what?"

"Yeah, I know I have a lot of explaining to do."

Alarms blared as the two climbed onto the back of the red dragon. Phoenix took off as lights and lasers came his way. One beam hit one of his feet, but it wasn't enough to stop him. Of course, Kero felt this as well on the bottom of her foot.

Phoenix hurried on through the howling wind and snow, over the towering walls of the prison. Darion turned his head around to see the fortress that held him for the past week. The time he spent there felt a lot longer. He turned around to see his younger sister in front of him.

"Yeah, you do have a lot of explaining to do," he curtly replied. Then, his voice softened as he said. "Thank you."

CHAPTER 17

The Betrayer

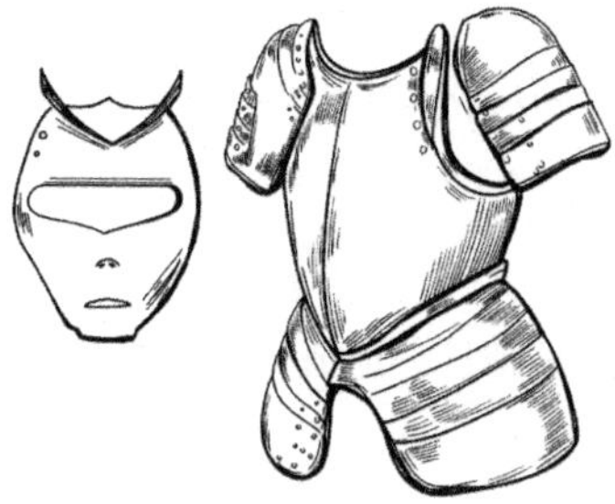

Blythe paced about while Eira watched her. It had been almost two hours since Kero left. Blythe stopped and turned towards Xan.

"You should ask if she's okay," Blythe insisted.

"I just talked to her. I don't want to call attention to her. It's best if she contacts me."

Blythe was about to protest when she heard massive wings flapping from up above. She peered upwards to see Kero riding on Phoenix. Someone else was with them. There was a rather handsome young man behind Kero. That had to be her brother. That meant that she succeeded in her mission. Blythe sighed with relief.

Phoenix landed. Kero and Darion dismounted as Blythe ran over to them.

"Glad you made it back," she said. "Is this your brother?"

"No, I just brought back some random guy," Kero quipped. Blythe raised an eyebrow to the sarcasm.

"She's such a smartass, isn't she?" Darion quipped.

"So, it seems you got what you want," Xan began.

Blythe turned to her longtime friend. "Uh, listen, when we last talked, you said that when we meet again, we were all going to discuss how we're going to take down the Empire. I met with Ramon in Isis and we flew over the wall on Eira." Blythe remembered that they dropped him off in the savannah very close to Athena actually. "He said he'd meet us outside of Gabriel–which is where we are now."

"Blythe," Xan said solemnly. "You shouldn't have done that. I told Ramon that I was coming back to Isis and he was supposed to wait for me."

"He wasn't safe there, Xan. He was hiding in some abandoned building, terrified that the Patrol might find him."

"Well, I hope he can make it over here. Why didn't you have him ride on the dragon with you?"

Blythe let out an aggravated sigh. "He didn't want to ride on the dragon," she almost yelled.

"Oh yeah, I forgot Ramon has a fear of heights. Well, don't worry. I have everything planned out. I'm going back to Gabriel, but you need to wait for me to contact you this time, okay?" He began walking away.

"How will you contact me?"

"Your friend still has the communication device I gave her." He kept walking.

"But, we have to open the gateway," Blythe replied. Xan turned to her.

"I don't know about this gateway business." He turned to

Eden. "Is this something we must do?"

"Yes, but we need Aeolus to return." She paused for a moment. "I'm concerned that it won't work though. Someone other than his original bonded awoke him and now he has a new bonded. I believe it has to be the same bonded from one thousand years ago."

Luckily, Kero had enough time on the flight from the tundra to fill Darion in with the mission of reuniting the Spirit Dragons.

"Why can't you just find the person who originally bonded with–what's his name?" the young man asked.

"Aeolus," Eden said. "We have a limited amount of time and it could be anyone on this planet."

"Right," Xan agreed. "Listen, I will contact Kero. I'm going to do some research to see if I can find Aeolus' former bonded. I'll contact you soon." Eden became a stream of green energy and flowed into the stone on top of Xan's ring.

Blythe stood, just watching her friend walk away. "Something isn't right. He's not acting like himself." Eira walked up behind her.

"He's hiding something," the dragon said.

"I know," Blythe replied. Blythe shook her head. Her usual joyful demeanor was replaced by despair. Kero was shocked by the sudden change. This girl didn't look like Blythe anymore. Her eyes just stared into space. She crouched down, cradling her arms around her legs.

"Blythe," Eira spoke softly. She didn't reply. "Everything will be okay."

"Yes," Phoenix agreed. "I'll contact Aeolus now."

The sun disappeared behind the trees. Kero glanced towards Blythe. She seemed to be coming out of her gloomy mood. She rose to her feet. Eira met her eyes.

"Let's finish what we began," she said. Blythe nodded and jumped onto the dragon's back. She seemed a little better, but she wasn't her usual toothy grin self either.

"That's strange," Phoenix said. "I can't connect with Aeolus. Something's wrong."

Before anyone could respond, their attention was drawn to a rustle in the bushes. Blythe turned around. "What's that?"

"Probably a rabbit or a bird," Kero replied.

Suddenly, a man with a long beard poked his head out, making a chirping sound. Blythe's eyes brightened.

"Ramon!" she yelled. She practically plowed over Kero as she rushed towards the man.

"Well, I'm here. Where's Xan?"

Blythe's smile turned into a frown. "He left," she said bitterly.

"Where'd he go?"

"Back to Gabriel."

Ramon shook his head. "I traveled all that way. It's not easy to get through the jungle and across a large body of water, ya know."

"Oh yeah, you had to cross the Etheric Ocean. How did you do that?"

"By stowing away on one of the Imperial cargo boats."

Such a simple answer for something that would no doubt

get Ramon imprisoned for life. Blythe returned a genuine glance to the man.

"Well, don't worry. We'll meet up with him again." Blythe's smile had returned.

"I'm still trying to connect with Aeolus," Phoenix said. "I keep getting some interference. There's this high pitch buzzing sound."

Suddenly, Kero cried out when she heard the same sound Phoenix mentioned. She tore the hearing device out of her ear.

"It's this thing," she said. She threw it onto the ground and was about to stomp on it, when Blythe stopped her.

"Wait! We need that so we can keep in contact with Xan!" Blythe shouted.

"I'm not happy with how this is going," Eira said. "And Eden just left with Xan. We're supposed to go and open the gateway."

While everyone stood around clueless of what to do, a large airship flew overhead, releasing a white substance that fell around the two dragons.

"What's that stuff?" Kero asked.

Suddenly, Phoenix collapsed onto the ground. Kero stared down at him, horrified.

"Phoenix!" Eira shouted. She tried to move towards her brother, but her legs felt frozen in place.

"Eira, you need to go–" Phoenix tried to speak, but he felt his eyes close.

"I cannot move my wings," she said slowly as her legs buckled from underneath her. It only took seconds for her eyes to close as well.

The airship landed and the drawbridge slowly descended to the ground. Two soldiers came out with General Kain himself behind them. He stared at the two dragons and their riders with glee.

"Look at this. I went from one prisoner to six. I must thank Dr. Hawthorne when I see him."

Blythe felt a chill go down her spine.

"What are you talking about? He'd never–"

"Never what?" Kain interjected. "Betray you?" He turned to Ramon. "You have been doing a great job avoiding my men," he said to the middle-aged man. "Looks like the chase is over."

"I'm not afraid of you," Ramon tossed back. "So ya found me. Good for you. Ya gonna arrest me now? Really sad how the Empire treats human beings. Like animals."

A smirk formed on General Kain's lips.

"Sadly, some animals need to be put down." Kain drew his gun and shot Ramon in the head. Blythe cried out as her friend fell to the ground. Blythe sobbed as she knelt beside the man's body. Kero felt a stab in her chest. She didn't know the man, but to see someone just get brutally murdered in front of her was a reminder of how her parents died.

Kero jumped off of the dragon.

"What are ya doing?" Darion called after her. Kero tried to make her sword appear, but nothing happened. A strange force blocked her. She felt it. Kain walked right up to her, staring her down.

"So, you thought you were going to come into my prison and take away your brother?"

"What did you do to Phoenix and Eira?" Kero asked, trying to keep her voice from shaking.

"You can't do this!" Blythe cried out. "These dragons have protected this planet for centuries!"

"Our Empress protects it now," the general spat back at her. A squad of soldiers joined the General.

"Kero, we need to get out of here," Darion said as he took his sister's hand.

"I have to make that sword appear!" Kero yelled.

"You won't be doing any more of your magic tricks, girl!" Kain threatened. It was then Kero noticed the general's arm was in a sleeve. He was still injured from her attack the last time they met. "That powder you saw dispels all magic. Just another invention from my dear friend, Dr. Hawthorne."

"He wouldn't do that!" Blythe screamed. "He wouldn't help you or the Empire!" Kain just smiled. The soldiers continued to put shackles around the necks of the two dragons.

Darion swore under his breath as the three of them were forced onto the airship. Kero thought about Aponi and A'keara. They didn't know that the Emerald Dragon was already bonded to someone. And unfortunately, that someone wasn't on their side. Even more terrifying, the Emerald Dragon may not be on their side either. Kero turned to see General Kain walk past them with his head high, like he accomplished some great feat.

Kero was forced into a cage with Blythe and her brother. She sat in a small cage, looking at her brother who was just as helpless as her. Then, her eyes went to Blythe. The girl looked broken. Tears formed in her eyes.

"Xan," she sobbed. "Why–?"

CHAPTER 18

The Meeting

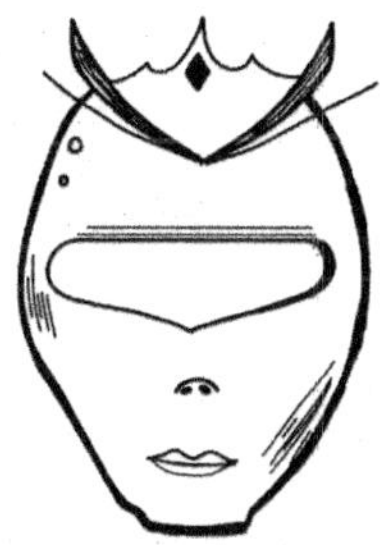

When Kero woke up, she found herself not in a dark jail cell, but on a soft mattress, covered by a sheet made of silk. She must have been knocked out, but she didn't recall when or how. Her eyes scanned the room. The white walls decorated with gold trim stood out the most. Across from her was a window with gold designed in a criss-crossed pattern across the glass panes. At least her prison was lovely to look at. Despite all that, she wondered why she was there. As if to answer her internal question, part of the wall slid open. Someone she wasn't expecting walked into the room. Kero met eyes with the Empress herself. This was the closest Kero had been to the Empress. The only time the ruler of Anu was shown was as an image from the airship projector. Up close, Kero saw the horned golden mask covering her face. Kero wondered if it was pure gold. If it were, wouldn't it be too heavy to wear?

"Hello my dear," her voice purred. "I hope you are feeling well." Kero tried to answer, but her mouth went dry. Was she dreaming? It had to be a dream. In reality, she was knocked out cold, lying in a filthy prison cell.

The Empress strolled over to the window. The gown she wore flowed behind her, giving the illusion of her floating across the floor. The Empress pushed open the window. Kero noticed the moon was full and glowed a vibrant color of violet.

"That's better. It was a bit stuffy in here."

Kero was beyond confused. Why was the Empress being nice to her?

"Where am I?" Kero demanded.

"You are in the palace of course. Where else would you be?"

Kero almost answered 'in prison,' but she didn't want to give any ideas to the woman.

"Where's my brother and my friend? What happened to the dragons?" The Empress returned a peculiar stare as if she didn't understand the questions Kero asked her.

"Who are you talking about, child?" Kero almost hit the ceiling as she jumped out of the bed.

"You know who I'm talking about!"

"All you need to know is that you're safe from those horrible dragons. Those beasts won't ever hurt anyone ever again."

"Beasts?" Kero spat out. "You're calling Phoenix and Eira beasts?" The Empress returned a sympathetic glance.

"Oh, you poor thing. You have no idea of the danger you were in. Those dragons manipulated your mind."

"I wasn't manipulated," Kero insisted.

"Why did you turn against the Empire then? You were

provided for back in Athena. You and your brother were safe there."

Kero remembered the incident that started this whole journey.

"My brother and I were taken by the Patrol because my brother killed a deer in the woods." Kero shook her head wondering why Darion chose to hunt on Harvest Day. "I know the Empire forbids civilians to hunt, but in our defense, the Empire demanded too much food from us. People were already starving and then we were told to give more food. If it wasn't for my brother, my neighbors and my friends would have died." Kero raised an accusing finger at the Empress. "Also, the Patrol killed my parents! My parents were innocent, but somehow were thought to be someone else, so they were killed right in front of my brother and me. The Empire doesn't protect anyone! You ordered them to do all that, so why should I believe that you care about me or anyone else on this planet?"

A long sigh came from behind the Empress' mask.

"More food is needed because the population of this planet is growing. If you want to be upset with someone, be upset at all those women in Isis getting pregnant from the random strangers they meet who flow into the city every day. I suppose you're right Kero. We should kill those women and their bastard children."

"No!" Kero yelled. "I don't mean that! I mean–" Kero stopped realizing the Empress was twisting her words.

"I am not the bad guy," the Empress spoke calmly. "All I want is for everyone to have enough food and live comfortably. It's hard. But don't worry, we will find a solution together." As she said that, two guards appeared at the door. "Now, if you'd follow me, please?"

In no way did Kero trust this woman, but what else could she do right now? She had the feeling that if she refused to go, she would be forced anyway. She followed the guards with the Empress on her heels. The guards led Kero down the long corridor until they reached a door that led through what appeared to be a glass tunnel. The white tiles on the floor remained the same, but the walls and ceiling were made of glass. Through the glass, Kero saw beautiful trees and flowers of all kinds.

"Do you like the garden?" the Empress asked.

Kero made a slight nod. The garden was very lovely, but she was too angry to give the witch of a woman a compliment.

They reached another door and this one led into a large foyer, which was where the golden doors of the throne room stood. The guards opened the doors to show a wonder of royalty. There was a golden border going around the room and golden statues stood in the corners. There was even gold woven into the violet carpet leading up to the golden throne encrusted with jewels. If the Empress wanted a solution to solve world hunger, she could use all the wealth that was in this room.

The Empress strolled up to her throne and sat properly upon it, crossing her legs.

"Kero," she spoke gently. "How do you feel taking in the glorious sight of this room?" Kero wanted to scream. This woman was so conceited and so ignorant. Did she realize what she was doing to the people who barely had anything?

The Empress hummed as she touched the side of the mask on her face.

"Is there anything you'd like to ask me?"

Kero stared at her for a moment. "Why do you wear that mask? Ya like hiding yer face? Is something wrong with it?" Kero asked mockingly.

The Empress never answered her questions. Instead, she let out a small laugh. "You are very smart and clever," she said. "I wish to offer you a position in my court."

Kero squinted her eyes suspiciously at the woman.

"You want me to serve the imperial court? Why?"

"I've been watching you. You have a lot of potential."

"I'm not going to serve in your court," Kero said haughtily.

The Empress stared daggers at Kero. "If you don't choose to work with me, then you will be sentenced to death for treason. However, if you do join my court, I will pardon you." Kero wasn't sure what she'd do as a court member. They did need to change food distribution and maybe give the people in her colony better farming equipment. But, she didn't like this. The Empress was giving her an ultimatum. Either become a court member or be sentenced to death. If she died, what would happen to Phoenix? What about her brother and Blythe?

"You never answered me about my brother and my friend? Are they still al–" Kero couldn't finish the word.

"They're fine. They're just in one of the holding cells under the palace. We can go see them, if you'd like."

"Okay," Kero answered slowly.

The Empress pulled a rope to her right, sounding a loud bell ring. Two guards walked into the throne room.

"Please escort our guest to her friends."

Blythe sat in the corner of the prison cell with her head down in her folded arms. Darion sat a few feet away. At least this time, he wasn't in a dark and freezing cell. They kept these holding cells warmer than the prison in the tundra. He looked up at the heating crystals on the ceiling. It pained him that Kero wasn't there. Where did they put her? Well, this time, he wasn't going to wait to be rescued. If anything happened to her, he would never forgive himself. His eyes moved to his cellmate.

"Are you okay?"

Blythe slowly lifted her head. "I'm sorry," she whispered.

"What are you apologizing for?"

"Huh?" Blythe turned to look at him as if she suddenly realized he was there.

"I asked why you're apologizing to me."

Blythe blinked a few times. "Oh, I was thinking out loud. But I do feel bad for what he did."

"He?"

"Xan. I still can't believe it. Something's wrong. He'd never betray me. He's the one who came up with our resistance group. He's the one who said we'd take the Empire down and free Anu–I just can't believe–"

"It's not your fault."

"Yes it is. I took Kero to Gabriel to meet him. I got her and everyone else involved. I thought he would help us."

"He did help me get out of that frozen prison," Darion pointed out.

"You're in prison now," she reminded him.

"Yeah," he admitted. "But, at least it's warmer here. Besides, I don't care what happens to me. I need to find Kero."

Then a little quieter. "I'm supposed to protect her."

Darion stood up and moved towards the door. The shackle around his ankle stopped him from moving any further, limiting his options for movement.

"Maybe we can get the guard to come in and then knock him out." Blythe looked up at Darion, surprised.

"How are you going to do that? We don't have any weapons. Well, I guess I do, but I can't use it with these on." She jingled the chain attached to the cuffs around her wrists.

"It's okay. I figured it out. Call the guard over here. When he opens the door, I'll punch him in the solar plexus."

"In the what?"

Darion shook his head. "Never mind." He looked at the big iron door. Cupping his hand around his mouth, he called out. "Hey! We need help!" He turned to Blythe. Lay on the floor and act like you're dead."

Blythe returned a skeptical glance, but followed along.

The door opened. The person's face was shrouded in shadow. Darion didn't wait to see who it was. He rushed up and threw a right hook right above the man's abdomen, a move taught to him by his father when he was a young teen. The punch landed and he heard the man cough and drop. Blythe's eyes went wide.

"Hey, it worked!" Darion exclaimed.

He looked down at the man he assaulted, but he wasn't a guard. "Who–"

Blythe climbed to her feet. "You hit Xan."

"Oh good! I didn't like that guy."

Blythe leaned over Xan and started taping the side of his face. Finally, he stirred. He looked up coldly at Darion. "What was that?"

"Don't yell at him," Blythe shot back. "You have a lot of explaining to do!"

"So do you. I came to rescue you guys and this is how you treat me?"

"Rescue?" Darion asked. "You got us put in here in the first place."

"He's right," Blythe agreed.

"Actually, I hoped you would have figured out I was just paying General Kain. I mean, come on! Really? You think I would betray you Blythe." She didn't say a word. Just stared at him with accusing eyes. "That stuff you made affected the dragons. It sounds like you've been making all sorts of things for the Empire to use!"

"Okay, the truth is–" He took a deep breath while clutching his stomach. "I was compromised. Actually, the white powder was supposed to be used for any large beast, not just for dragons. It was made for protecting soldiers while they were on patrols outside the colony walls." Blythe still stared at him with disbelief. "Listen, I told you that I might have to do things that went against my morals. Of course, they would kill me if I didn't follow orders. I didn't want everything I worked for to be for nothing. But, now that I'm bonded to Eden, I feel I have more of the upper hand."

"You can't die now anyways, because you are bonded to Eden," Blythe realized.

"Right," Xan answered. "If I die, Eden goes back into slumber."

Blythe nodded. They were both bonded to a dragon. Neither of them could make decisions for their own benefit.

"What about before you were bonded to a dragon? What was the plan, Xan? Pretend to follow the Empress' orders and have us captured? You know, we could have gone to where the gateway was going to open. The dragons can move faster than the ships."

"First of all, I didn't want you coming anywhere near Gabriel. I was planning on coming to meet you and Ramon in Isis."

"You know, that ID didn't even work," Blythe said haughtily. "I got arrested at the gate." She remembered that was how she met Kero. "But, I'm kinda glad I did get captured. That's how my whole journey began, meeting Kero, Aponi and A'keara. And learning about the dragons." Blythe moved closer, so she could see Xan's face in the tiny slit of light coming into the cell. "We can't stop now. We have to open the gateway."

Xan shook his head. "Eden told me that you haven't found all of the original humans who bonded with the dragons. You won't be able to open the gateway."

"But, our friend bonded with Aeolus," Blythe said.

"I'm sorry, Blythe, but it won't work."

"How do you know? We can at least try," she argued.

Xan let out an aggravated sigh. "Listen, Eden and I have a plan to bring an end to the Empire. I know what happened to the other members of our group. But, you, me and Ramon are all going to celebrate once the Empire is taken down."

Blythe's eyes saddened as they dropped to the floor.

"Xan," Blythe spoke softly. "He's dead."

Now Xan appeared distraught. "What?" Tears filled Blythe's eyes.

"Ramon–he showed up right after you left. And General Kain killed him!"

Darion, who had been watching the two discuss matters, suddenly felt saddened by the man's death.

Xan became eerily quiet. His breathing became heavy. Suddenly, he screamed in anger and turned away from Blythe.

"I knew this would happen! That's why I told him to stay in Isis." He let out another pained cry. "He never listened to me!"

As Xan leaned against the wall of the cell, he became lost in his feelings of regret and sadness. Before Blythe could say any words of comfort, two guards appeared behind Xan.

"Hey! What's taking so long?" One guard called out.

"Are they not cooperating'?" The other asked, pounding his fist into his palm.

"Everything is fine," Xan said to them. He turned back towards the prisoners. "I came to get you two because our presence has been requested by the Empress."

Blythe and Darion turned to each other in confusion. Xan turned to the guards.

"We're all ready to go."

Kero sat in a rather comfortable leather chair at an oval table in what the Empress called the conference room. She thought they were taking her to the prison cells to where they took Blythe and Darion. Instead, the guards brought her and just left her there. No. They locked her inside. She couldn't leave! Her eyes stayed glued onto the tall double doors. The woodwork was impressive.

All of those tiny lines made up an even larger design on the doorframe, just to look fancy. Kero honestly didn't see the point in it. It was a door. Who cares about what it looks like? However, the longer she stared at the design, the more it resembled a large eye. An eye on both doors. It appeared as if the door was looking at her. She quickly turned away.

She sat there for a moment before the doors opened and two guards came into the room. *Now what?* She thought to herself. Then, right after them, came Xan, Darion and Blythe. Kero stood up.

"You guys are okay." Blythe ran over and threw her arms around Kero, who returned the hug which surprised Blythe, who still welcomed it. Kero looked from her to Darion. She was surprised by his embrace too. Being hugged by her big brother made her feel like a child again. She suppressed the urge to cry. Then, her eyes landed on Xan and they went cold.

"What the hell is he doing here?" she demanded.

Blythe let out an aggravated sigh. "It's a long story. He was, what did you call it Xan? Compromised?"

Before he could answer, the doors opened again, and another familiar face walked into the room. All eyes focused on General Kain prancing into the room in his usual arrogant way.

"Well, well, I wasn't expecting all of you to be here," His eyes went to Darion. "You too, huh? You should be thanking the gods that you're not back in the tundra. I wonder what the occasion is for letting a bunch of traitors into the Empress' court?"

"Where is her majesty?" Xan asked.

"Be patient, doctor," he said coolly. He took a seat at the right chair next to the head of the table.

"Take a seat," one of the guards instructed. Xan strolled over and sat in the chair next to the General. Blythe sat across from Xan Kero sat to her left. This left two options for Darion, and he wasn't going to sit next to a man he barely knew and trusted even less. He took the empty seat next to Blythe.

A bell rang and the doors opened once again to show the Empress. The General and Xan stood. The others reluctantly followed. The Empress glided along the floor to the head of the table and sat down. Once there, she addressed everyone.

"Please be seated." Everyone took their seats. "Good. Everyone is here. Welcome to the Imperial Council. This is where every important decision that affects Anu is made."

"Decisions?" Blythe spat out. "You mean all the decisions to make the people of this planet poor while you stay in this palace?"

"Blythe," Xan said with a warning tone.

"It's alright," the Empress said calmly. "I know that not everyone is happy. That is why I asked for people like you to be on my council. You understand what suffering is." Her eyes went down the line to Kero. "And you felt it was unfair that people in your village are starving."

"Like you care," Kero said crossly. "Why are we really here?"

"I do care. Deeply," the Empress said. "I just want what's best for the people of Anu. You see, I saw potential in this little planet. My people either cultivate a planet or they just get rid of it."

"Your people?" Darion asked. "Who exactly are 'your' people?"

"They've explored many different planets. Have any of you ever wondered what's beyond the sky you see? I saw such potential in the people here, but *they* didn't. *They* wanted to destroy this planet, but I asked them–no, begged them to let me take care of it. I want what is best for all of the people because if they come back and see it hasn't flourished, well–everyone will die."

Kero had no idea how to respond to any of this. People from other planets came here? There was very little known about space exploration. Actually, it was just theories made by different scientists. No one really knew what was beyond the sky.

"So, what you're saying is that, you're from another planet and you came here to protect us?" Blythe asked. "I'm having a hard time believing this."

"Believe it, Blythe," Xan said.

"Oh yes," the Empress intercepted. "Dr. Hawthorne is in charge of the Space Exploration Experiment.

"Uh, yeah. I uh–I've been finding out some interesting things." His eyes focused on Blythe. "I'll have to let you in on it later."

"Don't be so shy," the Empress' voice hummed. "Tell them everything you've learned."

He sighed. "Uh, well, this planet is actually a dome-uh, that's a flat surface and a sphere around us–. Actually, you can't get to space using an airship. You actually have to create a hole in the fabric of space to move from one planet to another."

"I'm sorry, but all of this is mumbo jumbo to me," Kero admitted. "I just began to understand energy healing and dragons. Don't throw space into the mix."

"Ah yes, the dragons," General Kain said. "They come from another world too, right?" Kero wasn't sure what to say. She remembered Aponi saying that a portal to a higher dimension would open up once all four dragons were awakened. She supposed this higher dimension could be considered another world.

"I don't think any of them know much about that," the Empress said. "That knowledge comes from the old lady."

Old lady? She meant Aponi, Kero realized. She didn't want to give them any information about where Aponi and A'keara were right now. Maybe she could just play dumb.

"Uh yeah, I have no idea about that sort of stuff. I'm just a dumb farmgirl."

Blythe tossed her a peculiar glance.

"It doesn't matter!" General Kain spat out. "We know that the old lady and her granddaughter are looking for the last dragon. Once they find it, we can move on to the final stage of the plan." Blythe raised her eyebrows, then remembered what Xan said. No one knew he was bonded to Eden.

"What plan?" Darion asked. "After the dragons open the portal, you tyrants are done!"

Kain jumped up from his chair. "How dare you speak like that to our Imperial Highness!" He moved towards the young man with the intention of silencing the boy for saying such blasphemy.

"General Kain, please, these are our guests," the Empress said soothingly.

Kain actually returned to his seat. "My apologies, my Empress."

"There is more to the plan, Darion. You'll see. You will all see." She ended with a wide grin. "Oh, and please, call me Celise."

After the very uncomfortable meeting, Kero, Blythe and Darion, along with Xan, were escorted to the throne room. The General stood watch with two guards as the Empress sat on her throne. She turned to address Xan.

"Dr. Hawthorne, it's time to use your new invention."

The others turned to the man.

"Of course." He opened his bag and pulled out a headpiece made of black stone resembling a crown.

"What is that thing?" Blythe asked.

"Quiet!" the Empress hissed. She removed her golden, jewel encrusted tiara and placed the new one on her head.

For a moment, silence fell upon the room. The sound of large, flapping wings from outside interrupted the silence. The Empress slowly strolled over to the window. Kero saw the familiar scaly wings of a red dragon. She ran over to see Phoenix hovering just a few feet away. However, something changed within him. His usual fiery eyes were black.

"Phoenix!" she yelled to the dragon. He didn't reply. His eyes stared blankly outwards.

"I can hear the dragon's thoughts," Celise said. "He wants the girl to come to him," she said, pointing at Kero. "So sorry, my dear dragon, but we are bonded now." The Empress tried to take a step forward, only to discover that she couldn't move.

"What just happened? Why can't I move?!"

General Kain shot an icy stare at Xan. "What did you do?"

"Nothing," Xan replied.

"Don't give me that! The crown of obsidian is your invention." He pointed his finger at the man. "You sabotaged the Empress' plans!"

Xan shrugged his shoulders. "I don't know what to say. You're right, I did." Xan put on his ring. Putting the piece of jewelry to his lips, he whispered, "Eden." The Emerald colored energy flowed out of the tree agate stone. Eden materialized in front of everyone. General Kain almost lost his balance as he stumbled backwards.

"You're bonded to a dragon?" he gasped.

"Yes," Xan replied. He changed his glance to the Empress. "That crown I made paralyzes its wearer."

"Oh, that's a relief," Blythe said. "For a second, I thought you were actually going to help her."

"Don't worry Blythe. While it's true, she is not from this world, the crown will still work on her."

Suddenly, the Empress started to laugh. Everyone turned to her, alarmed. Her laughter continued and at the same time, the obsidian crown began to crack. The headpiece broke into pieces and fell onto the floor.

"You obviously didn't do your research, doctor," the Empress said mockingly. "I am stronger than you think."

Suddenly, Eden began tossing her head wildly and screeched.

"Eden? What's wrong?" Xan called to her. The dragon's emerald eyes suddenly changed black.

"Guard these humans while I address my subordinates," Celise said as she moved towards the window. She stared adoringly at Phoenix. "Now that I absorbed all the energy from that obsidian crown, I can control all four of the Spirit Dragons." She jumped onto the back of the red dragon. The dragon flew up into the sky. Blythe joined Kero by the window. As the two stared out at the sky, another winged creature joined the Empress. Blythe gasped as she saw the sapphire scales of the Crystal Dragon.

"Eira!" she yelled.

The four humans stood helplessly as Eden, now controlled by a malevolent force closed in on them.

CHAPTER 19

The Secret Room

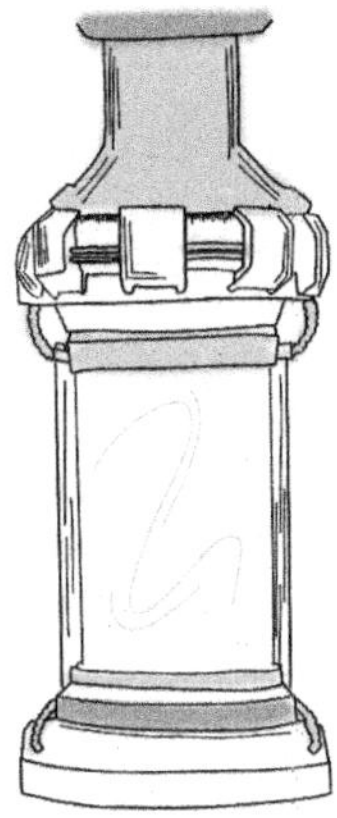

Eden let out another terrifying roar. Xan put up his hands in a calming manner.

"Eden, please–it's me."

The Emerald Dragon swung head around as if she were trying to shake something unwanted off of her.

"I think she's trying to break the control the Empress has on her," Xan said.

"But, the crown broke!" Kero pointed out. "How is she–"

"I have no idea," Xan replied. "Obsidian does have the power to enhance psychic ability, but–" He spoke a little quieter. "What did she mean when she said she absorbed the obsidian's energy? The crown was supposed to just trap her."

"We did find out that Celise is from another world," Kero pointed out.

"Uh guys?" Darion called. "What are we doing about

her?" he asked, pointing at Eden. The dragon stood, watching the four of them as if they were her prey.

"How wonderful, I get to watch the dragon eat all of you," Kain said menacingly.

Xan turned to General Kain, "She might eat you too."

He laughed. "You fool! Our imperial highness now controls the creature. Besides, she would never allow any harm to come to me." Kain sneered at Xan. "You've done your part, Doctor Hawthorne." He said the name mockingly. "Or should I use your other name, Alexander Stonewell."

Blythe's eyes widened. "He knows who you are?"

"I'm as shocked as you are," Xan replied.

"Oh please! I'm not stupid! All I had to do was match your picture to the one taken when you were younger. Also, you gave us a blood sample when you became a scientist."

Blythe narrowed her eyes at Xan. "I gave them the blood of a deer," Xan replied. Then his eyes grew big as he realized something. "My fingerprints–I couldn't fake those."

"You are an idiot, you know that, right?" Kain ranted. "I easily found out that the blood you gave me wasn't yours."

"Why would you give them your fingerprints?" Kero asked.

Xan shook his head. "I didn't. They already had them. The Empire has all our information." He changed his gaze to the General. "It's sad that you underestimate me."

Suddenly, a long staff appeared in Xan's hands. On top of the staff was a sharp piece of stone known as tree agate. Xan raised the staff and lightning erupted from the green stone, striking down the general and his soldiers. Xan didn't waste a second as he turned towards his bonded. Eden seemed distracted for the moment. She moved towards the window and flew out of the palace and into the sky.

Xan watched sadly as she flew away.

"What are we going to do?" Blythe asked.

Xan popped out of his daze. "Come on, follow me," he instructed. "I have to show you something." He rushed out of the room. Blythe followed. Kero was about to follow, but noticed that her brother stood in the same spot he had been in for the past few minutes.

"Darion! Come on!"

"I can't keep all of this straight," he said. "What the hell are we doin'?" He stared solemnly at Kero. "Do you know?"

Kero had no idea at this point. Phoenix, Eira and Eden were all being controlled. After a moment, she realized something.

"Aeolus! The Empress doesn't control the Golden Dragon. He's still with Aponi and A'keara. Hopefully, we'll all meet up together." She stared earnestly at her brother. "I know it's hard to trust people. I was afraid to trust Aponi when she told me there were dragons and I could actually bond with one. But, something told me to listen to her and now I feel that we need to follow Xan. He didn't betray us. He was just trapped."

"I don't know Kero," Darion said. He stared at General Kain. His chest moved up and down. It wouldn't be long before he woke up. "I guess we don't have any other choice, do we?" He grabbed his sister's hand. "Let's go."

Aeolus was really speeding through the air. A'keara held onto Aurora So she wouldn't fall off. Aponi glanced back to make sure her granddaughter was okay, then returned her eyes forward.

"We're almost there," Aeolus said. Aponi nodded.

Aeolus knew he was flying too fast for carrying two humans and a unicorn. Maybe he should slow down. He decreased his speed a little. As he did, he felt something pull at him to move faster again. The more he tried to slow down, the more he was forced to speed up. He began swaying right and left. Aponi gripped onto his neck.

"Aeolus! What are you doing?" she cried out.

His sand-colored eyes turned black. He raced forward with inhuman speed. The wind blew the two women and the mare backwards. Aponi leaned too far to the right and fell off the dragon's back. A'keara tried to grab her grandmother and fell off the same way.

It was at this moment that Aurora vanished suddenly. The mare reappeared under Aponi, catching her. She vanished again and reappeared under A'keara. The unicorn vanished once again, then reappeared on the ground. The two women stared up at Aeolus, stunned as he continued speeding through the sky.

"Grandmother! Are you alright?"

Aponi slowly dismounted Aurora. Her hand went for the broach on her cloak. It was gone!

"Aeolus– Something is wrong," she whispered.

High above in the sky, the Empress sat atop of the Crimson

Dragon. The Crystal Dragon and the Emerald Dragon hovered on either side of her. Celise gazed outward to see that the Golden Dragon flew towards her.

"Perfect. It's time for me to give my speech to all of Anu."

Back in the palace, Kero ran alongside her brother. Blythe was up ahead with Xan.

"Where is he takin' us?" Darion wondered. "We need to get out of here!"

They heard heavy footsteps of the soldiers coming for them.

"It's in here!" Xan shouted as he opened a metal door. The others followed. Once inside, Xan used his badge to lock the door.

"They won't be able to follow us," he said. "Come on! It's this way."

"Hey, hold on!" Blythe pressed. "How come you can use your spirit weapon so well?"

Xan met her glance with confusion. "My what?"

"That staff you made appear."

"Oh-I don't know. I don't have it now."

"Yeah, the weapons come and go," Kero said.

Blythe brought the conversation back to the matter at hand.

"So why did you bring us here, Xan?" Blythe asked.

Kero looked around the tiny room. One lone desk sat in the corner with a parchment and inkwell and quill. Behind the desk were four hardcover books.

"This is my private study," Xan explained. "No one, but me can come in here."

"Wow! The Empress made sure you were well equipped," Darion noted.

"Well, I made some of the best weapons and tools she's seen."

After those words, Blythe turned, pressing her lips together. "Yeah, about that– how long were you going to keep up this charade anyways?"

"I admit, this whole mission went a lot longer than I had planned," Xan said sheepishly. "However, I wanted to show these books to you." He pulled out a book with a thick, hard leather binder. "This book is about the law and order of the Drakens, a race of beings who like to invade planets and take their resources."

Blythe took the book from him. "The Snake People," she read. She opened it and began flipping through the pages. Kero watched her for a moment. Blythe looked up to see Kero's sour expression.

"What's wrong?"

"You said you didn't know how to read." Kero said.

Blythe glanced away. "Oh, I forgot I said that." She turned back around. "Xan taught me to read, but I don't tell anyone about that because–"

"I know. The Empire would have you killed." Kero's heart fell. It really was sad.

"It's always been a dumb law," Blythe continued. "Also, it's hypocritical as it's okay for doctors and scientists to read."

"This isn't much of a library," Kero noted. "There's only four books."

"True, but I feel this one stands out among the rest of them," Xan said, handing her a book with a plain brown cover.

Kero looked down at the plain brown cover. She opened it to see a colorful picture of a red dragon–Phoenix! She removed the brown cover to see the ball of light in the middle and the four colorful strips of red, gold, green and indigo. She read the title in golden letters, 'Tale of the Spirit Dragons.'

"This is my book. How did it get here?" she wondered.

"It was confiscated the day you and your brother were arrested," Xan explained. "The soldiers who took the book were going to burn it, but I stopped them."

Kero looked genuinely at Xan. "Thank you."

"Why did ya keep it?" Darion asked. Kero returned a peculiar glance. "Why not? Would you rather he threw it away?"

Darion furrowed his brow, "No. I'm just shocked a grown man would care enough to save a book like that."

"Well, if you must know," Xan replied. "I happen to like dragons. Also, I thought the Patrol took that book from a child and I was planning on returning it to them. Of course, I looked up the people who were arrested that day and realized it was a seventeen year old, but I still wanted to return the book to its original owner." Kero met Xan with a look of thanks. "One more thing, may I keep it in my bag?" he asked. Kero returned a peculiar stare. "I want to hide it until we're out of the city." Kero nodded. Xan easily fit the thin book into his bag.

The tender moment was ruined when numerous voices shouted from outside the door.

"They went in there, sir! The door is locked."

"Well what are you waiting for?" a louder voice boomed. "Break the door down!" That voice belonged to General Kain. Darion turned to the others.

"We've gotta find another way out!"

Xan nodded. "Don't worry, there's a reason why I brought

all of you in here." He reached under the desk and pushed a button. To the others' surprise, the floor opened up showing a descending staircase.

"This way," Xan said, heading down the staircase.

The other three ran to the opening in the floor, to where they found a descending staircase. Outside of the room came sounds of lasers cutting through the metal door. Everyone hurried down the steps. After they cleared the trapdoor, Xan pushed a button on the ceiling to close up the hole in the floor.

Continuing down a winding staircase, the four entered a strange round room with what appeared to be many long tubes covering the room's circumference.

What is this place?" Kero asked. Her eyes scanned the room. "This place–" An image of a child flashed inside her mind. The child was shoved into one of the tubes. The tube was some kind of machine. Kero grabbed her head. "Have I been here before?" More images flashed inside her mind. She saw the same child again. It was her. Six year-old Kero was dragged into the room and thrown into the machine. The images were replayed over and over. Then, she saw another child with light blonde hair. "Kero!" the other little girl cried.

Kero heard her younger self scream, "Eris!"

The images vanished. Kero still held her head.

"Kero?" she looked up at Blythe.

Kero breathed heavily for a moment. "Eris?"

Blythe backed away from her with an expression of confusion dressing her face.

"Kero, what's going on?" Darion asked with concern.

“Why are you holding your head like that?” Kero looked at the person she called her brother. “Who are you?” Then she turned to Blythe. “Eris, what happened to you?” Both Darion and Blythe exchange horrified stares.

“Kero–” Blythe tried.

Darion looked his sister in the eyes. “Kero, everything’s is going to be okay, please be okay.” He muttered.

He walked over to one of the tubes. “What are these things?” There were some switches on the side of the tube. “This is so weird. What?” Suddenly, images flashed inside his mind. At the age of ten, he was brought here with his older brother. Older brother? Where did that come from? Darion grabbed his head.

“What are they doing to us?” he whispered.

“Who are you talking to?” Blythe asked. He turned towards her.

“What?” he asked. He was unaware that he said anything. Blythe turned away, continuing to gaze at one of the machines. Images flashed through her mind. She saw Kero being shoved into a machine. She looked at Kero in real time. It took a moment, but she finally understood why Kero called her Eris… It was her real name.

“Kero, I’m sorry. I’m sorry I lied about who I am. I changed my name to Blythe after I left Luna.”

Kero’s eyes became focused and she came back to reality, realizing where she was in the present time.

“What?” she asked. Before Blythe spoke, Darion grabbed Kero by her shoulders.

“Kero! I have no idea what’s going on!”

“What are you doing?” she cried out, shoving him away from her. “Enough stuff is going on right now. I don’t need my older brother going crazy too!"

"Kero, You aren't my sister."

Kero just stared blankly at him.

By now, Xan realized that the effects of this room were already happening.

"You are all remembering who you are," he said. "I stumbled into this room a few months ago. My memories came back to me."

"I have no idea what the hell is going on!" Kero cried out. She looked at Blythe, a girl she met a few weeks ago and at the young man she believed she knew all her life.

"We've known each other since we were infants, Kero," Blythe said. "I knew something was familiar about you from the day we met. That's why– after I met you on the airship, I couldn't leave you–"

Then, a loud crash came from upstairs, followed by shouts and heavy footsteps.

"They're coming!" Xan shouted.

It only took a few moments before General Kain and his soldiers barrelled down the stairs and into the tiny room.

"Just kill all of them!" Kain ordered. The soldiers fired their weapons. Laser beams flew. Everyone ran and ducked behind a machine. Xan's staff materialized in his hands and he began shooting the soldiers with bolts of lightning. Blythe thought about summoning her own weapon.

"Xan, how do I get my ice disk to come to me?"

Xan gave her a quick sideways glance. "Uh–I'm not sure. What happened back in the throne room was unexpected." The staff appeared in Xan's hand. "Don't worry, I'll take care of these guys." Xan raised the staff to attack, but as he did, one of the ray blasts knocked the staff from his hand. The staff skidded across the floor, then disappeared. Blythe was so focused on the staff that she didn't realize that the soldiers were moving in on them. Xan pulled her back behind the machine. In his hands, the staff appeared again. Quickly, he stood up and held the staff out in the open. Lightning burst out from the stone, taking out two of the closest soldiers.

Meanwhile, Kero and Darion hid behind another machine on the other side of the room.

"I have no idea how to make that sword appear," Kero admitted.

"Even if you did, what use is a sword against a bunch of soldiers with ray guns?" Darion countered. Kero silently agreed.

From the side, a soldier came barreling towards Kero and Darion. The two were paying too much attention to the majority of the soldiers on the other side of the room. Darion stood in front of Kero, ready to take the brunt of the man's attack. The soldier came at him with full force, knocking him to the ground with the weapon in his hand. Darion peered upwards to see the man standing over him, pointing a long stick at him with a metal tip. Darion recognized the crude object as an electric rod, a weapon used on the prisoners back in the Sansin prison. He remembered when the guards prodded him with the weapon when he first arrived in the prison. He didn't want to go through that pain again.

Kero watched helplessly as the soldier pushed the rod into Darion's chest. He cried out as the electricity flowed through his body.

Come on you stupid sword! Appear already! Kero thought desperately.

The soldier proceeded to stab the weapon downwards onto Darion again. Kero did the only thing she thought she could and tried to tackle the man to the ground. Kero ran right into the soldier and instantly regretted it. With all the armor the soldier wore, it felt like running into a brick wall. The soldier laughed, picking Kero up and tossing her to the floor.

Darion was able to quickly climb to his feet before getting attacked. He rushed over to his sister. Kero groaned as she tried to move. Darion turned a hard glare towards the soldier pointing the electric rod at them. The soldier raced towards him. Darion side-stepped his attacker, grabbed part of the metal rod. In another motion, he twisted the tip of the weapon into the soldiers' face. The man cried out in pain before falling to the floor. He laid motionless.

"How did you do that?" Kero asked.

Darion stared down at the man. "Maybe it was the fighting technique dad taught me." He remembered attacking Xan earlier when he was in the prison under the city.

"Dad didn't know how to fight," Kero said. "What are ya talkin' about?"

Darion turned to her surprised. "I–" Then, he realized. Someone else on the farm taught him the move that he used on Xan. However, what he just did to the soldier came from somewhere else. He just couldn't remember who taught him how to fight like that.

Meanwhile, Xan continued to take out soldiers and Blythe still couldn't make her weapon appear. Blythe desperately waved her hands back and forth in front of her body, hoping the ice weapon would come to her. Just then, a ray blast struck Xan in the arm. He cried out and at the same time, his weapon disappeared.

"Xan!" Blythe screamed as she crouched down beside him.

"Don't worry, I'm fine," he said as he stood again.

Blythe tried once again to make the ice disk appear in her hands. She rhythmically moved her hands across her body. As the four soldiers closed in on the two, a large sheet of ice materialized around the men. They stood frozen in a block of ice. Now the only foe left was General Kain. He smeared at the group of rebels.

"This is not over!" he bellowed before turning his heels and running up the stairs.

Xan quickly moved towards the door to see the general fleeing up the stairs. Blythe joined him as well as Kero and Darion.

"We need to get out of Michael," Xan said. The others nodded.

Empress Celise sat tall on the Crimson Dragon, looking downward at all the people gathering in the streets. Everyone stared up at their queen in admiration, and in horror at her riding a dragon. Although no one could see Celise's expression under her gold mask, she was smiling triumphantly. Her face appeared in the sky as a hologram, projected above the city of Michael as well as the other six colonies.

"Greetings, my loyal subjects! I'm sure you are all surprised to see me here before you, riding this beast known as a dragon. I am pleased to tell everyone the evil that threatened you has been taken care of by your Empress. These beasts now are under my control. So, you need not worry. I will always be here for all of you. I love each and everyone one of you as my children."

Down below in the streets of Michael, Kero felt sick to her stomach, watching the Empress speak. Darion tugged on her sleeve.

"Come on! Everyone is distracted. Even the guards at the gate."

Kero followed the others towards the front gate. She realized that even if the guards tried to stop them, they still had their powers.

As Xan approached the two guards, they turned barring their weapons.

"Stop!" one cried out. Xan didn't flinch as he just used the staff to shoot lightning at the two men, making them fall.

Once outside the city walls, everyone relaxed a little, but was unsure of how to proceed. Kero finally addressed Blythe. Now would be the best opportunity she had to talk about what she saw back in that room.

"Why did you change your name?" Kero asked. Blythe turned away from her.

"Listen, I know you're not as happy as you want us to believe."

Blythe abruptly twisted her head around to face Kero.

"No! I'm not, okay! she shouted. Blythe calmed down after seeing Kero's stunned face. "I changed my name after joining The Hawks. It was a new start," she said. "I had to change my name because Eris Stone was now a traitor to the Empire for joining a resistance group." Blythe breathed in deeply. "Eris was a sad, insecure slave who got beat by her mother every day just because she existed. But as Blythe Krystal, I could do something to change the world."

Kero softened her expression. "I'm so sorry. I didn't know."

"No one knew. Once I became Blythe, I just kept a smile on my face."

"You don't have to do that," Kero said. "You don't have to pretend to be someone else–I mean, that woman wasn't your mother anyways. We had totally different lives before they reprogrammed us or whatever."

Blythe nodded, but a frown still stayed on her face.

"I'm just–really confused right now," she confessed.

"We were all reprogrammed," Xan broke into the conversation. "We had lives before the interdimensional beings came. We could travel freely and there weren't walls blocking the cities."

"So, you remember all of this?" Kero asked.

"Yes. After I bonded with Eden, not only did I remember my past life from a thousand years ago, but I remembered this planet's original state. I accidently discovered that laboratory under my study. The first time I went down there, I remembered who I was before being programmed. My name was still Alexander, but I had a different life. I grew up in Michael and the palace was a large house where I lived."

"That's crazy!" Darion replied. "I wonder what my life was like before going into that machine."

Kero tried to remember what happened the day she was stuffed into that machine, but something blocked her from those memories. She stared up at the image of the Empress in her sky. Her eyes hardened.

"Right now, we have other problems to worry about," she said finally. "There has to be a way to stop the Empress."

"I was thinking, why can't we talk to our dragons using our minds? We did it before." Blythe wondered.

"I've actually been trying to communicate with Phoenix,"

Kero said somberly. "I can't get through. There's something blocking me. I wish Aponi and A'keara were here. They understand this stuff way more than me."

"You understand a lot more than you think you do," Darion said. She returned a dubious glance to him. "Kero," Darion began. "I may not really be your biological brother, but I still have memories of us growing up together with mom and dad on the farm. You've always had your head in the clouds, but it's a good thing. You're a dreamer, Kero. Somehow, we have to get those dragons to join our side again."

"I definitely agree."

Everyone turned to the new voice. Kero's eyes softened as she saw Aponi and A'keara riding Aurora. The mare stopped letting her riders off. Kero didn't waste time as she ran to embrace the two women. Blythe followed suit.

"We are so glad to see you both!" Blythe greeted.

"So, what now?" Kero asked. "The Empress has all four dragons."

"We know," Aponi said gently. She looked at the others in the group. "I've spent a long time in meditation and now, I finally understand."

"What's a mediation?" Darion wondered. Aponi turned to the young man.

"Oh, a newcomer?"

"This is my brother," Kero said. Aponi returned a look of bewilderment.

Aponi studied the young man. "Oh, you found him. You know, you two look nothing alike."

"We know. It's because we're not really related," Kero admitted. "Aponi, do you know about all of the people on this planet having their memories wiped?"

"Not wiped Kero," Xan said. "You had new memories placed over the old ones."

Aponi squinted her eyes at Xan, then in a moment she realized what he was saying. Her eyes widened. "That's what happened!"

"What happened?" A'keara asked.

"Everyone had their memories altered. That's why no one knows their true heritage."

"That's right. I wish I could figure out how to use those machines to give everyone their true memories back."

"And who are you?" Aponi asked.

"This is my friend, Xan," Blythe said.

"Oh, the one who began the resistance group?" A'keara asked. Blythe nodded.

"Wait, you–" Aponi already felt his energy. It only took a moment to realize who he was. "You're the one who is supposed to bond with the Emerald Dragon."

Suddenly, both Aponi and A'keara saw all four dragons in the sky, with the Empress riding Phoenix.

"What is all that is good in Gaia is going on?" A'keara asked strongly.

"It's a long story," Xan admitted. "Long story short, I tried to stop the Empress from taking the dragons–and failed."

Aponi returned a sympathetic glance. "Do not worry. She

will not keep their power."

"That's right," A'keara agreed. "Don't forget, a dragon can only bond with one person."

Kero's eyes widened as she remembered what Eira said back on the mountain.

"Yeah, yer right! So how is she bonded to four dragons right now?"

"She's not bonded to them," Aponi replied. "She's using some sort of dark magic to control them."

Xan let out a long sigh as he had to come clean. "Unfortunately, I am responsible for this mess. I thought the obsidian crown I made would paralyze her, but maybe because of her origins, she was able to use the power to control the dragons."

"Crown of obsidian?" Aponi asked. She thought for a moment. "Where did you find obsidian?"

"A group of Kain's men found it in the mountains," Xan replied. "I was supposed to make armor that would protect the imperial soldiers from ferocious beasts like the yeti, but instead, I used it on the Empress." Blythe returned a look of sympathy.

"Don't blame yourself. At least you tried."

"I wish we could make it so everyone on the planet could wake up and realize that they had their memories altered."

"Now, we need to find a way to break this enchantment the Empress put on the Spirit Dragons," Aponi said. "We have all four humans who will bond with each dragon right here."

"Are you still acting as Aeous' bonded?" Blythe asked Aponi.

"I don't think that's my destiny anymore," Aponi replied. She turned to Darion. "I sense something special about you," she said.

Darion's glance wavered. "What are ya talkin' about?"

"Do you have any memories of your childhood?"

"Yeah, I remember Kero and I growing up together."

"I suspect you will remember more."

"Wait, are you sayin' that Darion is one of the bonded?" Kero asked. She glanced at her brother. Darion wasn't like her. He always fit in easier than she did in their village. He always rolled his eyes at her every time she talked about the dragons in her book. She turned to Xan. "You still have my book, right?" Xan's eyes widened and then he remembered.

"Here it is." He handed her the colorful hard covered book. Kero looked over it.

"Darion, you've never believed in stuff like dragons. You think all of this is childish, right?"

Darion shrugged his shoulders. "I've been through a lot in the past week. I don't know what to believe in anymore."

"Experiences change us," Aponi said. "The Empress is not bonded to any of the dragons. You cannot have more than one dragon. That was a rule set by the Elder Dragons. Also, you cannot use the dragons for malicious intent. Right now, the Empress is breaking a number of universal laws.

Kero looked up at the sky. Phoenix hovered above the palace with the Empress sitting on his back. The other three dragons flew in circles around him.

"It's time to get our planet back to the way it's supposed to be," Kero spoke confidently. "And we start by contacting our dragons."

"But, how do we do that? Blythe asked.

"I'm not sure," she admitted. "Maybe all of us need to try

talkin' to our dragons."

"I think that's a wonderful idea, Kero," Aponi replied. "All four of you need to sit in a circle and meditate, focusing on your bonded dragon."

"How do you know this?" Xan asked suspiciously.

"Please don't," A'keara interjected. "Just listen. She knows what she's talking about."

"So, which dragon is mine?" Darion asked.

Aponi turned to him. "Close your eyes and focus on your bonded. You'll see him."

The four dragon bonded sat in a circle on the soft grass. Darion felt strange sitting cross legged on the ground. He closed his eyes as the old lady instructed. He didn't see anything, but the woman started chanting.

Kero heard the chant and realized it was the same one Aponi did the night she first had the vision of Phoenix. Darion didn't know what he was supposed to do. His mind was blank because he didn't know what to focus on. He just listened to the chanting. Suddenly, memories flashed inside his mind. He saw himself riding on a creature with golden scales. As he focused more, he saw it was a dragon.

"What?" he whispered.

"Do you see your dragon?" Aponi asked. Darion, with his eyes still closed, nodded.

A'keara walked up beside her grandmother.

"Do you think they can join with their dragons?" she asked.

"It doesn't matter what I think. It matters what they think."

"So, you did all of this knowing that you would not stay bonded to a dragon," A'keara stated.

"We both knew from the start that we were not meant to be bonded to a spirit dragon, but we went on this journey anyway."

A'keara nodded. Suddenly, she felt bad for the childish way she acted before. Her grandmother was one of Etheria's elders and she should have shown the woman more respect.

"I'm sor–" Aponi put her hand up.

"Don't apologize." She put her arms around her granddaughter. "I'm just happy we all made it this far."

A'keara looked up at the violet moon in the sky. This was it. They would either succeed and be victorious or the world was done for. Either way, they all had a wonderful journey indeed.

CHAPTER 20

The Final Battle

Kero kept her thoughts on Phoenix. She thought about how they flew through the air together and the talks she had with him. Every time she tried to communicate with Phoenix, she got blocked by something. She tried again and again.

"Phoenix?" she called in her mind. *"I'm trying to connect with you. I found Aponi and A'keara. Blythe is here too. She's trying to connect to Eira."* She saw the red dragon in her mind, but her visions were only memories of what happened before. Then, something occurred to her. What if she thought of Phoenix where he was now? That was kind of frightening right now, as he was being controlled. Still, she pictured the dragon flying in circles with the other dragons and the Empress sitting on his back. She must've felt so much happiness and joy, having all of that power. It made Kero sick, but she kept imagining the woman in her gleeful moment.

"Phoenix," she called again.

Suddenly, she heard a strained voice reply. *K-e-r-o* It was Phoenix.

"Can you come to me? I'm outside the city walls."

It was silent. Then, *"T-this–cl-oud aroun-d my min-d–st-ops me fr-om th-ink-ing my own th-oughts– Ker-o, ke-ep talk-ing to–me."*

Keep talking to him? What was she supposed to say?"

"I'm meditating with Blythe, Darion and Xan. A lot just happened. I found out about my past. Darion and I aren't siblings. Blythe and I knew each other as kids–her name was not even Blythe. It's Eris."

Kero waited for a response. She probably just loaded his head with a bunch of information that he didn't need right now.

"Phoenix, is there any way you can stop the Empress?"

Phoenix stayed silent. *"Can you talk to the other dragons?"*

"I–will try," he replied.

Phoenix became aware of his surroundings. He felt the Empress on his back. Even though the woman was not very heavy in weight, she felt like a terrible burden to carry. Not only did he have to gain control of his mind, but his body too. His wings felt numb. He began moving the muscles inside them. He twisted his head to look at Eden.

"Eden! Wake up!" he yelled. All at once, he charged at her. He knew his attack would not greatly wound his sister, but it would definitely get her attention. His body collided with hers, pushing her back a little. The Empress was not ready for the attack and almost fell off of Phoenix. She smacked him in the back of his head.

"Stop that!" she growled. The Empress closed her eyes, using her thoughts to tell the dragon to obey her command. Phoenix felt his mind cloud over. He forgot where he was for a moment.

"Phoenix? What's going on?" He heard Kero's voice. Phoenix took control over his body and rushed at Eden again. Eden shook her head, realizing she was up in the air, even though she didn't remember flying up there. As she tried to understand her surroundings, she heard Xan's voice.

"Eden! Can you hear me?"

"Xan?" The Emerald Dragon looked around. Then, she saw the Empress sitting on Phoenix. "You witch! Get off of him!" Eden rammed into Phoenix. This time the woman lost her grip. She let out a blood curdling scream as she plummeted downwards.

Phoenix never saw her land, but something loosened up and he could think freely again. He looked into Eden's eyes, which had returned to their normal shade of green.

"Phoenix? Are you all right?" she asked.

"I think so," he replied.

"What about Aeolus and Eira?"

The other two dragons realized they were just flying in circles and came to a halt. Now all four dragons hovered in the air, gaining knowledge of their surroundings.

"What just happened?" Aeolus cried out.

"I feel so dizzy," Eira said.

"We were all under a spell," Phoenix replied. He peered downwards to see the Empress lying lifeless on the ground. The four dragons left the city and headed towards the grassy plains.

General Kain emerged from the palace to find the body of Empress Celise. She lay motionless in a pool of her own blood.

"What have those beasts done?!" Kain cried out with anguish. "How dare they?!" He stared down at the Empress. "My goddess–" He knelt down beside her. The photo of a woman with dark hair that sat on his desk, came his mind. Her eyes reminded him of the eyes of the Empress. "Mother," he whispered. Looking up at the night sky, he saw the four dragons flying away. "I won't let you get away with this!" he raged. "Do you hear me?" He stood up. "I will destroy every one of you monstrous beasts!" He stomped his way back into the palace and down a long corridor and descended a long flight of stairs until he reached the airship station. He touched the button on his personal radio. "All imperial soldiers report to the ship dock immediately!"

In the glassy plains outside the city wall, Kero still waited with the others. She felt a hand on her shoulder. Her eyes opened and she turned towards Darion.

"I'm not sure if we reached them or not," he said.

"Don't worry. We did," Kero assured him.

Blythe pointed in the sky. "Hey! They're coming this way!"

Phoenix and Eden landed together, then came Aeolus and Eira. Aponi watched everyone stand around awkwardly. They were all very weary from everything that had taken place.

"Wonderful! You're all here!" Aponi exclaimed.

"The Empress has fallen," Eden said.

Everyone's eyes flung wide open. Kero raised a skeptical eyebrow.

"Wait, are you serious? How?"

"I pushed her off of Phoenix and she fell to her death," Eden explained. "Sorry about that," she said to her brother. "I hope it didn't hurt too much."

Phoenix snorted. "I barely felt anything."

Kero couldn't believe it. That's it? The woman everyone deemed as all knowing and powerful met her end by just falling off a damn dragon?

"The Empress' only threat was that she had thousands of people following her," Aponi noted.

"That was scary," Blythe said. "I mean, I didn't know what to do when you four flew away with the Empress."

"Yeah, the Empress had all of your power," Darion agreed.

"Dragons are powerful, but our human riders have always given us the strength and endurance to see something through," Phoenix explained.

"I think I understand what Phoenix is saying," Kero began slowly. "You saw how the Empress took over their minds. Without us, they would have never come back."

"Dragons are strong and intelligent creatures, but humans remind us that we also have morals and obligations," Eden added. "It's a partnership."

"Hey, what about the gateway?" A'keara asked. "We shouldn't waste any more time."

"Yes," Aponi replied. "We should go now."

Just as she spoke those words, explosive blasts came from two laser cannons on an Imperial airship. Everyone looked up into the sky to see not one or two, but four airships coming towards them. General Kain stood in the front of the largest airship, glaring down at the four dragons and the humans below.

"Each airship will focus on taking down a dragon!" he instructed into the radio. "Do you hear me down there! All of you are finished! You might be dragons, but there's no way you can take down all of my ships!"

From the ground, everyone could hear the general's booming voice from the airship's loudspeaker.

"We don't have time to fight them!" Kero yelled. "Let's just go!" As she said that, all of the laser cannons from the four airships went off. Everyone ducked for cover so as not to get hit. Kero jumped behind a large bolder. She peered around it to see Aponi trying to run away from the blasts. A'keara rode on Aurora's back over to the old lady. After helping her on, the two rode on the unicorn towards the forest. They would be safe there.

Kero's eyes scanned the area until she saw Phoenix. He was flying alongside Aeolus who carried Darion. Before now, Kero never believed she'd ever see her brother on a dragon–or who she called her brother. She continued to look around for the others. Where were Blythe and Xan? Her eyes went up to the blue and green dragons above. They were riding on top of them.

Whoa! This is really happening. Kero realized as she watched Xan and Blythe ride their dragons. Without any delay, she came out of her hiding spot while the airships were distracted. She almost shouted to Phoenix when she realized that she didn't need to do that. Instead, she focused her thoughts on the red dragon.

"Phoenix. I'm down here. Come get me."

Phoenix was busy at the moment. He and Aeolus came up with the plan to use fire and wind together to take down the airship.

"I wish I could do something to help you," Darion said to Aeolus. Just as he spoke those words, something appeared in Darion's hand. He looked down to see a bow in his hand. It was similar to the one he always used to hunt, but a lot fancier. The wooden bow was also decorated with gold fabric and the edges of the handle were more defined. Then an arrow appeared in his opposite hand. Darion already had a lot of experience with a bow. He never hit an imperial airship before.

Darion aimed his bow and shot an arrow through the fire coming from the red dragon. He shot another arrow, then another.

"I've always wanted to shoot fire arrows," he said.

"Oh really?" Aeolus asked. "I've always wanted to breathe fire like Phoenix."

Darion readied another arrow. "Ya know, I've been wondering. How many dragons used to exist?"

"Used to? They still exist in the higher realms," Aeolus answered.

"And they breathe fire, ice, wind and lightning?"

"Actually, most of them breathe fire. A few in the north breathe ice, but not many breathe lightning and wind. Some have been known to breathe pure light. That's what comes from the Elder Dragons' breath."

"Light? That would be interesting to see." Darion wanted to imagine what it would look like. But he needs to focus on taking down the airships.

Phoenix broke into the conversation

"Aeolus, I need to get Kero. Can you manage on your own for a moment?"

"Of course," he replied. Darion became concerned.

"Wait! I don't want her up here!"

Phoenix turned a caring glance towards the young man. "She is more capable than you think." He flew towards the ground where the girl waited.

Kero ran towards Phoenix as he landed. She didn't waste any time climbing onto his back. As Phoenix ascended into the sky, she felt exhilarated.

They joined with Aeolus and Darion. The young man turned his glance towards the young woman he once knew as his sister.

"Are you sure you know what yer doin'?"

Kero didn't even return a glance. "I already did this before," she curtly answered.

The fire sword appeared in her hands. "Finally! Why didn't this thing come before?"

"You are able to summon your spirit weapon when you are confident in knowing what it is you must do," Phoenix replied.

"I think I actually understood that," she said. As Kero looked up, she saw the bright light of the laser cannon being aimed at them. Phoenix swerved the attack, continuing up above the aircraft. From there, he pelted the airship with fireballs, then released a long stream of fire.

Inside, the crew members were panicking, trying to put out the fire. There were sprinklers to put out engine fires, but they wouldn't be able to reach the very top of the airship. The captain saw the damage and realized it was too late..

"We're going down!" he reported into the radio.

General Kain stood on the other airship, watching the aircraft plummet down to the ground. His eyes locked onto the Crimson Dragon and his rider.

"Send out the air soldiers," he commanded. "We need to take down these dragons!"

Inside the remaining three airships, many soldiers armed

themselves with missiles and donned their jetpacks. The bay doors of the ships opened and about a dozen soldiers charged into battle.

Kero stared down at all the soldiers. Aside from the airships, they had to deal with them too.

"Phoenix–" Kero said, a little disheartened.

"This is not going to be easy," he replied. "Hold on."

Several feet away, Blythe sat atop of Eira, trying her best to throw her ice disk at the incoming enemies. Xan sat on Eden, holding his staff. Two air soldiers charged towards them. One of the soldiers fired his missile. Eden easily swooped out of the way. She returned with a few lightning bolts that, when connected with the soldier's jetpack, fried him. He fell like a rock. Eira released rocks of ice, which froze the other soldier. Even with their victory, Eden noticed that Xan looked uneasy.

"What is it?" she asked him.

"I'm wondering why they haven't used the powder yet?"

Eden stayed quiet for a moment. She knew that stuff would stop her and her siblings. "I only made so much of it, but–"

"I will be careful. And I'll warn the others," she said.

Blythe continued to fling her ice disk at the soldier closest to her and Eira. The violet blue dragon focused on the airship, taking out one laser cannon at a time. As Blythe threw the disk one more time, it froze the fuel tanks and the jetpack no longer worked. The soldier fell and that was the end of him. Eira took out the last cannon and now the two moved to the other side.

Eden and Xan continued fighting against the airship and stray soldiers coming from all directions. It would be easy to take down the air soldiers with one jolt of lightning, but getting a shot on them at once was more difficult. With the airship continuing to fire laser beams, along with the soldiers with jetpacks launching missiles at them, fluttering in the sky too long would not be wise. Eden flew through the air, twisting and turning to avoid all of the gunfire. Xan began to get a little dizzy.

Finally, Eden found a position where she could fire lightning at the soldier attacking them. Once he was out of the way, the dragon returned her focus to taking down the airship.

Eden shot bolts of lightning at the laser cannons, utterly obliterating them. Phoenix and Kero joined in with blazing fire. After many assaults of fire and lightning, the airship made an emergency landing.

Kain watched the second ship go down. He bit his lip. There was only one way to take down these creatures. There wasn't much of that white powder left, but maybe if it was timed right, he could get all four dragons at once. He spoke into his radio.

"Move in closer!" he commanded. "Yes sir!" the Captain responded.

In the air, everyone watched the two airships move closer together.

"What are they doing?" Kero asked. "I'm not sure," Phoenix replied. "Just be on your guard."

More air soldiers came out of the ships. Two had jetpacks and another one followed them, riding a flat white board. Blythe recognized the object.

"Hey! I rode one of those before," she said. "It's an airglider."

Eira studied the flat board connected to the soldier's feet.

"That thing looks flimsy. How is he staying on it?"

"There's a magnetic field that locks your feet on," Blythe explained.

"He's still a rather big target." She followed up by sending balls of ice at the soldier. He easily swerved around her attacks. Blythe saw something in his hand. It appeared to be a round clear object with white powder in it.

"What is–?" she never finished her sentence. The man tossed out the round orb. White powder exploded around them.

"No! Not this stuff!" Eira felt her wings go numb. Blythe felt the two of them descend. It quickly changed from floating to falling.

"Eira!" Blythe screeched. At that moment, Darion had noticed the other dragon.

"Aeolus, something's wrong with your friend."

Aeolus looked at his sister falling towards the ground. He swooped downwards, sending out a cyclone towards her. Eira fell into the wind. At first she panicked, then she realized that it gently lowered Blythe and her to the ground. Aeolus landed next to them.

"Eira!"

"I'm sorry. I won't be able to do anything. Blythe, go with them."

"What about you?"

"Don't worry. I'll be fine," she insisted.

"I can't just leave you!"

Aeolus stepped forward. He let out a few breaths, creating a wall of wind around his sister. "That should protect her. We need to at least take out the soldier with that weird powder."

Blythe swore silently. "Xan, why would you create that stuff?" She knew deep down that he was pushed into a corner by the Empire. It just showed how dumb his plan was in the first place. She sighed and mounted Aeolus.

Blythe realized that Aeolus was a little bigger than Eira. Also, Eira's scales were smoother, almost like glass. Aeolus' had scales that felt more like sand. The soldier who attacked Eira still hovered in the air. He prepared to launch another globe with the same white substance. Aeolus sent out a cyclone, engulfing the man, twirling him around until he became dizzy. Darion took his chance and readied his bow. He took aim at the soldier and fired. To his surprise, Blythe tossed her ice disk as well. The ice combined with Darion's arrow, crystalizing the tip. When the arrow hit its target, the soldier was frozen in a block of ice. Darion's mouth formed a wide grin.

"That was amazing!" he cried. He turned towards Blythe. "How did you do that?"

"I wasn't trying to do anything to your arrow. I just was getting that guy back for what he did to Eira."

"Can you do that again?" he asked.

"I think so," she replied.

"Darion, why don't you try shooting more than one arrow?" Aeolus suggested.

"I can do that?" he asked.

"Just picture in your mind more arrows coming to you."

Darion took a deep breath and did as he was told. Five arrows appeared on the bow and five arrows appeared on the bow. "Whoa!" he exclaimed. He drew back the arrows and released them towards the two airships. Blythe threw her disk again, turning the tips of the arrows into pure ice. Aeolus used his breath to send them deep into the airship's engine. The arrows hit their target and the gears of the engine froze.

Meanwhile, Phoenix and Eden took out the engines of the other airship, the one General Kain was aboard. The alarms went off and the crew members scurried to the emergency vessels.

"Where do you think you're going?" the general shouted. "The battle is not over!" No one listened as they saved themselves. "I won't let them beat me!" He grabbed a fully-armed jetpack and strapped it on. His fist pounded the switch to open the bay doors. Now standing on top of the airship deck, he flew up into the sky.

"I'll defeat all four dragons myself!"

As the last airship went down, Kero smiled. They did it! Her eyes went up to the violet-colored moon in the sky. It was the most beautiful moon she'd ever seen. It was so bright, that it was almost like looking at the sun.

"Kero, look!" Phoenix yelled.

She turned her head to see General Kain flying towards them. "What the hell is he doing?"

Kain laughed hysterically as he pointed a long canister at them. He fired a missile right at them. Phoenix avoided the attack, but the missile reached the city gates of Michael. The dragon and his rider turned to see broken pieces of the wall crumbling down. Multiple screams erupted from the city streets. Kain continued his demented laugh as he aimed another missile at the two and fired. Phoenix avoided the attack as well. The missile flew into the city and hit one of the palace towers, causing the stones to crumble and fall, burying part of the mammoth structure.

"He needs to stop!" Phoenix said urgently.

"Stop!" Kero yelled at the general.

Kain continued his maniacal laughter. "Stop? Stop?! *You* need to stop! You need to just die!" He took out a globe of white powder and tossed it at them. Suddenly, Kero swung her fire sword. The hilt of the sword connected with the circular object sending it back at Kain. The globe struck his chest and the white substance exploded around him. Kain lowered his hands to see the white powder on his uniform. A chuckle cracked from his throat.

"This stuff doesn't do anything to me!" As he spoke those words, the tiny jetpack engine on his back went out. The powder had clogged the engine. Kain fell with a cry of anguish.

By the time Phoenix landed in the field, Eden and Xan were already there. Xan stood over the general's body.

"Vincent–I wish you would have remembered your true self." He turned as Kero approached him.

"Once upon a time, Vincent and I were friends," he explained. "I lived in a large house where the palace was built. Vincent lived there too with his mother. I don't know what happened to his mother. After we got new memories, I still lived in the palace as a servant. This is why I decided to do the mission. I saw how poorly servants were treated."

"So, the Empress already knew who you were before you pretended to be someone else?"

Xan shook his head. "She never saw me when I was a servant. I worked in the dungeon with the prisoners. I gave them their food-or what they called food."

"Why did the Empire do all that? I mean, why were we put into those machines?"

"They did it to control us. Giving us new memories made us believe that the Empress has always been in charge. We wouldn't know anything different."

Finally, Kero understood. "Well, the Empress is gone now."

"Yes, but I wonder how the people are going to respond to her death."

Several feet away, Eira began to feel her wings again. Aeolus landed beside her.

"Hurry up and do something about this wind," she said.

"I know. Hold on," Aeolus replied haughtily to his sister's impatience. The golden dragon drew in his breath, taking away the wall of wind. Darion jumped off Aeolus and rushed over to Kero.

"Are you okay?" he asked.

Phoenix chuckled. "Of course she is," he responded.

As everyone gathered, Aponi and A'keara joined them, still riding on top of Aurora. Aponi dismounted Aurora to address the others.

"I am so grateful to you all," Aponi said. Her eyes swept across the four dragons and their riders. "And I mean, all of you." Her gaze ended on Xan and Eden.

"Hey, should we check on the people in Michael?" Kero asked. "That madman shot two missiles into the city."

"Well, he meant to hit us," Phoenix said. He cleared his throat. "I suppose we could spare a moment." They turned to the gates as two guards walked out of the city carrying the Empress' body. Many civilians followed. The two men put down the body and began digging a hole.

"The Empress–" Kero spoke quietly. Everyone wept as the two guards prepared a burial spot for the Empress.

Kero made her way over, with Phoenix close by. As Kero stared down at the body of the Empress, she noticed something was very odd about the blood. It was very dark red; almost black. On her face was the golden mask she always wore. Kero bent down and removed it. A startled cry escaped her lips. Darion walked up behind her. His eyes gazed down at the face of the Empress.

"What the hell? What is she?" he cried. Darion stared down at the true face of the woman who ruled over the planet. He was speechless. Everyone who saw the Empress' face stared at it in horror. There were numerous gasps and murmurs in the crowd.

The two guards hurried and tossed the woman's body into the hold and began covering it as fast as they could. Kero watched, wondering if this burial was too good for her. Xan walked up behind them.

"I know she said she was from another race, but I didn't expect her to look like that," Kero said.

"She is from a race known as Drakens," Xan said. "You saw the book in the library about the snake-like beings." Kero nodded.

"So, this is what she was talkin' about during that meeting?" Kero asked.

Xan nodded. The others joined them. Blythe looked down at the Empress in the hole.

"I never thought I'd actually see the day–" She turned to one of guards. "Maybe we should burn the body. I don't want her coming back."

"We can feed her to the dragons," Kero suggested.

At that moment, one of the guards, covering up the hole, turned with a sharp glare towards Kero.

"Hey! Show some respect! This woman took care of us."

Kero almost spat as she turned to speak to the man. "Excuse me? You call what she did as 'taking care of us'? She was a tyrant!" All of the people within earshot turned with gasps.

"Kero, they–they don't understand," Xan said sadly. "We should go now, okay?"

"Remember, Kero," Blythe spoke hastily. "These people live in Michael. They didn't have to suffer like us."

Kero stared daggers at the crowd. Finally, she turned away, disgusted by their presence.

As they walked back towards the group, Blythe addressed Xan.

"Why didn't you just tell us who she was?" she hastily asked.

Xan let out a long sigh. "I wanted to, but–I just couldn't get it out because I could hardly believe it myself. There are more of them out there," he said looking up at the sky. "I don't know what they'll do when they find out what just happened."

"How would they know?" Darion asked.

Aponi intervened at that moment. "I believe it is time to open the gateway," she said. "The energy violet moon won't be in the sky forever."

Xan took one last look at General Kain. He considered letting the guards know that they had another body to bury. He looked across the field to see a few soldiers coming their way. "We should go quickly," Xan said.

Kero climbed onto Phoenix, still having her head full of the excitement that just took place. She glanced at Blythe mounting

Eira and Darion on Aeolus.

"Are you alright?" Phoenix asked her.

She had to gather her thoughts for a second. "A lot just happened. And now we're about to do what we wanted to do from the start. Do you know what's going to happen? I mean, with the gateway opening and everything?"

"Unfortunately, none of us know exactly what is going to happen. We haven't connected with the Elder Dragons for eons. But, they are the wisest dragons in existence. They will know what we need to do next."

Xan had already mounted Eden. The Emerald Dragon took off into the sky; Phoenix followed her, then Aeolus and finally Eira. Aponi joined her granddaughter on Aurora's back. A'keara signaled for the unicorn to gallop after the dragons.

CHAPTER 21

The Elder Dragons

The deep violet moon began to fade. They had maybe a few hours left before it would be completely gone. Kero rode on top of Phoenix, feeling relieved that all of this would be over soon. Many questions filled her mind. What would she do after they opened the gateway into the higher realm? The Elder Dragons would come back and then what? What about the village? Would she and Darion go back and just do what they did before? But, there wasn't an Empire anymore. And Darion...he's not even her brother.

"Are you alright?" Phoenix asked.

"Phoenix, I don't know how everyone in my village is going to respond to a bunch of dragons showing up."

Phoenix laughed. "I guess we'll find out soon enough."

The ruins of Etheria were up ahead. The four dragons raced towards the direct center of the planet. They hovered in the sky for a moment. Aurora materialized on the ground below them. Aponi and A'keara let themselves become adjusted to the new environment.

"I'm still not used to that feeling," Aponi said.

"I know," A'keara agreed. "It's like your whole body gets compressed and then stretches back out again."

Aponi gazed up into the sky. "A'keara, look up." The elderly lady peered upwards to see the four dragons preparing to open the gateway.

"Ready?" Eden asked. The other three nodded. Eira and Phoenix faced each other as did Eden and Aeolus. Together, Eira and Phoenix flew upwards at a much faster speed than they've ever moved before. Kero thought she already let go and fell off, but a strong force kept her on Phoenix. He was just a stream of red, while Eira was a stream of blue. He and Eira twirled around each other. The two colors combined, making a vibrant violet light. Eden and Aeolus spun around each other, their colors of green and gold combining with the violet light. The streams of light became a silvery white ball in the sky.

Down below, A'keara and Aponi sat on Aurora, watching the ball of light in the sky grow bigger until it covered the moon. Great cries of victory came from within the light. Seven dragons emerged and flew across the sky, gracefully zigzagging down to the ground. The ball of light now grew smaller until it faded away. The silvery light separated back into the four colors of red, blue, gold and green, and then back into the four dragons.

By now, the violet moon had completely faded away, replaced by the rising sun. Now, the Elder Dragons finally arrived, scales shimmering in the sunlight.

"They look like crystals, they are truly majestic beings,"

A'keara said in awe. Aponi dismounted Aurora and approached the Elders. The one with deep red scales came forward.

"Greetings Dear One." The voice that came out of him was way deeper than Phoenix's. "My name is Alden. I am the head of the Elder Dragons Guild."

"Hello, I am Aponi. So, there are—" She counted their number. "Seven of you."

"Seven elders. Many more dragons back in our realm. So, the four humans who bonded with the Spirit Dragons have been found again. Wonderful!" Alden said as he looked around the supposedly familiar surroundings. "What happened here? Isn't this supposed to be Etheria?"

Aponi gazed sadly at him. "It was. Sadly, it was destroyed eleven years ago by the Empire."

"Uh, yes, the Empire. We will see to it that they are severely dealt with."

"No need," Eden said. "The empire is no more."

"Oh, you took care of the empire? So, why did you open the gateway?"

Everyone exchanged bewildered glances.

"Wasn't it you I talked to?" Aponi asked. "I did the sacred meditation and I believe you told me to awaken the dragons and open the gateway into the higher realm."

"I sent out the message. Yes. You must have been the one who received it. However, I thought you would open the gateway sooner so that we could take care of the Empress."

Kero had a wide grin on her face. "Hey, we took care of that witch by ourselves."

"Yeah, and her army is gone too," Blythe chimed in. "Well, the General is dead. There are some soldiers still left, but I don't think they'll be much of a threat."

"So you took care of the problem yourselves. It doesn't seem like you need us."

"We do need you," Aponi said. "I want to see a world where dragons and humans are reunited and live together in harmony."

Alden scoffed. "Humans and dragons live together in harmony? There is no such thing!"

Now everyone, especially the four Spirit Dragons turned around, stunned.

"What do you mean?" Eden asked. One thousand years ago, humans and dragons worked together to create a peaceful world."

"You must go back and study your history. It was not peaceful. It was a stressful mess." No one spoke. Alden looked around. "Let's start by cleaning up Etheria."

"What should we do?" Aponi asked.

Alden turned to her. "Your part is over, Etherian. We will rebuild this great city." An aurora formed around each of the seven elder dragons as they used telekinesis to move large pieces of rocks and stacked them onto each other. Some of the stone that eroded away was reformed. Pieces of gravel were reshaped to become rectangular blocks.

Everyone watched for a moment, still not sure what to do.

"I guess we can go home now?" Darion said.

Kero wasn't sure how to feel. When they defeated the Empress, she was on top of the world. However, now she felt empty.

"Darion, I don't know if I want to go back to Athena. I

mean, what exactly are we going to tell everyone?"

"We should at least see if everyone is okay," he replied.

Phoenix turned to Kero. "We should leave for now. We're not accomplishing anything by standing around." She nodded and climbed onto his back. Darion climbed onto Aeolus.

"So, where is this farm of yours?" Phoenix asked.

"We need to go south from here," Kero replied, "It's a small village."

"Actually, it's southwest," Darion said.

Phoenix turned towards the others. "Let's all go to Athena. Once there, we can get some much needed rest."

"That sounds lovely," A'keara replied.

Aponi looked at the Elder Dragons. "We'll just leave you to do your work. Hopefully, we can come to some sort of agreement on what should be done for the planet."

"Most definitely," Alden said.

After everyone left, Raya, the violet-colored dragon flew over to Alden.

"So, the Empress is dead," she said thoughtfully. "Which means she failed her mission."

"On the contrary," Alden hummed. "She accomplished her goal of making humans useful. However, now that she's gone, the rest of the Draken will come here and take the rest of the planet's resources. Then, they'll destroy Gaia."

"So, we have to stop the Draken then?"

"Who else is going to do it? The Spirit Dragons can't do it alone. And their bonded are still new to relearning their powers.

Plus, they have no idea of the dangers coming their way."

"True," Raya agreed. "We once again have to babysit the humans." She stayed quiet in thought for a moment. "Do any of the humans know about the Dragon Wars?"

"Hopefully not. Not even the Spirit Dragons remember. I made sure of that." Alden said sternly, briefly recalling what happened.

"Don't be too surprised when they find out." Raya warned.

"And how will they find out?" Alden challenged.

"Well, they passed your test and found a way to open the gateway."

Alden chuckled. "One human got my message. One."

"Yes, but she is a great influencer."

"Let's focus on other matters. We need to build a place to put all of the humans."

"So, they'll be safe, right?"

Alden went quiet for a moment. "Yes. of course."

Raya sighed. "Nothing has changed in one thousand years." She flew off, leaving Alden to ponder her parting words.

"No, not much has or ever will," he noted.

CHAPTER 22

Gaia Restored

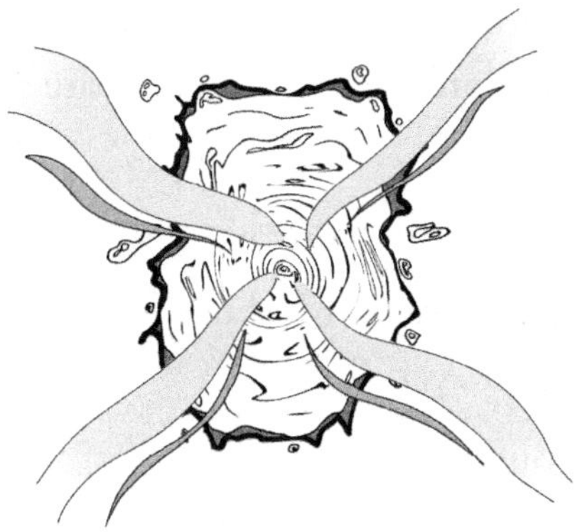

Kero didn't know what to expect when she returned home. *Please let everyone be okay*. She thought. After a few hours of flying, Kero saw the open fields of the farmland. Many of the villagers down in the field looked up as four dragons and their riders soared towards them. A few dropped their tools and ran for cover.

Arthur Daniels looked up from where he stood. His eyes narrowed as he tried to comprehend what he was looking at. Then, he recognized a familiar looking girl on top of the red dragon.

"Kero?" Then, he looked at the other riders. Two he didn't recognize, but one he definitely did. "And Darion?"

The four dragons landed by the cornfield. Mr. Daniels ran towards the dragons as others were running away. Even the two guards at the gate ran and hid. Mr. Daniel maneuvered around the fearful group of workers, but he finally reached where Phoenix stood. He gazed up at the creature with wonder.

"Oh my– A dragon? A real dragon?" He stared in awe.

"Hi," Kero said, waving to him. "Don't 'hi' me! What's all this? How?" Mr. Daniels said trying to understand what was happening.

Darion hopped off of Aeolus.

"Hi Mr. Daniels, uh— yeah, so I guess we have a lot to explain. First of all, don't be scared. These are the Spirit Dragons and they're our friends."

"Okay. Why are you two riding dragons?"

Darion put a hand on his shoulder. "Take a break. Let's go inside and I'll explain everything."

"A break? But, we can't just—"

"Trust me. No one is comin' here to tell us what to do anymore."

Arthur twisted his face into confusion. He followed Darion towards the farmhouse.

Kero led Blythe and Xan to the front door of her home. Xan took Kero's book out of his bag.

"Here ya go," he said as he handed it to her. Kero took the book and held it out, looking at the cover.

"Ya know, this is the only copy in the whole world. Aponi wrote it and it was once in the Etherian library."

Xan raised his eyebrows. "Really?"

Blythe looked around at the small living area, connected to the tiny kitchen. A large pot sat on a pile of logs in the fireplace. There were four chairs set up around the small square table. The staircase leading up to the rooms looked pretty old with rotting wood.

"Still better than where I grew up," she said with a shrug.

"Um, so I'm not sure where everyone is going to sleep. My brother–I mean Darion and I each had a room and the third room was our parents–" Kero became quiet. This whole business with them learning about their true history was really messing with her head right now. If her memories were false, did she really lose her parents? They were two people acting as her parents, she realized.

Kero led the way upstairs. She gave a quick look to Darion who was talking to Arthur at the table about their adventure. The man in his fifties sat with his mouth agape and his eyes squinted, trying to understand everything being said to him. Kero sighed, realizing that many were going to have that same reaction when they learned the truth about what the Empire did.

When Kero reached the top of the stairs, she headed right into her bedroom. The loose floorboard that she used to hide her book had been ripped out of the floor. She held her book in her hand. She had to find a new hiding spot for her book. Then again, maybe she didn't. Without the Empress, that law was abolished. People could read books again. Kero read this book so many times. She turned to Blythe.

"Do you want to read this book?"

Blythe looked over the colorful cover. "Uh, sure." Blythe took it.

Kero pointed to the door across the hallway. "That's Darion's room." Then, she looked straight ahead. Slowly, she walked towards the door at the end of the short hallway. She put a hand on the door and closed her eyes. She hadn't been in there since her parents were killed. However, after learning about the reprogramming of every person on Anu, they may not have been her real parents...

Turning the doorknob, she pushed open the old wooden door. The two girls stepped into a humble bedroom with two worn out mattresses by the far wall and a wardrobe across from it. Kero lost her words for a moment. Xan walked up behind the girls. Kero turned to him.

"Uh–this room is available if you want to sleep here. We'll have to get more mattresses for Aponi and A'keara." Aurora couldn't teleport to Athena since the unicorn had never been there before and there was no one there she had a bond with. It would be a few days before they reached the farm.

"Where can I sleep?" Blythe asked.

"Uh, there are two mattresses in here. You can take one."

Blythe returned a peculiar stare. "Or, I can put it in my room. It's just it's really cramped so-"

"It's fine. I'll sleep in here with Xan."

When Aponi and A'keara arrived two days later, everyone was already acquainted with the story of their journey. To the women's surprise, everyone stood, and applauded them as they rode on top of Aurora.

"What's all this?" Aponi asked. Shouts of 'thank you' and other admiration erupted from everyone.

"I guess we're heroes now," A'keara said. "Strange, I didn't expect all of this."

That night, four dragons and their riders had a huge celebration with all the villagers in Athena. Kero even read her book to everyone. Some of the children looked at the pictures and wanted to learn how to read. Phoenix sat with his siblings, feeling at peace which he hadn't felt in a long time. He turned to Eden sitting next to him.

"I pray the Elder Dragons get their work done. Maybe we should go help them."

"Actually, Xan and I are going to see them tomorrow," Eden replied.

"Oh, do you need us–"

"No," Eden answered a bit sharply.

Phoenix drew back.

"I mean, It is not necessary. Just relax and–have fun."

Phoenix wasn't sure how to do that. "I'll try," he said.

Aeolus looked around at everyone staring at him in admiration.

"Well, I'm just glad these people like us. Not like those people on the island."

"Yes," Eira agreed. "And I want it to stay this way." She turned a cautious glance to the others. "It will stay this way, right?"

"Believe me," Phoenix spoke strongly. "We won't be separated again. I won't let that happen."

"None of us will let that happen," Eden finished.

Kero sat between Blythe and Darion, just enjoying herself. The villagers prepared a wild boar and another deer. Since all of the Empress' laws were abolished, the people could hunt for their food.

"Kero, do you know that there are more creatures besides dragons in the higher realm?" Phoenix asked her.

Kero shook her head. "Like what?"

"The higher realm is home to other mythological creatures,

like unicorns, gnomes and fairies, who all want to be helpful to humankind."

Blythe was taken aback. "Wait, there are more unicorns, like Aurora? And what are gnomes and fairies?"

"Gnomes are tiny men and women who live in the forest and make things out of wood. They only help you if you can trade with them, but they like humans. Fairies are winged creatures who also lived in the forest, but in a different section than gnomes. They are a little mischievous, but will help in whatever situation as long as it benefits the planet," Eden explained.

"Can we go through the gateway, into their world?" Kero asked.

"Unfortunately, humans cannot survive in the higher realm. But don't worry, they will be coming here. We need to unite all of humans first. There is no doubt going to be a lot of confusion since the Empire fell."

Xan, who had been listening to the conversation added, "Many of the soldiers who worked for the Empire will have one of two reactions to this situation. Either they will join the rest of us to create a new life on this planet or hold onto the belief that they have to still protect an Empire that no longer exists and they'll fight those who disagree."

"What about other people who live in places like Michael and Gabriel?" Kero asked. "They worshiped the Empress. You saw those people from Michael. They were sad when the Empress died."

"We should start with the people who want change. Then, we'll worry about the others," Phoenix stated.

The fire burned brilliantly with high flames reaching up into the night sky. There were many twinkling stars that anyone could gaze upon. Except one. It was a craft, hovering in the sky, trying to blend in. Within the craft, a few creatures with skin like a snake. One of them sat at a monitor, looking at the people having the celebration. He turned and spoke with the one piloting the craft.

"I'm recording everything going on with the humans who bonded with the dragons. Is this enough proof to show to the council?"

The pilot nodded. "Send it to them. They need to know that Celise failed and now the planet has no one to lead it."

He pushed a few buttons until a message came up that the video was sent.

"It's a shame really. This planet has a lot of nice resources." He looked at the pilot again. "What do you think? Will they destroy it? What will happen to the inhabitants of this planet?"

The pilot turned around, "Stop asking so many questions!" he snapped. "Just do your job."

"Fine," the other one spoke, defeated.

In a large room full of podiums, a council of thirteen members sat and watched the videos sent to them. The video of Empress Celise falling from the dragon was played over and over. It seemed to amuse everyone. They also watched the dragons and their riders fighting against General Kain and the four airships. The camera went from Xan on top of Eden, to Darion, then Blythe and finally on Kero. The tape froze on Kero and Phoenix. A Draken by the name of Khanan stood in front of the council.

"Humans are not supposed to be this capable," he sneered. "So, how did these humans escape our trap?" He turned to his council who didn't appear to have an answer. "I called this meeting of the council so that we can discuss the fate of the planet known as Anu or its former name, Gaia. Celise is dead, so the planet has no one to rule it. What will your decision be on how to proceed? Should we find a new ruler or destroy the planet?"

Many murmurs came from the twelve council members. Finally, one member rose to his feet.

"As the speaker of the council, I believe we need to discuss the matter more before we make a decision."

"Alright. You have exactly seven days to make a decision. If one is not made, we will just destroy the planet." Khanan turned and exited the doors. He continued down the hallway, towards a large throne room where two guards stood.

Once in his throne room, Khanan sat upon his throne and put his hand to his chin in thought. "Celise is dead. I'm not surprised, but the fact that she had the power of four dragons and lost control of them–" A small chuckle escaped from his throat. "Well, I guess it's my turn now."

Back on Gaia, morning came. Kero wasn't ready to go back out adventuring just yet.

"Can't we just wait a few more days?" she asked Phoenix.

"It's been over a week since you came home," he replied. "We have to speak with the Elder Dragons and I figured you'd want to be part of that discussion."

"I don't see why we're in a rush. We're safe now. The whole planet is safe."

"Yes, but we have to make sure it stays that way," he said. Kero groaned.

"Come on, don't be so down!" Blythe said. "We're going

to reunite everyone. We can really do some great things now. Besides, Xan and Eden left a few days ago. I want to make sure they're okay."

"Fine," Kero said. The two mounted their dragons and took off towards the skies. Kero started to feel more energized as she rode on Phoenix. She looked over at Blythe who screeched with glee. Kero began to relax and have fun too. No more Empire. No more people starving. No more division of social class or feeling like you don't belong. The gateway to Gaia had been restored and all of humanity was free. At least, that's what everyone wishes.

DID YOU LOVE BOOK 1?

Leave a review.
heatherjeannovels.com

AUTHOR'S NOTE

WARNING: DO NOT READ THIS PART BEFORE READING THE BOOK!

Dragons have always fascinated me. When I was in college, I played a video game that featured a woman warrior bonding with a dragon. I remember the game was given to me as a gift. A few years later, I played the sequel, which I still own today. Soon, after beating the game, I felt inspired to write a story about people who bond with dragons. I put the setting in medieval times and began writing the story. However, I never finished it. In 2023, I felt inspired to rewrite the story I never finished. Instead of using a medieval setting, which many books about dragons often have, I made the setting on another planet with a post apocalyptic scenario. I really liked the type of setting that was used for the Hunger Games, a book series I loved reading. I liked the idea of a dictatorship running a planet and having the protagonist go on a journey to find the dragons who would free the people living under the evil government. When I first began writing this book, I was going to call it Gateway to Gaia because the goal of the main characters was to open a gateway and restore the planet, which was originally named Gaia. However, after my husband, Tony, read my manuscript, he said the book needed a stronger title and he came up with Dragon Wars. We both loved the title. Thus, Dragon Wars was born!

The Planet Anu

Nowadays, many people are getting more interested in conspiracy theories. Many wonder if the Earth is really flat or if alien reptiles are ruling over us and we just don't know about it. We already have stories that dabble in the idea that a one world government will soon become a reality. In this story, the planet's name is Anu. It may be obvious to you where I got the name. It comes from the word, Annunaki. The Annunaki are known as a group of deities who decide the fate of humanity. Some believe they created humanity. While I am not sure if I will use these beings in later stories, I felt led to use the word Anu as the planet's name.

So, hopefully, you heeded my warning at the beginning and you read the book before reading this letter. The Empress came from a race of snake-like beings, called 'Draken.' There is a whole planet full of these beings. It is possible they worship Annunaki and renamed the planet Anu to honor their gods. Our heroes learn that the true name of the planet was Gaia and learn that the technology used to rewrite the memories of the people came from Draken technology. This idea is another conspiracy theory where people believe that we don't remember our true selves and 'put up' with living on a slave planet.

The Main Character and her Dragon

Kero Embers began as a girl with long dark hair the first time I tried writing this story. I didn't even have a last name for her. When I was in college, I used to draw my characters so I could get a good visual of them. Kero wore red armor to match her red dragon. In Dragon Wars, she has copper red hair and gold eyes, and she wears a red shirt and black pants with black boots. Originally, she was supposed to be the leader of a group called Dragon Knights, which was a potential title for the book. I didn't get too far into the plot, however. I had five different dragon riders and dragons. The dragons still had their elements of fire, water (not ice), earth, air, and lightning. In the current story, there are only four elements that match with the four seasons of winter, summer, spring and autumn.

The Spirit Dragons

I don't recall the name of Kero's dragon in the original story, but the name Phoenix popped into my head, just as the name Kero had. Eden was also a name that just came to me. I thought about the Garden of Eden, and how it was a place that represents paradise and the most beautiful garden you will ever see. For the names, Eira and Aeolus, I researched names that meant either snow or ice, and names that meant wind. Eira is a Welsh name that means 'snow.' In fact, the way to pronounce the name Eira is, 'Ay-ra.' The name Aeolus, for the Golden Dragon, is a Greek name that means god of the winds.

The Empress and her Army

Everyone loves a good villain. When I thought about who the main antagonist would be, I thought of someone the main characters would see as a formidable foe. The reader would hopefully find this character to be appalling or horrifying. They would say to themselves, "I wouldn't want to have to go against that person."

Actually, there are two big villains in this story. There is the Empress and there is General Kain. Our heroes go up against the general more than the Empress. He is seen as the main obstacle. The Empress has her moment to shine too, but she isn't a brute nor does she appear threatening. She is more cunning and manipulative. She plays more mind games. In both cases, the Empress and the general meet their end in the same way, by underestimating the heroes.

The Helper Characters

The first friend Kero meets is Blythe. Blythe, a name that means 'cheerful,' 'joyous' or 'pleasant,' tells you the personality of this character. Blythe befriends Kero and the two begin their journey to escape the Empire. They meet Aponi and A'keara by fate. Aponi and A'keara also play a huge role in helping Kero and Blythe on their journey. Aponi is our wise character who helps Kero and Blythe learn about who they really are and the power they possess.

The City of Etheria

The city of Etheria, where Aponi and A'keara came from can be seen as the great city of Atlantis. Atlantis was known as a city with great technology where the people lived a lot longer and happier lives. Many have speculated how Atlantis fell, but I for one, believe it was taken away from us. What if the people of Atlantis made a deal with beings from another world and everything went wrong. Or they could have just been invaded by someone stronger than them. In the book, Etheira was invaded by 'newcomers,' but perhaps there is more to the story that you will read in later books.

I hope you enjoyed reading, "Dragon Wars: The Awakening." Please keep a look out for Book 2.

BOOK 2 SNEAK PEEK

Turn the page to continue

STAY TUNED!
DRAGON WARS
2
COMING SOON
DRAGON WARS
DRAGON WARS

CHAPTER SNEAK PEEK

As Kero approached her house, she noticed three young boys standing about ten feet away from Phoenix. The Crimson Dragon was curled up around an orange tree, fast asleep. Kero hoped the kids wouldn't disturb him.

"Uh, excuse me," Kero said. The three boys spun around, surprised by her presence. "What cha up to?" she asked.

The tallest boy in the middle turned his gaze up to her.

"Does your dragon eat people?"

Kero rolled her eyes. "No, he doesn't. But, you'd better leave him alone. It's not good to disturb a sleeping dragon."

"He looks like he's guarding the oranges," another boy said.

"Yeah, the third one chimed in. "He's guarding the magical oranges," he said with a laugh." Kero realized these boys were no older than maybe nine or ten. She could only imagine the fantasies all the children on the farm were coming up with in their heads after seeing the four Spirit Dragons.

"Well, like I said, just leave the dragon alone," Kero said before walking into the farmhouse.

When Kero entered her home, her nose caught the aroma of something sweet coming from the pot on the fire. No one was tending to the pot however. Kero peered into the steaming pot to see some stew cooking. Maybe it was deer meat.

"Darion?" she called. No answer. Kero grabbed the wooden ladle and stirred the pot. She lifted the utensil to see meat and some berries. The only person she knew who made berries and meat together was A'keara. The Etherian woman was known for leaving a pot when she was in the middle of cooking.

Kero climbed up the staircase. As she approached the top of the steps, she heard voices coming from her parents' room. Kero walked down the hallway, and stopped, staring at the doorknob. Even though she knew the truth about her parents, it still felt weird to go into their room. She knew all those memories were false, but something still kept her from totally freeing herself from the feelings those memories had.

Kero decided to knock on the door.

"Hold on!" she heard A'keara's voice. The door opened and Kero was surprised to see all the faces inside the room. Darion, Xan, Aponi and A'keara all stood in various places.

"What is everyone doing in here?" Kero couldn't help that her voice came out sounding a bit annoyed.

"Having a meeting," Xan said. Do you remember when Eden and I talked to Alden, the leader of the Elder Dragons?"

Kero shrugged her shoulders. "Yeah, so?"

"Well, I was just telling everyone about the visit. Oh, I'm sorry I wasn't able to invite you to join us. But please do." Xan said, gesturing her to come inside the room.

Kero stared back at Xan with a gleam in her eye. After Phoenix told her to get up so they could go meet Xan and Eden, Eden spoke to Phoenix telepathically. She said, "Change of plans, don't worry about coming to meet us. We're heading back now. Tell you everything when we come back to Athena."

"So, what happened?" Kero asked.

"Well–" Xan sniffed the air. "I think something is burning."

A'keara gasped. Aponi turned to her granddaughter.

"The pot! You left it too long!" A'keara hurried out of the room and down the stairs.

"Here's the gist of the story," Xan said. "Alden and the rest of the Elder Dragons are almost done rebuilding Etheria."

"Really? It's only been three weeks since we opened the gateway," Kero said.

"Actually, it's been over a month," Xan corrected her. "Eden and Aeolus are there now. Eden is telling me all about how Etheria looks all new, like it had never been destroyed." Kero turned to Aponi.

"Well, you must be happy."

"Oh, 'happy' isn't enough to describe what I feel," Aponi said. "I can't believe–I never thought I'd ever see Etheria like it was before the invasion."

Kero smiled at Aponi. Turning to Xan, she said, "Well, when are we going to see it?"

"Oh, here's the best part. They want us to bring everyone to see it. Everyone on this planet."

"Everyone on the planet?" Kero asked.

"I don't think everyone is ready to see dragons," Darion said. "And I don't think anyone cares to see a city that they've never heard of before."

"I think the six of us should go. Or eight of us, counting Phoenix and Eira," Aponi suggested.

"Right, as soon as Blythe and Eira are done patrolling the skies, we can leave," Xan said.

"Who is going to guard the farm until we get back?" Kero asked. If all of us go with our dragons, no one will be here to make sure everyone stays safe."

Everyone eyed each other in silence.

"Well, I can stay here," Xan said.

"I can too," Darion added.

"You're going to be here without your dragons?" Kero asked.

"It's fine. Remember, we do have our spirit weapons," Xan replied. "I've been practicing," Xan closed his eyes and breathed in deeply. The long staff with the green agate crystal on top appeared in his hands.

"I'm still working on making my bow to appear," Darion said. "But I know how to use a normal crossbow, so I'll be able to fight anyone or anything that comes into the colony."

Kero gritted her teeth. "I thought we weren't calling it that anymore."

"Oh, right," Darion said. "Uh, are we just calling this place 'the farm' then?"

"I always have," Kero replied.

The group met downstairs where A'keara served her berry blend into bowls for everyone.

"Oh good, lunch is ready," Aponi said.

Everyone sat around the small wooden table. Well, Aponi, A'keara and Xan sat down. There was one chair left, but Kero remained standing.

"Go sit down," Darion said to her. He stood by the wall, eating the stew. Kero sat next to Xan. "Is Blythe going to eat?"

Just as she said that, the blonde pranced through the door. Her nose caught the aroma of the sweet berries, and cinnamon, mixed with deer meat.

"Berry Blend!" she cried. She rushed over and grabbed the empty bowl on the table. Darion set down his bowl.

"Here, let me help you." Darion used the ladle to pour the stew into her bowl. Blythe took the bowl, but not before exchanging a quick smile with Darion. The two stood next to each other, enjoying the tasty mix of sweet berries and savory meat.

Outside, Eira walked over to where Phoenix slept. She blew some of her ice breath into his face. Phoenix jolted up. His eyes focused on his sister. Her blue and violet crystal scales glistened in the sunlight.

"What do you want?" he asked haughtily.

"We are going to meet Aeolus and Eden in the new Etheria.

"New Etheria?" he asked.

"Oh, yeah, you've been sleeping all day, so you haven't heard the news. The Elder Dragons rebuilt Etheria."

Phoenix squinted his eyes at Eira. "There's no way they could rebuild the city that fast!"

"Well, in any case, I guess the plan is to go pay them all a visit. They requested the presence of you, and me, and our bonded to come.

"And who is going to guard the farm?"

"Uh, good question." She glanced around the farm, seeing everyone at work. "Also, I'm hungry. I smell the stew that A'keara cooked."

"There's not enough for us," Phoenix said as he stood. "We can stop in the savannah to grab something to eat."

At that moment, the front door of the farmhouse opened and the six humans walked out, showing satisfied smiles on their faces. Kero pranced over to Phoenix.

"Hey, ready for a trip. You've had a long nap."

"Yes. I heard we're going to see Etheria, apparently."

Kero nodded. "Yup." She mounted the dragon. As she did this, she noticed the same three boys she saw earlier. The tallest boy waved.

"Hey! I want a ride!"

"Yeah, me too!" the other two chimed in.

"Uh, I'm not sure you three are ready to ride a dragon," Kero said. "Besides, we have someplace we need to be."

Blythe jumped onto Eira's back. "Is it okay if Phoenix and I eat on the way there?" the crystal scaled dragon asked.

Blythe shrugged her shoulders. "That's fine."

Aponi walked up to Phoenix.

"Kero, I can either ride with you or A'keara can."

"Either way is fine. So, Xan and my bro-I mean Darion are staying here? I hope they'll be alright."

"I think they'll be fine." Kero helped Aponi up onto Phoenix. A'keara hopped onto Eira. Blythe turned her head around to face A'keara.

"Is Aurora doing okay?"

A'keara nodded. "Yes. She's enjoying her time with the horses."

"I don't think the horses even know that she's different from them. Does she know she's different?"

A'keara smiled. "Of course. Oh, and don't worry about her mating with any of the horses. Aurora is very particular. She will only mate with a male unicorn." Her eyes saddened. "Unfortunately, I don't know if that will ever happen as she's the only unicorn left on the planet."

"What about the gateway opening? Can more creatures from the higher realm come through?"

A'keara narrowed her eyes in thought. "I'm not really sure."

Kero waved to Darion. "You'll be okay, right?"

Darion laughed. "Yeah, it'll be fine. The Empire is gone. I don't think we'll have any problems."

Phoenix and Eira took off into the sky, leaving Xan and Darion on the ground.

"Let's go help the guard at the gate," Xan said.

"I still can't believe he's helpin' us," Darion replied. "He was actually happy when we told him what happened to the Empress."

"He was a slave too," Xan replied.

Everyone on the farm was so busy that they didn't notice a young man in his late teens limping onto the farm. He suddenly collapsed. Mr. Daniels rushed over. The man's eyes stared upwards. Tyrian brought over a flask of water. Mr. Daniels helped the nineteen year-old sit up, while Tyrian tipped up the flask, pouring fresh water into the mouth of the young adult. When he gained control of his body, the young man finally spoke.

"Ammon, our speaker sent me from Isis–we haven't gotten any new shipments in the last few weeks. Why has production stopped?" He ended his sentence in a fit of coughing.

Mr. Daniels stared down at the teen, unsure of how to respond.

"Uh, well–"

Before the man could say anything else, a large shadow loomed over the farm. Mr. Daniels and Tyrian gazed upwards to see a most terrifying sight. A large imperial ship. The eyes of the middle-aged man and the teenager went wide.

"I thought we didn't have to worry about the Empire anymore!" Tyrian yelled.

Xan and Darion stood by the gate of the colony. Their eyes stared up at the sight of the airship.

"Yeah, maybe one of the dragons should have stayed with us," Darion said.

Printed in Great Britain
by Amazon

56959440R00209